✯ ✯ ✯

A Journey SPARED

JACKSON'S STORY

Book One in the Journey Series

Cover design by germancreative
Edited by Cayla Cavalletto

The Journey Series is a steamy, closed-door romance.
Book 1 Content Warnings: Coarse language, suicide (off page), PTSD, loss/
grief, rape (off page), and violence. Jackson's story has hardships, pain,
heartbreak, and raw emotions. But there is even more inspiration, hope,
sweetness, perseverance, and unconditional love to balance it out. Enjoy!

Follow me on Instagram, TikTok and Facebook:
@authoralexandragrace

Website: https://authoralexandragrace.carrd.co

The Journey Series
by Alexandra Grace

The series is best read in the below order.

Prequel Novella
(Sydney & Will's Story)

A JOURNEY WORTH TAKING

(Jackson's Trilogy)

A JOURNEY SPARED

A JOURNEY TO LOVE

A JOURNEY HOME

(Sydney's Story)

A JOURNEY BEYOND

Journey Series Spin-off

(Nora & Jordan's Story)

MAKE YOU LOVE ME

(Hayes & Josie's Story)

HOW YOU SEE ME

*To my husband for his patience and encouragement
while I took this journey to write my first book series
and realize a dream.*

*To Lindsay for her friendship, great advice, generous
giving of time and love for this story.*

Chapter One

✫ ✫ ✫

Jackson

The view from the open, passenger side window of Jackson's ride was saturated with a rainbow of vibrant colors. Typical Virginia spring scents of freshly cut grass and cheerful blossoms assaulted his senses.

Looking up, he searched for a few ominous, gray clouds in the distance. A rolling thunderstorm would better match his mood and the shambles his life had become. Still, the beautiful April morning paid him no mind.

Ironic since not that long ago, he would've given anything to be ignored. And per usual, what he wanted didn't seem to matter.

"Jax."

Surprised, he turned toward Aiden, his friend and fellow Marine, in the driver's seat.

"Where were you just now? I said your name three times."

"Sorry." Glancing at the small wooden box in his hands, the one he'd been squeezing hard enough for his joints to ache, he dropped it and rubbed his fingers. "I was thinking I don't know how to do this."

"Do what?"

"Be here."

"I know," was all Aiden could say, and he couldn't blame him. They'd both seen it countless times in others and knew what would come next—debilitating pain, suffocating guilt, confusion, and roaming without purpose through the days. Some turned to alcohol or drugs. Many disappeared without a trace.

Aiden had always been clear about getting out of the service before he lost himself. He'd spent four years in the Marines, most of them serving under Jackson, and he wanted no more. He was proud of his service, often talking about his gratitude for the experience, but he never intended to make the military a lifelong career or let it define him as Jackson had.

"Remember when we arrived in Afghanistan the first time?" Aiden asked, trying to distract Jackson from the raw emotions he struggled to control and understand. "We'd barely wiped the sand out of our eyes before we were attacked. I was terrified, and you had no patience for it. You told me the world would not wait for me to decide what type of man I wanted to be."

Tuning him out, Jackson focused on the passing landscape outside. He knew where this impromptu story time would end and wasn't impressed.

Undeterred, Aiden continued to fill the awkward silence and make his point. "I wanted to punch you then, but I'll never forget it. Whenever things got unbearably difficult— as they often did—and I could feel myself slipping into the darkness…" He paused when Jackson's gaze cut to his.

Since his brush with death, Jackson had become acutely acquainted with unforgiving darkness and how it can consume the mind.

"I had to make the conscious decision to be the person needed in each moment to survive and keep the shadows at bay. Now it's your turn, Jax."

"I shouldn't be here."

"No, you shouldn't, but somehow you are. Don't waste it." He flashed a toothy smile over his shoulder when Jackson had nothing to say, then returned his attention to the road.

As the pair made their way down Virginia's I-95 toward Richmond, Aiden attempted to keep him distracted with conversation, avoiding topics that might remind him of their comrades or Jackson's three closest friends: Billy, Will, and Josh. But that didn't matter. He could think of nothing else 24/7.

He pointed toward the Richmond exit and rolled his shoulders at the injection of new tension. For eight years, he'd avoided his childhood home. Well, the place hadn't felt like home since his mother died, and he had zero business showing up like this.

He directed Aiden through the city and down a private road lined with meticulously trimmed shrubbery and flowers—Eleanor's doing, no doubt, he thought with a rare surge of anticipation. She'd been the only reason he went through with this ridiculous plan. Other than missing her, he needed her usual guidance and steadfast love to get through whatever hell came next.

Aiden pulled to a stop next to the black box housing the gate's keypad and punched in the code Jackson provided.

The ancient iron gate hitched into motion.

"Something funny?" Aiden asked when Jackson puffed out a cynical chuckle.

"It's been almost fifteen years. You'd think the old bastard would've changed the security code."

"Maybe he wanted to make sure you could always come home."

Jackson scoffed at his friend's innocent optimism and couldn't blame him. Aiden had a profound respect for, and close relationship with *his* father—things Jackson could never have with his own. The Great Grayson Vane had always been unreachable, and their already fragile relationship only turned volatile and vanished before his mother was laid to rest. If Eleanor hadn't been working as the estate's caretaker at the time, Jackson would have ended up in foster care or fending for himself at twelve years old.

The car hitched into motion, bringing his focus back to the present.

"Be right there," Aiden promised after setting the car in park.

Jackson leaned back against the headrest and waited for the worst part. When Aiden appeared, he took out his frustration over the fate he'd been dealt on the door and accepted Aiden's help into the wheelchair.

There is no other choice, now is there? He could accept that every movement following multiple major surgeries to repair his shattered legs would be excruciating, but he couldn't get past the dependency it created. Whenever he needed help with basic tasks like getting out of a car, someone might as well jab his heart with a dull butter knife. Feeling like a burden felt the same, and he despised nothing more.

"Alright, Jax. Let's get you home."

While they traveled up the driveway, a silence fell over Aiden as he admired the dignified colonial house where Jackson grew up. A stunning example of his father's affinity for showing off, it was a sight not easily forgotten.

Most visitors marveled over the expansive, two-story structure with its smokey gray stone and authentic historic features, but he gravitated more toward the natural elements: the classic hanging fern baskets between the wide white columns on the porch, the wisteria blooming in lively shades of purple and blue along the inside corners of the wings on each side. All Eleanor's doing. It was her presence, her laughter, her caring touch that made this otherwise cold and heartless place into a home.

"This will work," Jackson finally said when they came to the small roundabout with a garden of shaped bushes and flowers circling a central water fountain.

Noticing the side, ground-level entrance door—a more accessible entrance for the wheelchair—Aiden headed that way. They didn't get far before the screen door flew open, revealing Eleanor in all her glory. Seeing her in a white apron over a flowing yellow dress with her dark gray hair tied up with a ribbon on top of her head took him back in time. She looked just as he remembered and hadn't aged a minute since he last saw her over a year ago.

"Hi, Eleanor," Jackson greeted.

A shaky grin was all he could assemble as she stood motionless, her hands clasped over her mouth. It took a moment for her to wade through waves of shock, relief, and emotion, tears springing to her dark blue eyes. Then, she rushed to him and bent to wrap him in a hug.

Now, he was home.

With her hands on his face, she kissed his forehead and cheeks before straightening to study him, her hands on her hips. "Why didn't you tell me you were coming back today?"

"Surprise."

She clicked her tongue in disapproval, but he knew better. "Best one ever," she said, her love for him coming through, as expected. "Oh, how I've missed you."

"Stop doing that," he scolded gently, as she took him in.

"Stop what?"

"Making a mental list of all the ways you're going to fix this." He waved a hand over his frail body. He'd lost most of his muscle, and even he could see how pale and sickly he looked. Four months in a hospital bed would do that to anyone—even Marines.

"You're too skinny," she complained with her standard sass to cover her concern. "Didn't they feed you over there?"

"Hospital food makes me lose my appetite, and since it wasn't your cooking, it wasn't worth eating."

"Such a charmer." Pulling herself away, Eleanor turned to the stranger standing behind him. Knowing Eleanor, Aiden wouldn't have that title for long. "Who's this handsome fella?"

"I'm Aiden, Jackson's chauffeur, staff sergeant, and friend." He reached out his hand, but she stepped around the wheelchair and swallowed him in a hug before he could react.

"Any friend of Jackson's is a friend of mine." She gave him a loud kiss on the cheek. "Please come in and relax a bit. You must be worn out from your flight."

Coughing, Aiden folded his arms and leaned on the back of the wheelchair. "You could have warned me," he whispered, teeth clenched as he refilled his lungs.

"And miss out on seeing that look on your face? Not a chance."

Eleanor held the door for Aiden to push Jackson inside, then led them through a large mudroom on the way to the eat-in kitchen. The antique, off-white cabinets surrounding the bright, cheerful room looked the same as he remembered, but the marble countertops with tan, gray, and gold specks were new. The center island, where Jackson used to sit and help Eleanor cook, seemed smaller now, even though it took up half the open space and provided enough seating for four.

Following Eleanor down an adjacent hallway, he tried not to despise the ornate and boastful magnificence of his father's gaudy taste: oil paintings, Oriental rugs, sculptures, and vintage furniture in bright, eclectic patterns. Too grand for his taste, it overshadowed the classic components that he appreciated, like the curved wooden staircase, layered crown molding, and original wide plank hardwood floors.

After depositing him in a bedroom as Eleanor instructed, Aiden returned to the car to retrieve Jackson's bag.

"Please stop worrying, Eleanor," he pleaded when she started fluttering around the room, moving breakables and small pieces of furniture to clear a path for the damn wheelchair he was strapped to. "I'm not dangerous in this thing."

"I know. I only want you to be comfortable."

"I'll be fine." At least, he hoped to be one day.

With a long sigh, she sat on the bed to face him. Everyone Jackson knew understood how much he wanted to be a Marine, but Eleanor most of all. They'd talked about his dreams at length since he was a boy. Serving was as much a part of him as his friends were. Coming to terms with all he'd lost and his new circumstances would not come easy.

"When we first heard what happened, I thought we'd lost you." She lowered her gaze and pulled a tissue out of her apron pocket for the tears that were sure to follow. "We had no idea where you were. All we knew was what we heard from others, and while it wasn't much, none of it was good."

She blotted her eyes. "I'm so sorry about Josh and Billy. I know how much they meant to you. Such sweet boys." She shook her head, catching a glimpse of Aiden in the doorway.

"I'm going to head out. I've got a couple more hours of driving ahead of me," he said awkwardly, knowing he had interrupted something, and crossed the room. "Jax, I know you'll get back to your old self soon. Nothing can keep you down for long."

If only he could believe that, too. He'd never been one to give up but moving forward only got more difficult by the day. So did finding a reason to keep trying.

"Sergeant Vane, it was an honor to serve with you." Aiden clicked his heels together and held a formal salute. Then, he looked down at Jackson with his eyes only and grinned.

"I'm not your sergeant anymore."

Aiden dropped his hand to shake Jackson's. "Maybe not, but I will always respect and honor you as I did when you were. Glad you're alive, Jax. Now, stay that way."

Not having the words, Jackson nodded and returned to the window. Several minutes later, he watched Aiden's car disappear around the bend, symbolizing the end of his life as he once knew it.

Although his heart still pumped and his lungs still took in air, everything was broken, and nothing was as it should be.

Chapter Two

✮ ✮ ✮

Jackson

Alone in his room, Jackson pulled himself onto the bed and removed the smooth wooden box he slipped into the side pocket of the wheelchair when they arrived. He hadn't opened it since it was given to him at a small ceremony in Washington, D.C., and tried not to loathe the contents.

He should take pride in what it represented, but he could muster nothing more than a profound desire to smash and bury it. How could something so small pack such a devastating punch to the gut?

To get it over with, he flipped open the lid. Sunlight, streaming through the double windows, reflected in the gold edges of the medal, and stabbed at his eyes. Absently, he traced the gentle heart shape with his finger and thought of the day that earned him the so-called award.

———

It started like every other morning in the unforgiving desert. No strange activity or warning signals. No gut telling him to take caution. Just the normal routine of physical training at five, lukewarm MREs for breakfast, and breaking down camp before traveling to their next mission.

While loading the Humvees, the usual rousing and laughter rose above the clang of metal with the same topics at the center—the previous night's card games, who snored and kept everyone up, plans for their next leave, items in their care latest packages from family.

Later that afternoon, the distant horizon vibrated in the heat under a setting sun, painting the endless sky with indescribable warm colors. He could still smell the stinging combination of diesel, sweat, and gunpowder and remember the feel of soft desert sand on his skin. Those were memories to be grateful for.

But he would give anything to forget how the missiles bleached the black night and launched his vehicle over a tidal wave of sand. Blinded, he could only ride the crest into the dark void and hope he was deposited in one piece. The brutal landing tossed him and others across the cabin like a pinball, his bones snapping on contact. He screamed but heard nothing.

The silence provided a reprieve, albeit fleeting. While the vehicle crashed and rolled, shards of glass rained over him and sliced both fabric and skin. Sand mixed with open wounds. His entire body burned with a pain unlike any he'd ever experienced.

Then, rapid gunfire echoed across the vast terrain, replacing the ringing in his ears. Frantic, he felt around for his rifle, only to discover a thick liquid—either oil or blood, possibly both—coated most of his body. Everything he touched felt hot and gritty.

He attempted to sit up, and his head took off, spinning out of control, and his stomach rolled. Blood ran into his eyes and mouth. Smoke filled his lungs, choking him and burning his throat. The last thing he heard before he fell into the dark obscurity of death was the shrieks of his brothers in pain.

If this was the end, at least they would die together.

––––––

He relived that chaos in vivid detail—fear, pain, heartbreak, and helplessness clashed at debilitating levels every day now.

Here we go again, he thought when the freight train slammed into his head. He slapped the box closed and threw it inside the bedside table drawer in one fluid motion. He didn't need another tangible reminder of what he'd lost, sitting around in plain sight. He had enough of those already.

Lying back, he threw a pillow over his face and begged for the blinding pain at his temples to ease soon. The migraines usually lasted only an hour if he could find a dark, quiet space to wait it out. He used that time to search for the trigger in hopes of preventing future attacks, but he had a sinking feeling that everything was a trigger these days.

Damn, he hated the quiet darkness.

Refocusing his thoughts, he listened to the creaks and moans of an old house settling for the night instead of the war raging in his head. It was much calmer than the barracks, and infinitely more soothing than his hospital room with its incessant beeping, carts rolling up and down halls, and the never-ending conversations of nurses outside his door. He preferred almost any noise over the clatter of a hospital at work.

The familiar sound of Eleanor humming as she cooked lulled him into a restful state until a slamming door catapulted his heart into his throat. Startled, he pushed up to an elbow and heard muffled voices in a room down the hall. As the conversation heated, he listened to determine if he recognized anyone before remembering he couldn't care less.

He threw himself back against the pillow and let out a long, shuttered breath. At least the throbbing in his head had lessened to a dull roar, something he could manage. Headaches were the new normal, but he didn't bother with painkillers. After having them pumped into his veins for months on end in the hospital, he welcomed being able to feel again. Even if the only sensation he got now was pain.

A few moments later, the screen door slammed, followed by the roar of an engine and the screech of tires taking off down the driveway. Well, the unidentified visitor left either in a hurry or in anger.

Good riddance.

Being his first night back, his mood didn't allow for entertaining visitors or pretending everything he'd been through hadn't changed him. Placing his arm over his eyes, he attempted to relax and regain that elusive relaxation he found earlier.

"Jackson, sweetie." Eleanor's timid knock sounded through the silence before she opened the door and stood in its frame.

He shot up, remembering the abrupt departure of the unidentified guest and identifying the concern in her voice. "Is everything okay?" he asked, despite how utterly useless he'd be if she needed him—another dagger through the chest.

"Yes, sweetie. Everything's fine." Sitting on the bed, she laid her hand on his. He jumped, too on edge to stop the reflex, and the resulting sympathy in her eyes added a dose of vinegar to his open wounds. "I was wondering if you were hungry, dear. I made your favorite—roasted chicken and asparagus with garlic potatoes."

At the thought of eating real food, Jackson's stomach rumbled.

"I'll take that as a yes." Eleanor tapped her leg and rose off the bed with determination. "Now, let's get you out of this bed and some food in your belly. You need it."

Although it stung a bit, he allowed her to help him into the wheelchair. At this stage in their lives, he should be taking care of her. Not the other way around.

"Well, that's what months in a hospital bed will do to you." He tried to make light of it for her benefit, but it was another touchy subject.

His entire adult life, he prided himself on his fitness routine. Five days a week, he'd rise at dawn and run ten to fifteen miles, stopping several times to work in some calisthenics. He ate healthy and was in the best shape of his life.

Now, after four surgeries to repair his damaged bones, doctors weren't optimistic that he'd ever walk again. The old Jackson would have said *bullshit*. The long journey of physical work would have been a welcome challenge. But his life had taken a turn, and his motivation was lackluster at best.

Some days, it took all the strength he had not to end his suffering for good. It wouldn't take much since part of him was already buried under a mound of anger, sorrow, and regret. But every time the thought crept into his mind, so did the faces of the people he loved—Eleanor, Will, Josh, Billy, and his friends' parents, who had been there for him all his life.

The Jackson they knew would fight, crawl, claw, do whatever was necessary to live life to the fullest, and he couldn't bear to disappoint any of them. That would be worse than the pain. Worse than death. He chose to live for them, trying to take advantage of this second chance. After all, he'd survived when so many others hadn't.

And why was that? Why were he and Will the only souls spared in the blasts? That one question haunted him the most.

"Someone joining us?" he asked when he saw six white candles positioned evenly down the center of the long, mahogany dining room table. Eleanor only lit candles when guests were expected for dinner.

"No. Not tonight." Frustrated with herself, she rushed around Jackson and collected the third setting.

"Eleanor, who was here earlier?"

She paused at the question but ignored it and continued resetting the table to her liking. "Let's get you settled."

He said nothing as she removed a chair, pushed the wheelchair to the table, and set the brake. But when she started toward the kitchen, he gently took hold of her arm to stop her.

"Who was here, Eleanor? Who is no longer coming for dinner?"

"I wanted to do something nice to celebrate your return home. I've missed you so much. I'm sorry, Jackson. I didn't mean to upset you." Tears spilled down her soft cheeks.

He released her arm, angry with himself for making her cry. "So, Grayson came home, found out I was here, got angry, and left to avoid the inconvenience."

It was the reaction he expected from his father and why he wished he had somewhere else to go. The transformative family reunion she'd dreamed about would never happen. Grayson Vane had no interest in playing dad to a twenty-six-year-old, disabled veteran. He'd never wanted a role in Jackson's life, and his current situation wouldn't change that, except their inevitable run-ins would be more hazardous now. This would be the first time he would face his father as an adult, and he was more than equipped to defend himself—dead legs or not.

"Jackson," she began, disappointment overwhelming her tone and posture.

"Dinner smells delicious, Eleanor. Let's eat. I want to hear about all you've been up to since we last spoke."

She smiled down at him, understanding he needed to focus on something other than his father, and hurried to the kitchen to collect the food. After a few quick trips, her eyes were dry, and dinner was displayed magnificently on the table in serving dishes of varying colors and sizes. Candles still flickered only for him.

Over the next hour, they ate, talked, and enjoyed being back together again. Eleanor updated him on her daughter and grandchildren in southern Virginia and how she hoped to visit them soon. She didn't mention her son-in-law, Jackson noticed but wasn't surprised. He'd never liked the guy and his lack of concern for anyone but himself. It was unbearable watching Eleanor constantly search for the good in him when there wasn't any.

To ensure her son-in-law didn't enter the conversation, she quickly changed the subject and talked about her vacation last June to see her sisters in Maryland. She also repainted her rooms a cheerful yellow and planted another garden beside the back porch.

"I like to stay busy. It gets pretty lonely here."

"What about the man of the house?" Jackson couldn't say his name a second time.

"You know he lives at the apartment full time. I only see him when he wants something or throws a party here, so that's plenty enough for me. Plus, he isn't very chatty unless he brings company. Then, it's just him showing off."

He rolled his eyes. "Eleanor, why haven't you left? You don't deserve the way he treats you."

"This is my home, sweetheart. Heather has her own life in Stony Creek. I'd be in the way or twiddling my thumbs in my own little house there." She shrugged and leaned back in her chair. "At least I have a purpose here, and the hard labor keeps me young and fit." She kept her gaze on him until a deep belly laugh snorted out.

"It was a valiant effort."

"I tried to say it with a straight face." She wiped the happy tears from her face before another laughing fit took over.

She leaned on the table to catch her breath, and he patted her hand. "Maybe next time you'll pull it off."

"I doubt it. It's about the same odds as your father giving up his work, whiskey, or women."

"I thought he preferred brandy."

"I was being dramatic, deary. Try to keep up."

Holding up a hand in surrender, he grinned. "Brain's a little slower these days."

"You do look tired," she observed when he sunk into his thoughts.

"I'm still on London time, I guess."

"In that case, I propose we continue catching up tomorrow. You need some sleep."

"That would be nice. Dinner was wonderful, Eleanor. Better than a five-star restaurant."

"You flatter me, and I love you for it." She helped him move away from the table, then pointed him toward the doorway.

"Eleanor," he said, looking over his shoulder. "Thank you."

"You're welcome, sweetheart. I'll see you in the morning. If there's anything you need, please holler."

Chapter Three

✦ ✦ ✦

Jackson

While Jackson stared at the ceiling the following morning, wondering if he'd ever get a good night's sleep again, the house phone rang. Eleanor answered it from the kitchen.

"Yes, he's here. Sure. One moment. I'll get him." He heard her voice above the sound of her hasty footsteps on the hardwood floors.

"Jackson, sweetie," she called through the door before turning the knob. "It's your doctor calling."

Adjusting the pillow, he sat up and accepted the phone. Still nothing from the leg department, he noticed with a sigh.

"Hi, Doc."

"Jackson, it's so good to hear your voice."

The familiar, British accent boomed through the receiver. Dr. Evans had the distinct and commanding voice of a drill instructor converted into a kindergarten teacher, and Jackson missed him deeply. They had grown close over his last month in the hospital, but the journey hadn't been easy. His anger over what happened to his unit got the better of him, and he was uncooperative during most of his recovery. He begged to be left alone to wallow in his misery, but Dr. Evans wasn't easily swayed. He stayed by Jackson's side, finally winning him over with patient persistence.

"How are you?"

"I've been better," he answered honestly.

"Understandable. All the nurses miss you around here."

"Ha." He scrubbed a hand over his beard, still not appreciating the inside joke. He loathed both dependency and attention.

"Anyway, I have a list of physical therapists in your area, and I want you to schedule an appointment this week. You need to start working those muscles and get the blood flowing. I can email them to you. What's your address?"

"I would give it to you, but I no longer have a cell phone or computer to check it. I've been out of commission for too long."

"What about a pen and paper?"

He scanned the room. "Sorry, Doc."

"Fine. I'll wait until you get with the century and send me your email address. Now, go take care of that problem, you damn caveman." Without waiting for a response, Dr. Evans hung up, his laughter fading into silence.

"Thanks a lot, Doc," he murmured as Eleanor appeared in the doorway. "Do you have plans today?" he asked her, pushing his legs off the edge of the bed.

She crossed the room to steady the wheelchair for him to slide into. "Is there something I can do for you?" she asked, pushing him out the door.

"I realized that I need some things. Would you mind driving me to a few stores?"

"Of course not. You know how much I love shopping. What about a haircut while you're out?"

His fingers dug through his hair. a few inches longer than his usual buzz cut. He'd barely looked in a mirror over the last four months. Could barely stand to see who he'd become.

"I was thinking about growing it out. No need to keep it short without—"

Eleanor responded with a hum, knowing it was best to let the comment float away unfinished.

After a hearty breakfast, the pair climbed into Grayson's SUV. The big trunk would make getting the wheelchair in and out easier.

"He prefers his fancy, little sports car. I have no idea why he bought this monstrosity," Eleanor complained and heaved herself inside. The inside still smelled new, and dust covered the hood as if it had never been driven. She gave Jackson a wide smile before pushing the button to open the garage door. "Ready?"

"As ready as I can be."

"Good. But let's get a heavy-duty razor while we're out. You can grow your hair long, but that unruly beard of yours is freaking me out."

"Deal."

It took three hours to get everything he needed. Before returning to the estate, they stopped by their favorite restaurant for lunch.

"Welcome back," the waitress sang cheerfully and set down their regular drinks without them having to order. "Do you two know what you want to order, or do you need a few minutes?"

"Just a few."

"What's so amusing?" he asked, suspicious of Eleanor's wide smile.

"You didn't notice our waitress undressing you with her eyes?"

"You just can't help yourself, can you?"

"No, and why would I? Young lust is such a glorious thing."

"Lust?" With a huff, he rolled his eyes and returned to the menu. "You're unbelievable."

"You may be experienced and educated in the ways of the world, Jackson Vane, but you're oblivious to so many things."

He dropped his menu, challenging her. "Like what?"

"How beautiful you are."

"Eleanor." He'd heard her opinion about his lack of a normal life a hundred times over the years. It was sweet of her to want that for him but insignificant in the grand scheme of things. He just wanted to live peacefully without distractions and with the people he loved, especially when he had only a fraction of them left.

"You have the soul of an angel—humble and kind, selfless and strong—and you love with all your heart. I'm just trying to get you to put the rest of you to good use, so you'd have someone other than an old lady to keep you company. Like those incredible blue eyes that make women stop in their tracks."

"First of all, that doesn't happen." He glared at her when she scoffed. "Second, I prefer your company and don't need anyone else's."

The arrival of their waitress interrupted her next tease. "She just couldn't stay away," Eleanor mumbled, causing his scolding eyes to dart in her direction.

After ordering, Eleanor carried on as if she hadn't embarrassed him a minute before, placing a loving hand on his. "Tell me, my boy. Do you know what you'll do next?"

He looked down at their hands—his dark and rough from years of sun and training and hers weathered from age and hard work—and realized he hadn't been touched by someone he cared about in so long. Although he'd been surrounded by hospital staff for months, he'd never felt lonelier there—no visitors, no family or friends who understood him, no one except Dr. Evans to talk to. But that had been his choice, and he had to live with it.

With a sigh, he returned his attention to Eleanor. "To be honest, I have no idea. I'm twenty-six years old and washed up with no real-world skills or working legs. What prospects could I possibly have?"

"Now, you listen here, child. You are anything but washed up. From here on out, you're going to get up every morning and thank the good Lord that He spared you in that desert. He is giving you a lesson in perseverance, and you will listen. You have your entire life ahead of you. If you put your mind to it, you will learn to walk again and find your new purpose in life. If anyone can do it, you can." She squeezed his hand, then sat back in her chair, arms crossed and proud of herself.

Her words cut deep, and he wanted to believe her. He'd do anything to forget, turn off the memories, and find happiness again. He just couldn't see the path that would take him there.

She continued gauging him, her eyes shimmering with enough mysterious mischief to make him uneasy. Picking up his glass of water, he studied her back.

Then, her crooked grin made sense when she uttered the words, "What about sex?"

He choked on the water he'd been drinking, coughing to clear his lungs. "Jesus, Eleanor!" Snatching up his napkin, he wiped his lips and glared at her. Were there no boundaries? "Where did that come from?"

"I'm not a prude. I know men sometimes need a little action to get their juices flowing…and women." She wiggled her brow at the dumbfounded look plastered on his face. "Our waitress is cute and has a thing for you. Maybe you should ask her out."

"Absolutely not." He could no longer stifle a laugh. "You're crazy, you old bat."

Thankfully, their food soon arrived and diverted the bizarre conversation toward a less embarrassing topic. While they ate, they talked about potential maneuverability improvements they could make to his bedroom suite.

"But you won't be in that wheelchair for long." She pointed that all-knowing finger at him. "You're going to be walking—no, running soon—so we just need to make sure you can get around the house until then."

"Speaking of walking, we'll start there. Dr. Evans is sending me a list of physical therapists to call. He hasn't been optimistic that it will work, but—" He stopped when Eleanor's finger waved in his direction again.

"You tell that doctor to stick it. It's going to work. You need to believe it and give it all you've got."

She'd preached that his entire life. *Believe in yourself and give it one hundred percent*, she'd demand. *Anything less is cheating yourself.* In everything he'd ever done, he worked hard and practiced until he ached. It was all or nothing for her and for himself.

But things were different now, and he couldn't help wondering if this was more than he could handle.

———

Later that evening, after his new laptop, phone, and wireless router were set up, he sent Dr. Evans his email address and cell phone number. Within ten minutes, he received the promised list of physical therapists and strict instructions to ensure he attended every appointment. It was 2:15 a.m. in London. What in the hell was he doing up?

With slight annoyance, Jackson saved the document and closed the laptop.

Next, he texted Will his number and invited him to stop by when he had time. Although it would be hard to talk about what happened, he needed to see his best friend and the man who saved his life. Risking his own safety, Will pulled him from the burning wreckage after the explosion. And while he was unconscious, hidden away in a nearby ditch, Will returned to rescue two more wounded Marines while taking three bullets himself. He applied tourniquets, bandaged wounds, and kept them all safe until the search and rescue team arrived hours later.

Of course, Jackson knew none of that when he awoke from the coma following his first surgery. He asked the hospital staff daily about his friends and the rest of his squad. No one ever had the answers he demanded, and their attempts to appease him with empty promises only agitated him further.

Several weeks passed before he learned that Will had been the only other survivor. The missiles hit two Humvees head-on, instantly killing all souls on board, including Josh and Billy. The other Marines he rescued succumbed to their injuries within days. Will spent two weeks in recovery before getting shipped home with crisp new bandages on his wounds and a shiny medal for his bravery.

They'd both been through hell, and although Will's physical recovery was shorter, Jackson hoped he wasn't struggling to cope with the aftermath. He wanted to believe Will had found himself again. That he was happy and enjoying life, lighting up rooms with his infectious energy like old times.

But what if Will didn't want to see him? Although he'd understand, he couldn't bear losing another friend.

He just couldn't.

Chapter Four

✮ ✮ ✮

Jackson

Unable to turn off his mind long enough to stop worrying about Will, Jackson gave up trying to rest at the first light of day. Exhaustion weighed down every limb.

He could see no end to the torture. Navigating a stone maze at night with no light, no map, and no tools seemed easier. At least in the maze, he could use his training and skills to find a solution. Laid up in his father's house, unable to fend for himself, let alone walk, he could do nothing. Hell, the person fate forced him to become *was* nothing.

Sitting up, he placed a hand over his racing heart. His skin felt damp, and air wouldn't fill his lungs. He gulped faster, searching the room for a way to escape from a future that had him in a chokehold. The past beat him down, and now his bleak future was burying him alive.

He looked up at the ceiling and beyond. *Is this my life now?* Frantic fits of anxiety, suffocating memories, fear, heartaches, and regrets randomly attacking him between blinding migraines? Oh, and not to mention two dead fish for legs.

With that, he threw his legs over the side of the bed with a force that matched his frustration, sending the rest of his body crashing to the floor. He landed hard, sending bolts of pain through his hips and spine. A shriek escaped his lips before he realized what happened.

Eleanor came running when she heard the commotion and found him sprawled on the floor, face down on the rug, writhing in pain. The wheelchair, pushed up against the window, teetered on two wheels.

"Fuck," he yelled, agony stealing his manners.

To soothe him, she rubbed his back. "Honey, are you okay? Can you move?"

No. He couldn't fucking move. His legs were distorted, and while he drew in one shuddered breath after another through his teeth, he gripped the shaggy rug in each fist. His lower body burned as if stuck in an electric current. Sensing his struggle, Eleanor stepped closer to help, but his hand shot up to stop her. He needed to do this on his own.

It took everything he had to make the agonizing adjustments, but soon, he was leaning against the bed with his eyes closed and his dead fish lying straight out in front of him. Finally able to breathe again, he angled his head toward Eleanor and apologized for the foul language.

"Oh, sweetie. I've lived with your father all these years. Believe me, my ears are no longer innocent."

Despite himself, he grinned at her and motioned toward the wheelchair. "Would you mind grabbing that?"

After some maneuvering and more exertion than either of them was accustomed to, he made it into the detested wheelchair without further incident. Exhausted, he allowed Eleanor to push him out of the room.

"Are you kicking me out?" he asked when they passed the dining room. "I said I was sorry."

"Ha. I'm not kicking you out. Not right now, anyway," she teased. "I know how much you love the outdoors, and it's a beautiful morning. We're going to eat breakfast on the back porch and breathe in the fresh air."

Together, they worked to safely lower the chair down the short stoop and onto the back porch overlooking the lake a short distance away. The sun, still low behind the house, cast bright strokes of orange and pink across the sky and reflected in the water.

While she hurried to the kitchen to collect the food, he poured her a glass of orange juice and filled another for himself. Calm mornings like these were Eleanor's favorite. A mild sixty-eight-degree temperature with a gentle breeze barely enough to jostle a leaf. Birds sang happily from every angle, and not one gnat or mosquito floated around. Another perfect, spring day in Virginia, and he couldn't help wondering, with slight irritation, if he would ever stop despising it all.

After circling the dock, a lone duck landed on the smooth water, reminding him of the time he'd spent there with his friends. The lake and the surrounding wooded acres were ideal for young boys who sought adventure.

They'd go swimming, search for new trees to climb, chase small creatures that crossed their path, play football or war with pretend guns, fish on the bank, or sail boats made from items around the house. Eleanor was always there, watching over them and bringing them snacks and fresh lemonade whenever their empty stomachs caused a detour.

Eleanor setting two full plates on the table and taking his hand for grace interrupted his flashback. She praised God for their food and again for Jackson's safe return. While His plan unfolded in the months ahead, she asked Him to help Jackson find patience and peace through the challenges.

"You really believe that, don't you?"

"Believe what, sweetie?" she asked before taking a bite of buttered rye toast.

"That God has a plan for me, and this all happened for reasons I have yet to discover."

"With all my heart. You're meant for greatness, Jackson. And that potential, we now know, was not meant to be fully achieved in the military."

"I wish I had your faith." Wouldn't it make his days and night so much easier?

"You'll find your purpose," she assured him with a pat on his arm. "And it will bring you more joy than you could ever imagine."

————

"Jackson, sweetie," Eleanor said softly, opening the back door. She'd taken the dirty dishes inside, leaving him on the porch. "Someone's here to see you."

"Wow. What'd you do?" Will asked, raking his eyes over Jackson as he stood over him. "Roll straight out of bed and into the wheelchair? You look like hell."

"And you have a way of making a guy feel special, asshole."

Slapping hands, Jackson yanked him down to his level for a hug. "It's so good to see you, man." Better than good, actually. His friend looked healthy and sounded like the same overzealous, life of the party he remembered.

He glanced behind him for Eleanor. He needed her direct connection to the heavens to give God more praise. Divine intervention was the only explanation he could imagine for how Will walked away from the explosion nearly unscathed.

"I heard you were transported to London," Will said, sitting opposite him at the table. "But they discharged me and shipped me home so fast, I couldn't get any details." He looked down at his hands and rubbed them together, the uncharacteristic motion making Jackson uneasy. "For the longest time, I had no idea if you survived."

"I almost didn't, or so they tell me. I'm here because of you and the doctors who didn't give up on me. Now, I need to find a way past the aftermath and get my legs back." Jackson looked down, daring his legs to do something and give him hope. They answered with more of the same.

"What do the doctors say? About your legs, I mean."

"They're not optimistic that I'll be able to walk again."

"They don't know you, do they?"

The person Will still considered him to be no longer existed, and he wondered how Will continued to smile through it.

Snatching up Jackson's glass, Will refilled it halfway with juice and drained it. "There's something that can help, right?"

"Physical therapy."

"That's it?"

"Last option."

"Well, in that case, you might as well get the best." Will grinned. "You remember my cousin, Avery, don't you?"

"Yeah. I haven't seen her since high school. Why?"

"She moved back into town late last year, and she's a physical therapist now." Will's guilty grin was suspicious.

"Is she really a therapist, or are you trying to set me up?"

"Of course, she's a therapist. Just because she's hot—runs in the family—doesn't mean I'm trying to set you up."

He narrowed his eyes at his oldest, and last remaining friend. Well, if he couldn't trust Will, who could he trust? "Text me her information, and I'll give her a call."

When Will's smile widened, showcasing all his perfect white teeth—it was shocking he hadn't had those punched out yet—he clarified. "To schedule an appointment."

After that, the conversation switched to life after discharge. Will lived with his parents while he searched for a job. Apparently, being a war hero didn't translate to real-world experience as Jackson feared. Will had trouble sleeping. The nightmares, he said, started about eleven weeks ago and were so vivid that he'd wake up screaming. Jackson could empathize and wasn't pleased to learn that his friend struggled with them, too. He'd hoped to be the only one. Will's parents were worried and sent him to multiple psychiatrists. It hadn't helped. The only good in his life was a woman.

"Wait a minute. Are you telling me that you're in an actual, committed relationship?" *The explosion must have altered Will's personality*, he considered jokingly.

"Yeah, and get this, we met before our last deployment. I haven't been with anyone else since," he added proudly.

"I'm speechless." Will had taken himself off the market—the female population was going to be devastated. "Well, she must be special."

"She's the only thing keeping me going. My shrink says I have PTSD." He rubbed his hands together, then scrubbed them over his short brown hair. "Throughout your career, you hear about it but never think it will happen to you. It's fuckin' hell."

He could relate and saw the all-too-familiar hopelessness flash over his friend's face. "What's her name?" he asked for a distraction.

"Sydney."

"I can't wait to meet her."

―――――

The following week mirrored the one before—breakfast, lunch, and dinner with Eleanor and spending time with Will on his good days. Jackson went fishing whenever the weather allowed, but he didn't enjoy it as much as he'd hoped. Alone in the tranquility, his mind wandered to dangerous places deep within his memories.

The replays of war and survival intensified when his surroundings were quiet, and he'd yet to find an off switch. Every day he spent at the estate felt like a long wait—for what he didn't know—which didn't help with the boredom.

With his motivation waning, he packed the supplies to head back to the house. Reaching over the side of the chair for the tackle box, an unexpected jolt shot through his left leg, sending him and the wheelchair flying backward.

He landed hard on his back but didn't notice. He was too busy fighting through the muscle spasms and sensations radiating from his hip down to his ankle. Dragging himself up, he repositioned his legs and massaged everywhere within reach.

Damn, he hoped this meant his legs were coming to life again. Electric shocks soon dulled to tiny needles—thousands of them repeatedly poking all over his leg while his muscles continued to spasm. Lying back on the grass, he concentrated on every needle prick. Although it was uncomfortable, it gave him what he wanted—hope.

Basking in his newfound appreciation for the pain, he didn't hear Eleanor approaching until she appeared beside him.

"Jackson, are you okay?" Her voice was frantic as she knelt beside him.

"Better than okay. My leg's dancing a jig."

"What? Is that a good thing?"

"Eleanor, my legs have been dead for months." He sat up again. "And now my muscles are moving."

Excitement shone in her eyes, warming his core. "That's wonderful, dear."

"It's only my left leg, but it's something."

She placed a hand on his cheek and beamed. "This calls for a celebration. Let's pop open a bottle of your father's expensive champagne." She tapped him on the leg.

"Oww."

"Oh, my gosh. I'm so sorry. Did I—"

"Gotcha." He grinned, accepting the scolding smack she delivered to his shoulder.

"Don't you mess with me." She stood with fists perched on her hips. "If you don't watch it, I will save all that bubbly for myself."

"You wouldn't dare."

Her booming laugh echoed over the lake. "So true. If I'm going to be naughty, I'd much rather have company."

Chapter Five

★ ★ ★

Jackson

D espite lying awake all night daring his legs to come to life again to no avail, hope still lingered. Plus, the sweet aroma of Eleanor's eggs and maple bacon oozing into his room under his door provided all the motivation needed to start the day.

"Good morning, sweetie," she greeted from the kitchen stove while she tossed the eggs and skillfully added her special seasonings at the same time. "Hungry?"

"Always when you're cooking."

With a satisfied grin, she scooped the pan's contents into a bright red serving dish and set it on his lap.

"We'll eat in the kitchen today," she declared, collecting the bacon and fresh fruit.

He led the way to the oak table that had been in the Vane family for nearly a century and waited for her to take a seat beside him.

While he filled his plate, he could feel her watching.

"What?" he asked without pausing.

"I like the new sparkle in your eyes. Is that from yesterday?"

"Yeah. I hope more happens today."

"Me, too, sweetheart."

Ignoring his empty stomach, he waited for Eleanor to scoop herself a portion of eggs, pick a few pieces of bacon, and fill two glasses with orange juice. Years of having his hand slapped as a child taught him to ignore everything until she'd said grace.

"So," she began after she'd asked for the blessing, "what's on the schedule today?"

"Nothing much." At the first bite, he nearly groaned with pleasure. She had a way of turning ordinary scrambled eggs into a culinary masterpiece. "Will is coming over this afternoon."

"Wonderful. What will you boys be getting into?"

"I'm not sure. Guess we'll go fishing."

"Make sure you invite him to stay for dinner," she insisted. "I miss the antics that ensue when you two are together."

"Alright. He won't be able to turn down one of your meals."

"I'll make something special tonight. Will he be bringing the angel that settled him down?"

"Not this time." He snatched another slice of bacon. "He said she had class and then work."

"Darn. I was hoping to…did you hear that?" Eleanor's eyes went wide as she sat frozen in her seat.

Her smile melted into panic, and when she jumped up from the table, quickly putting away dirty pots and dishes, he knew what that meant. Moving his full plate to his lap, he backed away from the table. "I'll eat in my room."

"Sweetie, please. You two need to talk."

"I have nothing to say to him. Plus, he doesn't want to see me, and I'm fine with that."

"Jackson, don't go," she pleaded to his back.

Disappointing her didn't feel great, but he had no interest in ruining his good mood.

"Mr. Grayson. It's so nice to see you," he heard her say with too much sweetness and rolled his eyes. His father didn't deserve her kindness.

"I'm in a hurry." The sharpness lining his father's tone had Jackson's wheelchair rolling to a stop in the hallway. "Is my white tuxedo back from the dry cleaners?"

"No. I'm sorry. I wasn't aware you needed it cleaned this soon."

"Damn it, Eleanor. If you'd get out of Jackson's ass long enough, you'd see the note I left on my—" A deep, choking cough interrupted the rude complaint.

"Is everything okay, Mr. Vane? You're looking pale."

"For fuck's sake, Eleanor. I'm fine."

Grayson's hard footsteps grew louder as he stalked out of the kitchen.

"Wear a different tux." Jackson pushed his chair toward his father and watched his expression switch from raging mad to amused in an instant. "And don't talk to her like that ever again."

"I will do as I goddamn please in my own house. The one I'm *graciously* allowing you to stay in right now."

He planted his feet and glared down his perfectly sculpted nose. What he wouldn't give to punch that smug face just one time.

"She does everything for you, more than she should, without protest. She doesn't deserve to be treated like a slave." He kept his cool, as his training taught him, but his hands ached from squeezing the wheels on his chair as though they were his father's neck.

"That's what I pay her to do. You're welcome to go elsewhere if you don't like it." With a quick pivot, he headed down the hall.

"Why do you do this?"

Grayson stopped outside his office, then came back to him, poised for battle. "Do what, son?"

"Don't call me that. You were never a father to me."

"Oh really?" Grayson smiled. "Without me, you wouldn't be here."

"What does that mean?"

"Your mother never wanted a child. I'm the only reason you were born." He took a step forward, enjoying Jackson's pained surprise. "What? You didn't know?"

No, he didn't. Of all the hateful things Grayson had said over the years, none had been as terrible as saying his beautiful mother hadn't wanted him either.

"I'm the one that convinced her not to go through with the abortion. I hired Eleanor to raise you. I made sure you were properly educated and provided for. Your mother did nothing but bring you into this world."

Jackson's head pounded hard and loud in his ears. Had the few good memories he had of his mother been figments of his imagination?

"If that's true, why do you hate me so much?" The words slipped out before he could stop them. Although he'd always been curious about the answer, he never uttered the question, refusing to grant his father any real or implied power.

Grayson stood a few feet away now, his cheeks flushed and eyes bright with either delight or anger. Jackson wasn't sure which, but he also didn't care. With the words floating out in the open, the time had come to put his curiosity to rest.

"Let me enlighten you about the person your mother truly was—who she became after you were born."

"That's not what I asked."

Ignoring him, Grayson continued. "She resented me for getting her pregnant and for the marks it left on her body. We fought constantly, but she was able to hide her hatred for me when we were out. You see, she enjoyed the privileges that came with being my wife, but her love came with conditions."

With his temper rising, Grayson paced, his hands balled into fists inside his pockets.

"We had a strong relationship in the beginning. She was stunning, passionate, and fearless. You got all that from her, by the way, and her blue eyes." He shook his head and stopped to address Jackson directly, old resentments simmering back to the surface.

"Do you know how difficult it was to look at you when all her affection and desire for me came to a fucking halt?" Lost in the memory, he didn't wait for a response. "Damn, she hated me and took great pleasure in making me suffer in true Jacqueline fashion. She poured herself and the love she once had for me into her volunteer work and her ludicrous affair."

A sinister grin curled his lips. "Oh, they were masterful at sneaking around, but I knew. They'd meet up while I was out of town or slip away during her supposed mission trips to God knows where."

He tossed his arm out to the side in frustration. "Hell, she eventually started talking about him in front of me, throwing the affair in my face. I tried to make her forget him, but nothing I did was good enough."

Another painful memory punched Grayson in the gut, and he stumbled backward. Grabbing the handrail on the staircase, he took several jagged breaths. "She left me for that asshole...all because of you."

"I was a child!"

"Irrelevant. It all started after you were born. But she came crawling back, as I knew she would. Sneaking around wasn't as exciting without my bank account." He smiled, knowing he'd won there. "We tried to make it work, but I couldn't get him touching her out of my mind, and she still hated me for what I did."

"What did you do?" Jackson managed, his mind reeling from the new insight.

"When she refused to have my child, I switched out her birth control pills."

He'd always known his father to be dreadful, egotistical, and demanding, but what he did went beyond contempt. No wonder his mother despised him and didn't want the child he forced upon her.

"After she returned to me, it wasn't long before she was diagnosed. Fuck!" He bent over as he yelled it, releasing the tension. Then, he stood, threw his head back, and dragged a hand down his face. "What am I doing? I don't have time for this shit."

Spinning, he headed up the stairs, stopping midway to glare down at Jackson. "Moral of the story here…you are who you are because of me. Don't you ever forget that."

"You're wrong. I am who I am despite you."

"Keep thinking that…son." He rolled his lips into a sarcastic grin before continuing up the stairs. The sound of his victory came in the form of the bedroom door slamming behind him.

Grayson *had* won, accomplishing precisely what he set out to do. He'd hurt Jackson again by stealing the few good memories of his mother he managed to collect. But the more he thought about it, not much had changed as a result. The strange conversation simply confirmed what he'd always suspected—his parents were absent in his life because they never loved him, and he barely knew or understood either of them.

Manipulation, affairs, revenge, secrets. The truth was much worse than he could have imagined, and he was the innocent victim caught in the crossfire. At least he'd discovered one thing to help put the whole ordeal behind him—no matter what he'd done, accomplished, or said, or how perfect he'd tried to be growing up, it wouldn't have been enough.

In a way, Grayson had given him a gift and set him free from all the anger and hurt he'd harbored through the years. As far as he was concerned, both his parents were dead—ghosts of a past he'd rather forget. The only memories he wanted to remember were with the people who loved and supported him when his own parents wouldn't.

Speaking of his true family, he spun the chair around to check on Eleanor. Her forgiving heart would undoubtedly be broken over the cruel things Grayson so effortlessly said. Blood or not, he was her child. She'd given him a beautiful childhood and made him into the man he was—not Grayson.

And if his father ever again spoke to her the way he did that morning, he wouldn't hold back again. He'd be ready for the next fighting round. All Grayson had to do was step into the ring.

———

"Is that roast beef I smell?" Will asked, entering the kitchen and breathing deep. He'd let himself in the side door, as he would when he came over in high school.

"What else would it be? It's your favorite, isn't it?" Eleanor took her hand.

Setting down the cooler he'd brought, he lowered to one knee. "Eleanor, will you marry me?"

"Ha! If I was thirty years younger, I'd take you up on that offer." After accepting his hug, she swatted his rear with her towel on the way out of the kitchen to continue her chores.

Jackson, who'd watched the entire scene from the kitchen table, shook his head. "You haven't changed a bit."

"I love that woman with all my soul."

Smiling, Jackson spun the wheelchair toward the door. "Get in line."

He grabbed the box of worms Eleanor picked up for them and motioned for Will to follow. After collecting the cooler, fishing rods, a chair for Will, and the bag of snacks she insisted on packing, the friends headed to the lake. They set up on the wide dock and cast their lines before Will broke the silence.

"I can tell something's bothering you. Out with it." He removed a beer from the cooler and handed it to Jackson before grabbing one for himself.

Leaning the rod on the wheel, Jackson twisted off the cap and took a long pull. The last time he'd had a beer was with Billy and Josh before being deployed for the third and final time. Will was busy, and now he knew Sydney had been the reason he ditched them that night.

The three friends stayed out until dawn, crashed at Billy's house, then left for the base later that afternoon. It wasn't the smartest thing they'd ever done, but it wasn't the worst, either. Of course, Will made fun of their red eyes and hangovers for days.

"Jackson."

"Sorry. I was thinking about Billy and Josh. The last time I had one of these was with them." He held up the bottle before grabbing his fishing rod.

"As I recall, you had more than one."

"Like you'd let me forget."

"Never." With a mischievous smile, he raised the bottle to his lips and drained it. "So, what's got you on edge today?"

"Saw the man that calls himself my father this morning."

"Shit." Will removed another beer from the cooler, opened it, and drank. "What did he do?"

"Nothing, except throw a few new punches. Apparently, my mother almost had an abortion." He nodded when Will's eyes darted to him. "He claims he stopped her and that I owe him."

"Fuck him."

"Agreed. He took credit for raising me and said Mom did nothing except cook up ways to get back at him. Did you know she had an affair?"

Will puffed and shook his head in disbelief. Jackson had yet to fully process it either. "Wow. Yet another twist in the Vane saga. Although not entirely shocking, but I don't recall your mother doing *nothing*. She wasn't here much, but she was nice to you, at least when I was around."

"Yeah, but he claims she knew how to turn it on when it would benefit her. I don't know how much to believe. He showed up ready to fight anyone who got in the way."

"Not Eleanor?" Will's body shifted into battle mode, his inner armor forming in Eleanor's defense, and Jackson loved him for it.

"Started with her."

"Why does he act like that? I've never understood his motives."

"Who knows?" Gazing into the full bottle in his hands, he desperately wanted to gulp it down, get sloppy drunk, and forget, but he just didn't have the energy. "And I don't care. I've got enough to deal with right now."

"I feel ya." Will emptied his bottle and set it aside. "I don't think I've slept more than an hour since I got back."

"It takes a toll, doesn't it?"

"I'm surprised Sydney is still around. I'm too tired to do anything. Then, the visions…" He looked at Jackson, someone he knew would understand without further explanation. "And I have these outbursts now that I can't control. Sometimes, I don't know it's happening until it's over."

"What kind of outbursts?"

"You name it. It doesn't take much to set me off, and I cry all the fucking time." He rolled his eyes.

Twisting in his seat, Jackson faced him squarely. "You?"

"I know. I'm not proud of it."

"I don't think I've ever seen you cry." That was concerning. Will was the happiest person Jackson had ever known, and his smile and loud belly laugh were always at the ready, no matter the circumstances.

"Usually happens after I come out of a rage fest and realize my outbursts have hurt someone." He reached for another beer and looked out over the lake.

That day, the water's smooth surface reflected the bright white clouds of the sky above, and he knew what was on Will's mind. He had the same thoughts every day he came to the dock. For his emotions to take on the same qualities as the water—peaceful, calm, predictable.

"What's a rage fest?" he asked to break into Will's thoughts. He'd gone silent, and Jackson knew from experience that never ended well.

"My chaotic cycle of yelling, punching, or breaking things, and storming away."

His gaze shifted to the raw knuckles on Will's hand clutching the beer bottle.

"Don't worry," he answered before Jackson could ask. "I haven't hit anyone."

"I didn't think you would."

"Good. Even during fits of rage, I still have boundaries. Although, I don't think Sydney shares your confidence in me. I'm afraid she won't be able to take much more."

"I'm sure she's stronger than you think, and if she hasn't left already, she's not going anywhere."

"I hope you're right. I knew she was different the second I saw her, and I couldn't do any of this without her." Suddenly fidgety, he ran shaky fingers through his hair, then chugged his beer. "She's amazing."

"She better be." He smiled and waited for Will's questioning gaze to find him. "You're the most amazing person I know, besides Eleanor, of course."

"Of course."

"And you deserve an equally amazing woman that loves you back."

"Thanks, man. That means more than you know."

"I have some idea." He didn't like the familiar turmoil he noticed flash in Will's eyes before he hid behind sunglasses. And he knew exactly how to distract him from it. "Plus, you, of all people, should know I don't waste time with douchebags."

"Whatever." With that indignant exclamation, the hard line between Will's eyebrows and the veins in his neck loosened. Leaning back in his chair, he reeled in his line and cast it out again, causing a ripple on the water's surface. "What about that guy you adopted in the eighth grade?"

"Who? Tanner?"

"Yeah. He was a total douchebag."

"No, he wasn't." He laughed when Will tilted his head and glared at him over the dark aviator glasses.

"He picked a fight with Josh. The only one of us that would save a fly from drowning in this fucking lake."

"Okay. I'll give you that one. It was the final straw, but I felt sorry for him before that. He had a tough life, and he needed a friend."

"He needed a lot more than a friend. You were too busy trying to save him to notice. He was like an orphaned puppy to you."

"I wonder where he is now."

"Probably in jail," Will joked and finished the beer as his rod jerked, surprising them both.

The reel spun fast, but he snagged it before the rod shot into the lake. Turning the reel with the beer pinched between his legs, he leaned back to pull the fish closer. Over and over, he reeled and yanked with little progress.

"What kind of fish do you have in here? Fuckin' tuna?" Will complained.

Jackson could only laugh as his friend struggled with the line. "You act like you've never fished before, and I know that's not true."

"Shut up! The bastard weighs more than I do."

"I can't wait to see this one." He tossed the worm he'd picked from the box into the water. "Keep it up. I'm enjoying the show."

Will narrowed his eyes at him as determination reshaped his expression. The next yank of the rod must have been too hard, and the line snapped. The motion threw Will backward, he and his chair landing on the unforgiving wood dock with a thump.

The impact knocked the air out of his lungs, and he didn't notice Jackson's uncontrollable laughter until he stopped coughing. He pretended to be offended at first, but it didn't last. The disapproving glare merged into deep belly laughs, matching Jackson's.

"I can't remember the last time I laughed like—"

Will shot up and felt around the top of his head as he swiveled in a frantic search. "Where are my sunglasses? Do you see them?" he asked.

Jackson couldn't wrangle in his amusement long enough to answer. Another fit of laughter took over as he pointed at the glasses, floating on the water. Will jumped to his feet, ran to the edge of the dock, and dropped to his stomach to reach over the side. His finger grazed the gold rim before they sank to the bottom.

"What are you doing?" he asked when Will sat back on his heels with a scowl. "I've never seen you shy away from a challenge."

"You're right!" Standing, Will kicked off his flip-flops, and yanked off his shirt and shorts. Puffing out his chest, he grabbed the waistband of his boxers with a toothy grin.

Jackson pointed at him, all amusement gone. "Don't even think about it."

"Consider this payback for all those times you made me run or do more push-ups than the others." He slowly inched the boxers down his hips until Jackson held up his hands.

"Wait. Let's talk about this. I was your squad leader, and you snuck away in the middle of a scouting mission. You nearly blew our cover."

"I was hungry."

"We were all hungry, jackass." He could laugh about it now, but at the time, he wanted to strangle his friend and do more than give him a few more miles to run when they got back to safety.

"Alright. I kind of deserved it," he retreated and left the boxers in place. Sprinting past Jackson, he jumped off the dock, clutched his knees to his chest, and landed in the water with a loud splash. He rose to the surface soon after and took a long breath before disappearing under the water again.

Seconds collected into minutes, and concern started to grow heavy in Jackson's gut. He pushed to the edge of his seat to see more area around the dock and searched for his friend, but the water was too dark and dense.

A hand, holding sunglasses, shot out of the water off to the side, and the rest of Will soon followed.

"Victory is mine." Throwing his head back to float on the cool water, he slid the glasses into place.

"Nice to see your water survival training finally being put to good use."

"I knew it would come in handy one day. Nowhere to swim in the desert."

"See that tuna while you were down there?"

"Damn it. No, but I'm going to catch that fucker." A sly grin pulled at Will's cheeks, but the rest of him remained still on the water's surface.

"Maybe next time."

"Yeah." He sighed. "Next time."

Chapter Six

★ ★ ★

Jackson

If he never got used to the incessant boredom that consumed his days as a civilian, it would be too soon. In the military, and when his legs worked, he was constantly stimulated. Now, he could do nothing except sit around all day, deteriorating like rotting fruit.

He wanted to be excited about his physical therapy appointment later, but the tingling, spasms, and movement hadn't lingered in his leg, and neither had his positivity.

Skipping it had crossed his mind multiple times while the minutes dragged by, but he'd have to answer to Dr. Evans, and he literally had nothing else to do. Having no other choice only amplified his grumbling. He let out his displeasure multiple times on the way there, once as Eleanor helped him transfer from the SUV to the wheelchair and another after he checked in with the receptionist. But since no one heard that last one, it didn't count.

While he sat in an open area in the lobby, he surveyed his surroundings to pass the time. Photos of the office's physical therapists and doctors hung on the wall to his right, but he didn't recognize Avery among them. He'd known her since they were kids yet remembered very little about her—other than she seemed to be persistently underfoot. At parties, track meets, football games, Will's house…she was always there.

Of course, Will never protested. He thought of her more like a sister than a cousin—that huge, accepting heart of his never resting. Always positive. Always showing his love and appreciation for others.

Noticing he'd been slipping in those areas, he promised to be better. Promised to show his friends still on this side of the dirt, and especially Eleanor how much he appreciated them. As soon as he felt better, he'd work on getting back to his old self and following Will's lead.

————

Avery

Avery saw him first, sitting by the front window in the lobby, and nearly tripped over her feet. Jackson Vane had lived rent-free in her heart since her seventh birthday party, and no other man had lived up to him ever since. Without knowing it, he had shaped her opinion of what a man should be, and through the years, she had many failed relationships because of it. Dreams etched in stone weren't easily broken and seeing him again only confirmed what she already knew.

She was still hopelessly in love with him.

Running her fingers through her wavy brown hair, she wished she'd done more with it that morning. A pretty clip. Some styling mousse to calm the flyaways. Hell, she'd have sprinkled in some glitter if she had some. Her gorgeous destiny didn't glide through the front door every day, and she planned to make the most of this opportunity. Bad hair day or not.

In a desperate attempt to keep her heart from wiggling its giddy self into her throat, she took a few deep breaths and made her way to him.

"Hi, Jackson. I can't believe you're here. We haven't seen each other in what? Seven, eight years?" She knew exactly how many years, days, and hours it had been—too many.

"Avery? Wow. You're not a—sorry." He held out his hand, and she took it. "We were teenagers, I believe. Was that really eight years ago?"

"Yeah. A little hard to accept." She reluctantly released his hand and assumed a stance that she hoped made her appear confident. "You look great."

"You lie, but I appreciate it nonetheless."

The awkward small talk continued along the way to an evaluation room. Once inside, she rolled a stool closer to his wheelchair.

"So," she began, dropping the notepad in her lap. The long list of things she wanted to say had gathered into organized piles as she prepared for his appointment. Now, sitting across from him, those Caribbean blue eyes filled her mind with unspeakable things, shuffling her professional to-do list like confetti in a windstorm. "I, uh, like to take time when I start a new patient to get to know them. We have somewhat of an advantage, but we were kids then. Why don't you tell me about yourself and what brought you here?"

His gaze dropped to his hands as he rubbed them together, and she wished to take back the insensitive question. She knew about Will's struggles and would have considered Jackson's had she not been so selfish and flustered. The misery in his eyes said it all.

"Jackson, I'm sorry. We don't have to get into the details, just anything you think would add to your treatment."

She placed a hand on his to comfort him, but his flinch flung an arrow through her heart. The Jackson she remembered was affectionate, joyful, confident, and never fearful. She wanted to make it better for him. To say something profound to take his apprehension and anxiety away. Yet, the words wouldn't form.

"Thank you," he said and took a deep breath. "I was discharged a couple of weeks ago after spending about four months in surgery and recovery at a London hospital. I'm sure Will has told you what happened, and I assume you have my medical information from Dr. Evans."

"Yes, I read your chart, and the doctors' notes. What happened to you breaks my heart."

Rubbing at his temple, he closed his eyes, and she silently kicked herself for adding another layer of stress.

"If you're ready, I'd like to go over the initial schedule for your program," she said to change the subject. "Then, we can get started."

Over the next several minutes, she reviewed the chart she'd meticulously prepared the week prior. After this first session, he would have two weekly appointments and a home exercise routine. Based on his progress after a month, she'd amend it as needed.

The physical evaluation began once he was settled on an examination table adjacent to the fitness room. She tested his flexibility and posture, joint and muscle movement by rotating his ankles, legs, back, and hips. He was quiet while she worked on his right side, his back to her, only speaking when she prompted him with a question.

"Everything okay?" she asked, his earlier reaction to her touch on his mind. With his nod, she continued the exercises. "Let me know if you need a break."

To ease the tension, she talked about whatever popped into her thoughts. It was an excruciating exercise in mind control, but she had to do something to distract herself from the feel of his body under her palms. He wasn't as muscular as she remembered seeing in photos Will showed her, but the Greek God shape that always made her stutter was still there.

She'd often fantasized about touching those muscles and pressing her body against his. That day, the fantasy replayed in high definition, and she had to keep reminding herself of their professional arrangement. He was her patient, and she had a job to do. But damn, he made one hell of a distraction.

"Left side now," she instructed. "Like before, tell me if you feel any pain or need me to stop."

He rolled to face her and adjusted his legs. Working up from his ankle to his thigh, she started with testing his range of motion. When she pressed on his back and hip, he jerked, and his leg slipped out of her hands. He buried his face in the pillow and pounded his fist on the table.

Backing away to give him space, she waited and watched. He rocked and growled through whatever had consumed him like a rabid fire, and it took everything in her not to go to him. Not to wrap him in her arms and do whatever she could to take away the pain.

"I'll be right back."

When she returned minutes later, Jackson had sat up to rub his leg. She stepped closer, and his eyes, bright and energized, fell on her. He flashed her the smile she'd missed and always hoped would one day be accompanied by his love.

"Avery, I can move my leg."

Rushing to the table, she handed him the water bottle she grabbed while away and took over massaging. "That's wonderful. Has this happened before?"

"Once, and I almost broke my neck when it knocked me out of the wheelchair." He laughed. "I want to try to stand. Will you help me?"

Breathless from the intimacy in his voice, she nodded and waited for him to swing his legs over the side of the table. His hands steady on her shoulders, she pulled him forward until he could balance upright on both feet.

"Well?" She raised her gaze to find his bright with hope. "How does it feel?"

"Amazing."

He held on for a few more seconds before his knee gave out. Slapping his left hand on the table, his right arm fell over her shoulder to keep from falling. His breath warmed her cheek as he steadied himself, sending a chill over her skin.

"I've got you." She helped him back onto the table and waited for him to settle. "By the way, I asked another therapist to take my next appointment."

He lifted his head, and between labored breaths, asked, "Why?"

"You were hurting, and I didn't know how long it would last." She shrugged and resumed massaging his legs. "I couldn't leave you like that. Now that you're feeling better, we can continue—if you feel up to it, of course. I don't want to push you."

He considered the idea for a beat. "I can keep going, but I need to let Eleanor know. Would you mind grabbing my phone?"

For the next hour, she continued stretching, testing, and exercising his legs. He could raise his left foot and leg a few inches by the end, uplifting his mood. It warmed her heart to see him smiling and wiggling his toes while talking about his excitement for future therapy sessions.

Beautiful moments like these were the reason she chose this profession, but sharing in Jackson's triumph meant far more than another accomplishment at work. It meant she was no longer a faceless spectator, watching his life from the sidelines. She'd played a part in bringing that sparkle back to his eyes and giving him hope.

For as long as she could remember, she'd longed for the chance to be more to him than just his best friend's cousin. To share life's ups and downs alongside him. To be truly seen and loved by him. Maybe that chance had come.

When Eleanor arrived, Avery walked beside his wheelchair to the lobby.

"Thank you," he said, stopping at the door. "I know I wasn't the best patient today."

"You weren't that bad." She winked to punctuate the playful jab.

"I can't promise I'll be better next time, but I'm ready to work."

"Good. Keep up your home routine, and you'll start to feel stronger soon. You're unstoppable. Never forget that."

As she watched him roll to Eleanor's vehicle and drag himself into the passenger seat, she thought about fate and the past twenty years. Seeing him again dug up and exposed feelings she hadn't buried as deep as she intended when she tucked them away after college. He'd always possessed a special place in her heart, and she'd accepted that she would always love him. But with no other choice with him so far away, she moved on and let go of her dreams. At least, she thought she had.

After touching him and seeing his eyes light up and focus on her, those dreams crawled back to the surface, latched on with titanium claws, and burrowed in for the long haul. She couldn't have stopped it. Not when everything she'd ever wanted was finally within reach.

———

Jackson

"This calls for a celebration," Eleanor announced after he told her about the appointment. "I picked up some steaks at the market earlier. We can grill out, turn up the music, and have a good time. Why don't you invite Will to join us?"

"Great idea."

Marveling at his toes wiggling inside his shoe, he texted Will. He added a suggestion to bring Sydney, shaking his head as he typed it. It would take a while to get used to that one.

Entering through the gate of the Vane residence, a red convertible came into view. Eleanor parked behind it.

"Shit," was all Jackson could say as Grayson unfolded his tall, lean body from the driver's side of the little sportscar. He leaned against the door and crossed his arms.

Eleanor parked behind it and turned to him. "I didn't know he was coming, or I would have warned you."

"Not your responsibility, Eleanor. This is his house, and we've said all there is to say." He patted her arm. "Don't worry."

"Can't help it with you two. I'll get the chair."

While she helped him into the wheelchair, his father never moved from his spot to greet them or offer help. Not that Jackson would have accepted it, but Eleanor would be disappointed.

"Mr. Vane, Jackson had his first physical therapy session today, and he's made terrific progress already. Isn't that great?"

Based on Grayson's expressionless features, her efforts to mend their fractured relationship fell on deaf ears. His eyes stayed on Jackson, daring him to say something, but he had no idea who he so recklessly challenged, or how far Jackson would go to ensure another heated argument didn't happen in front of Eleanor. When Grayson altered his stance and shifted his annoyed gaze to Eleanor, Jackson considered it a win.

"I'm planning a party here this weekend. Make sure the house is spotless," he barked. "I left instructions for dinner and drinks on my desk, and I'll need my dark gray suit dry cleaned."

"Yes, sir," Eleanor said amicably, making Jackson's blood boil.

Opening the car door, Grayson paused with one foot on the floorboard. "Oh, and make sure you stay out of sight," he instructed Jackson over his shoulder before dropping into the seat. With a swift touch of the gas, he circled the roundabout and sped down the driveway.

"Well, that was fun," he joked. "Recognize the flavor of the week in the passenger seat?"

Irked, Eleanor puffed out a breath and took hold of the wheelchair handles.

"Let me know what I can do to help get ready for the…dinner party." He motioned quotation marks and enunciated *dinner party* in an elegant British accent he picked up from Dr. Evans, making Eleanor laugh. "There's my girl," he said, reaching back for her hand to kiss the top.

While Eleanor prepared the steaks, Jackson tried calling Will since he hadn't responded to his earlier text messages. After a trying, yet stimulating day, he looked forward to the impromptu get together and hopefully, meeting Sydney.

But something didn't feel right when Will didn't answer. He dialed again.

"Jackson? Is that you?" a female voice answered.

"Yes. Who is this?"

"Oh, my God. Jackson…"

Her choking sobs echoed through the phone, and his stomach rolled with fear.

"Avery, is that you? What is it? What's wrong?"

Eleanor heard his raised, frantic voice and rushed to his side.

"Tell me. Where's Will?" Panic rushed over him. "Avery."

"He's…"

"He's what?"

No answer.

"Avery!"

"How is this happening?" She sucked in a shaky breath, but it burst out of her throat with more sobs.

"What's happened?"

"Oh, my God. Jackson, he's gone."

"Gone? Where?"

"He's dead."

Avery's uncontrollable cries boomed through the phone. Eleanor's voice filled his other ear with questions, but he couldn't comprehend any of it. He didn't feel Eleanor removing the phone from his rigid hand or his soul being ripped from his body.

Chapter Seven

✯ ✯ ✯

Jackson

Time passed by in a blur. While Jackson spent each day in the dark, the sun rose and fell without his acknowledgment or care. He lay curled against the assault of his sorrow, leaving the curtains drawn. Lamps and overhead lights never came on. Pillows often covered his pounding head. Doing anything beyond merely existing felt like a chore, and his last thread of motivation to remain above ground strained and frayed in response to the pressure.

"Jackson, sweetie." Eleanor opened the door, allowing light from the windows flanking the long hallway outside his bedroom to stream in. The pale sunlight landed on him in bed and burned his eyes. Reflex had him burying his face, but he hoped it also sent the usual message.

Not today.

"We need to leave for the funeral soon."

Will's funeral. Damn.

Ignoring him, she began searching through his closet. Hangers scraped against the metal bar with angry screeches, until she stormed out without a word.

Good, Jackson thought. Maybe she'd leave him be. After all, he didn't know how to drag himself out of bed, much less face Will's parents—two people he adored almost as much as Eleanor. Caroline and Jonathan Mason were surrogate parents to him, as were Billy's parents, Harrison and Sophia. How could he look at any of them that day or any day? His heart was riddled with holes. Seeing their agony would sever the last few pieces of himself still clinging together through the grief.

"It's a good thing you and your father are about the same size," she said, reentering the room. "These will have to do."

A soft thud of something landing on the vinyl seat of the wheelchair sounded before her determined footsteps. She soon sat on the bed beside him.

"Jackson, I know this is hard, but you need to go." She ran the back of her hand over his cheek. "They want you to say a few words, remember?"

He turned his eyes, already blurry with unshed tears, on her, and held her hand to his chest.

"I know, sweetheart." Leaning down, she kissed his forehead. "I know."

———

It took some coaxing, but Eleanor got him out of bed and dressed. He sat motionless while she brushed his hair and pushed him to the driveway. He said nothing on the way to the funeral home or when ushers escorted them to the front of the room to Will's family.

At the sight of him, Will's mother rose to greet him, but since there were no words to make their hearts hurt any less, their arms and sobs said it all.

"He loved you so much," she finally said, pulling back and resting her hands on his shoulders. Her mouth opened like she wanted to say more, but emotion caught in her throat. Cupping her hand over her mouth, she hurried back to her seat, leaving Jackson alone in the aisle.

This was all too much—too impossible to go on alone. His head dropped into his hands, and he didn't notice Eleanor had pulled the chair into his spot in the aisle until she rested a hand on his leg.

When the ceremony began, he couldn't focus. His mind kept jumping from one memory to the next. Memories with Will, Billy, and Josh when they were kids and traveling around the world. Basic training, his mother, Eleanor, and war. The destructive chaos pounded against his skull.

Sinking fast, he longed to scream how unfair it was. How could all three of his closest friends be gone? Why was he still alive when he felt so dead inside?

"Sweetie, it's time." Eleanor stood and pushed him to the front of the room without waiting for a response.

With Will's lifeless body in the casket behind him, he had no choice but to accept reality. No more questioning or wondering. No escaping it. Sweat began to bead on his forehead as a headache raged, nausea rolled, and an all too familiar ache pounded against his ribcage. Rocking in his seat, he pressed the base of his palm to the concentrated source of the throbbing and stared blankly ahead.

"Will was more than a friend. He was my brother." Closing his eyes, he took a deep breath. "He always had my back both in life and in service, and he'd do the same for anyone else. You could always count on him to be there."

Tears stung his eyes at the thought of never feeling that security again.

"I know he's still here with us. At least, I hope he is." He swallowed hard. "There are no adequate words to describe how much his friendship meant to me. So much love poured out of that huge heart of his." He wiped at the tears now flowing freely and darkening his suit.

"Honoring that, maybe I could tell you what I loved most about Will. I love how he's been my best friend since the first day of kindergarten. I love our many adventures and how he was always up for anything. All any of us had to do was ask. I love that we had the same dream and pursued it together. I love how he always followed his heart and did the right thing, no matter the consequences. I love how he supported the people he cared about and stood by them, even when we didn't deserve it. I love the scar he gave me when we were twelve so I can think of him whenever I look in the mirror. I love that he never lost his smile, not even when taking a beating from the drill sergeant or after learning that smile was the reason for the punishment. I love how he always knew what to say in every situation, and I love all the unforgettable memories I have because of him."

By then, his voice was barely more than a whisper.

"Caroline and Jon, thank you for raising such an amazing person. All our lives are better having had him in it. Will's memory will live on through us." He paused and looked up. "Will, I'll never forget you, buddy. I love you."

Ready to escape the sea of sorrow staring back at him, he headed toward his spot in the audience, stopping at the end of the aisle next to Caroline and Jonathan. He accepted a hug from them both and noticed Avery sitting in the same row, her face red from crying.

She raised her gaze to him, the emptiness he felt mirrored in her eyes. At first, he couldn't look away. She reminded him so much of Will, both in appearance and personality, and his heart was drawn to her. Then, just as easily as those qualities comforted, they gripped him by the throat and tore him in two.

———

Time continued to be inconsequential in his new reality, but that week, he noticed the world, moving on without him, had shifted. Eleanor stopped by his room less often than usual, and when she brought him food, she didn't linger. She'd been hustling around the house, running the vacuum, rummaging through cabinets, and cooking more than usual.

By dusk on Friday, he knew why. Eleanor's bustling sounds had evolved into rowdy conversations over upbeat music. Metal utensils clanking against fine china and ice cubes dropping into crystal glasses rang like bells through the house. Another legendary Grayson Vane dinner party.

His father's demand to stay out of sight on such an occasion came to mind, and he had a sudden urge to behave like a disobedient teenager. Part of him wanted to waltz into the room in nothing but his boxers and help himself to a drink or ten. He could drown the pain in a vintage bottle of Scotch and forget for a few drunken hours.

Wouldn't Grayson be appalled? And wouldn't it be a sight to see him fumble to explain the embarrassment that was his son? But as with everything else, he couldn't muster the energy to go through with it. He'd already canceled all physical therapy appointments, and he couldn't remember the last time he got out of bed to do anything other than to take care of normal bodily functions. Even that was exhausting.

"Jackson," he heard someone call from outside of the door. "It's Avery. Can I come in?" She didn't wait for an answer and pushed open the door. "Eleanor said I would find you here."

He scrubbed a hand over his face before rolling over. The hallway light shining into the room acted like a spotlight, shining on his vulnerabilities, and aggravating his weary eyes. Squinting against it, he held up his hand to block the source.

At first, he could see only her silhouette in the doorway. She was wearing a long, dark dress that framed her shapely figure and held a sparkling glass in each hand. As his eyes adjusted, he noticed the dress had a wide slit that exposed her left leg from the top of her thigh to her shoes. She wore her hair down and wavy this time, the right side pinned up with a silver clip.

"I could use some company if you're up for it," she said, filling the silence. "Why are you here and not enjoying the party?"

He dragged himself up to lean against the headboard. "I wasn't invited, nor would I attend."

"What's the matter? Stuffy dinner parties not your style? Don't answer. I already know." Crossing the room, she motioned toward the bed. "May I?"

She sat on the edge when he nodded, then handed him the extra drink. He took it but didn't sip.

"How are you?" she asked, nervous fingers twisting the ring on her left thumb.

"Why are you here, Avery?"

"At the party or knocking on your door?"

"Both."

His sharp tone had her taking a moment to think about her next words, her anxious eyes darting to her hands, to him, and back again. "I wanted to see you. Eleanor said that you could use a friend, and frankly, so could I. When a colleague asked if I wanted to come with him tonight, not as a date or—"

"What about Will?"

"What about him?"

"Everyone is going about their life like nothing happened while I'm drowning in grief." Part of him felt guilty for lashing out at her, but exhaustion had trumped patience. "He's been gone only…what? A couple of weeks?"

"Jackson, it's been *five* weeks, and no one has forgotten what happened. Especially me. I was there, remember? Sydney and I were the ones who found him."

She stood and faced him, strong and fearless, and he admired her for it.

"Avery, I'm sorry." He held out a hand, but she stared down at him, her arms crossed—pissed at him for the inconsiderate attack, as he deserved. "Please."

Conceding, she slid her free hand into his and slumped onto the bed again. "I'm tired, Jackson," she said with a long sigh. "I'm tired of being sad all the time and constantly thinking about what we lost. I loved him, too." Although her body shuddered, her voice remained steady. "He was like a brother to me, but he took his own life, Jackson. He left *us*."

"What?" His head spun out of control. How could Will give up? He'd assumed Will had been fighting and would forever push back against what was pulling him under. That something else happened to yank him away from them.

"You didn't know."

"No." He fought the urge to lash out again. "Or I don't remember. It's all a blur."

"Oh, Jackson." She scooted closer, and in meeting his gaze, her eyes softened.

"How could he do it?"

"You lived through that hell with him. You tell me."

His hands tunneled through his hair and clutched handfuls as he rocked. "I can't do this. I can't do this without him."

"Yes, you can." Lacing her fingers together, she cupped the back of his neck and brought him closer. She smelled of vanilla and lavender, comfort and tranquility. "You can do anything, Jackson. It's who you are."

His head shook in disagreement. "It feels like I'm next, and I don't know how to stop it. I'm not sure I want to."

"Think of Josh and Billy. They'd want you here, living life to the fullest. So would Will."

"How?" He jerked up and let his heavy arms drop into his lap. "Show me how to do that because I can't see it."

"I don't know, but I'll help you." When he trembled, she drew him close, cradling him as she soothed. "We'll figure it out together."

His forehead fell to her shoulder, weakened from treading an ocean of emotions for too long. It constantly ebbed, flowed, and pulled him under with no end in sight. He couldn't remember what it felt like to not hurt. To not be angry, lost, and in absolute misery, physically and emotionally.

Circling his arms around her waist, he let it go for the first time since the incident. Sinking into her embrace, he felt the tension that had compounded over the past five weeks finally leave his body.

———

Avery

Jackson's breathing stabilized into a restful pattern after only ten minutes. He desperately needed to sleep, but she wouldn't be able to hold up his heavy body for much longer. For support, she shifted to rest her back against the headboard, and his head slid into her lap.

She froze, waiting to see if he reacted to the commotion, but his breathing only deepened. To think about anything other than being in his bed, she brushed away the hair that had fallen into his face and let her mind wander.

She still remembered the very first time he touched her. She was seven years old and had tripped over a rock, trying to keep up with him and Will in the backyard. Her dirty knees dripped with blood through the new hole in her favorite leggings. While Will went inside to retrieve his mother for help, Jackson took off his shirt to press the soft fabric against the wounds. He hadn't told her to stop crying. He hadn't looked at her like she was a stupid girl as the boys in her class usually did. The gentle softness in his voice and blue eyes melted her young heart, she was forever changed.

Relaxing into her memories, she leaned back. Her love and appreciation for Jackson only soared through middle and high school. Rarely did he acknowledge her, but he was kind and gorgeous and could make her heart flutter over the simplest things. Like when he—

Her heart took off when an urgent rhythm of footsteps sounded down the hall. She didn't care who saw them in bed together, but she preferred those footsteps, walking with intention, to not belong to Jackson's father.

"Avery?" Eleanor whispered, shock evident in her voice. "I was coming to check on Jackson, but I can see he's in good hands." She moved closer to keep from waking him.

"Eleanor, I'm worried. He had no idea how long it's been since Will's funeral or how he died."

"I'm not surprised." Eleanor took Avery's hand and looked down at Jackson. "He hardly eats, doesn't sleep, and nothing I say or do works. I'm not even sure he hears me half the time. It pains me to see him hurting this way."

"Me too. Before he fell asleep, he was overwhelmed with emotion."

"He's been in a deep depression and won't talk about it. He needs to let it out so some good can come in. Maybe he will with you."

"I hope so. If it's okay with you, I'm going to stay. I'm afraid if I move, he'll wake up."

"That's sweet of you, dear." Eleanor patted Avery's hand before releasing it. "Of course, you can stay. This sleep will do him a world of good. Can I get you anything?"

"No, thank you, but would you mind telling Bradley Morgan that I won't need a ride home tonight?" The message was a moot point since they weren't on a date. Still, she didn't want to leave any perceived obligation open-ended. "If he hasn't already left."

"Sure. I'd be happy to." Eleanor rose. "You got here just in time, Avery girl."

———

After the last of the party guests departed, the house grew eerily quiet, except for the various creaks, moans, and pops the old house made in the night. It wasn't enough to keep Avery from dozing, later awakening to an intense wash of sunlight on her face and two numb legs.

Shielding her eyes, she looked down at Jackson. He still slept in her lap, content and tranquil with his arms wrapped around her.

I did that, she thought proudly, then winced. If she didn't return the blood to her lower half soon...

With a slight shift of her hips, she attempted to bring the feeling back to her legs without disturbing Jackson, but she was unsuccessful on all attempts.

The motion had him lifting his head and pushing up to lean against the headboard beside her. He looked over his shoulder, and the disjointed, puzzled expression on his face had her biting back a smile.

"Good morning, sleepyhead."

"Did I...did you..." He ran his fingers through his hair—the reason for his unexpected bed companion not registering.

"Yes. You fell asleep while we were talking last night. You must have found me a real bore," she joked, but his sleepy eyes, nearly translucent in the morning sun, made her want to do something other than laugh.

"Avery, I—"

"It's okay. You seemed to need the rest, and I didn't want to interrupt. But I believe congratulations are in order."

"For what?"

"You slept all night." She pointed both thumbs at herself and winked. "Lucky charm."

He chuckled, and it was music to her ears.

"I can't remember the last time I slept for over an hour. Thank you."

She nudged his shoulder. "No problem."

"Does Eleanor know you're here?"

"Yep, she came to check on you last night."

"Oh." With a weighted sigh, his gaze shifted to his hands.

"Don't worry. All your secrets are safe."

They sat in awkward silence until Jackson spoke.

"I need to know how you did it. How did you move on and forget how much it hurts?"

His eyes begged her to save him, and she was lost again.

Swallowing hard, he pushed back emotions he didn't want to feel. "I don't know how long I can live like this."

She turned to face him and slid a hand under his, bringing it to her chest. He didn't flinch or move away, warming her to the core.

"I haven't forgotten. I just learned to think differently. For weeks, I laid awake at night, crying, cursing him, or reliving our memories together. Mostly cursing," she flashed him a fleeting grin, "because those memories would turn on me too many times, and I'd hear Will's voice. I ignored it at first and kept cursing him like a sailor."

He smirked.

"What?"

"We both know Marines are better at that…as with everything else."

"My mistake." God, he was adorable. "As I was saying, once the anger subsided, I could hear him telling me to live. Jackson, we never know how long we have left. We must choose to make the most of every day, and that's what I'm doing."

Peering into his eyes as they studied her, there was no denying her feelings for him. If only her body could function properly in his presence. She'd love to slide her other hand to his cheek and pull his lips to hers. If she were brave, she would tell him how she'd always loved him. If only those words didn't seem so impossible to say after all these years. Then again, when it came to Jackson, *if only* was the story of her life.

"You make it sound so—" He stopped when Eleanor knocked and opened the door.

She smiled, taking in the view of them sitting close together, Jackson's hand in Avery's. "Breakfast is ready if you're hungry," she informed them before spinning and hurrying away, her skirt billowing with the motion.

Jackson stayed silent, staring through the empty door frame with suspicion.

Breaking into his thoughts, Avery jumped up and rolled the wheelchair to the bed. "I'm famished. Shall we go eat?" She stood behind the chair and smiled, enjoying the view of him rumpled and shirtless in bed as if they'd done more than just sleep over the last eight hours.

"I can't."

She rushed around the chair to his side, sitting on mattress. "Why not? Is something wrong?"

"I'm underdressed." The corners of his mouth curled up when he motioned to her dress.

She'd forgotten about the make-Jackson-notice dress she'd selected for the mission. Nice to know it worked.

"Well, we can fix that." Feeling encouraged, she crossed the room to the closet. "There must be something in here you can wear to our fancy breakfast shindig." Seeing no other option, she selected the only collared shirt in the closet and tossed it to him.

Once he was dressed and comfortable in the wheelchair, they headed toward the dining room. But instead of entering, Jackson stopped in the hallway outside the doorway and spun the wheelchair to face her.

Surprised, she tossed up her hands and jumped back to save her legs from getting smacked with his. "Whoa, there, cowboy."

"I wanted to tell you something."

"Yes?" she managed, her heart still in her throat from how he looked at her with a sly smile and eyes alight with mischief. It was a look she could get used to.

"I can still move my left leg a little, and last week, I had sharp tingles in my right leg. I can move that leg now, too. Some, anyway."

"Jackson, that's wonderful. Now, we need to continue your program and keep making progress." She bent down and placed both hands on his knees. "Are you ready?"

He thought about what she'd said earlier—healing could come through living. Damn, he hoped so. He had to try, even if he wasn't convinced it was possible. "I'm ready."

"That's the spirit."

———

Jackson

After breakfast, Avery shifted in her seat to face him. "What do you say about starting your next session here today?"

"You want to work out today? In that dress?"

"Good point. I'll go home to change and be back here within the hour." She held out her hand for his promise. "Deal?"

What about warming up to it? Getting back in the swing of things at an introductory pace? Under normal circumstances, he'd respect the full-speed-ahead approach. But...

But nothing. He had no reason to delay the work and couldn't bring himself to disappoint her. And wasn't she offering the one thing he needed most? A chance.

With hesitation, he took the deal. After all, he'd already said he was ready, and his word was all he had.

Chapter Eight

✯ ✯ ✯

Avery

For the next three months after work, Avery met Jackson at the estate for his therapy sessions. They used the fitness equipment in his father's gym or whatever they could find around the estate. Being outdoors lifted his spirits, so whenever he rested, she walked the grounds to find new areas to use or researched exercises she could modify for outdoors.

Spending time at the estate, in acres of beautiful gardens or at the lake with Jackson's undivided attention, had become her refuge—her second home. Without the constraints of appointment schedules, she could be creative and spend more time on exercises when he needed it.

The new program was working. Jackson's strength and mobility had made considerable progress, and he could now stand on his own. With Avery's support, he could even take a few steps. Although it was painful, he didn't shy away from the work, but the walking exercises took the most out of him.

"How'd the workout go today?" Eleanor asked Avery one evening. After Jackson's sessions, Avery would often help her in the kitchen while he rested, then stay for dinner.

"I'm so proud of how hard he tries. He took a few more steps today."

"Praise the Lord. I bet he's so relieved and excited."

"I wish I could say he was. I can't read him. He doesn't show much emotion, and he's often distracted," Avery confided as she finished cutting the last carrot for the stir-fry. "Did anything happen recently to upset him?"

Eleanor set down her knife. "He did have another run-in with his father yesterday. It was ugly." She cringed. "And it shook him more than he'd ever admit. Plus, he's been struggling with nightmares. He puts on a brave face when you're here but hasn't improved mentally as much as he hoped. I think he assumed his mind would improve as his body did."

"He told me about the horrible noises and images that come with the migraines. I can't imagine what that's like. I wish I could help."

"Oh, honey. You are helping. You're getting him out of his room and back into shape. You're also giving him hope and someone his age to talk to." She saw Avery's shoulders droop and reached over the counter to pat her arm. "I know you want more but be patient."

Pressing her lips together, she hid her disappointment with a grin. Despite spending three months, many late nights, and countless hours together, their relationship hadn't progressed past being therapist and patient. He hadn't tried to kiss or touch her in any way remotely romantic, and he hadn't said a word about how he felt.

"For as long as I can remember, my heart's been his."

"Have you told him? He's not good with recognizing these things."

"No. I don't want to push him, but I'm going crazy wondering what he feels for me. If anything." She let out a long breath. "If he needs time, I can wait. However long it takes, but it would be nice to know what I'm waiting for. Does he want more, as I do?"

"He cares for you, sweetie. That's easy to see. He's just dealing with so much right now. Simply rising each morning and getting through his workouts without giving up is a victory. When things settle, he'll be able to focus on more than just surviving each day."

Avery nodded, then slumped into her thoughts.

"I have an idea." Eleanor circled an arm around Avery's waist and leaned closer. "Why don't you ask him out?"

"I can't do that."

"Why not?" She smacked Avery on the hip and reached for the wok. "It would do him some good to get out of this house and have some alone time to explore who you are together when you're not therapist and patient."

"Eleanor, you naughty girl. Do you have some magical mind-reading powers I don't know about?"

"What do you mean?"

"I was thinking about how our relationship is still strictly professional and stuck in the friend zone…for months." She laughed to keep her frustration in check.

"Then, do something about it. He knows good and well how I feel."

"Feel about what? Eleanor." Avery joined her at the stove when she tucked her smile away and pretended not to hear. "You can't say something like that and not elaborate."

"It's just a little motherly advice. He was so down and lonely when he came home, so I might have encouraged him to date or at least…you know." She winked for clarity.

Avery gasped. "Eleanor, you *are* a naughty girl, and I love how you think." She turned toward the island, pleased to have Eleanor's support, then scooted back to Eleanor's side. "But he didn't follow that advice, did he?" God, she couldn't bear thinking of him with another woman.

"Not yet." Eleanor winked again and returned to the stove.

After dinner, Avery couldn't bring herself to linger as she normally did. Jackson escorted her to the door, always the perfect gentleman, and her heart ached for him.

"Jackson?" Stopping in the doorway, she shoved her trembling hands in her pockets and couldn't force a smile. "Some friends and I are going out on Saturday. Would you like to join us? It'll be low-key. Just dinner and drinks."

"Sure."

"Really?"

He grinned. "I don't know what kind of company I'll be, but it might be nice to get out."

"Okay. Great. I'll pick you up at six."

———

Jackson

On Saturday afternoon, Eleanor found him reading on the back porch. "I got you something."

"What's this?" he asked when she dropped a white paper bag in his lap.

"Open it."

He reached in and pulled out a new pair of jeans and a red collared shirt.

"Thanks, Eleanor, but what's it for?"

"Your date tonight."

"It's not a date."

"A pretty girl asked you to join her for dinner. Sounds like a date to me."

With a scoff, he returned the clothes to the bag. "I appreciate the thought, but it wasn't necessary."

"I wanted to do something nice for you. You've been so down lately, and now you're going on a…" She grinned. "However you youngins label it, I'm happy for you." She patted his hand and surveyed him. "Jackson, can I ask you something?"

He raised his eyes to her and nodded.

"How do you feel about Avery?"

"She's great." A tilt of her head told him that he'd given the wrong answer. "What are you really asking me, Eleanor?"

"She has feelings for you. Deep ones that go back to when you were kids."

"I know," he said, looking out at the lake in the distance and wishing he was there not having this conversation. "That's why I'm going tonight."

"Then you feel the same?"

"No, I don't, but I owe it to her to try." Maybe feelings would grow if he could find the energy to focus on her instead of the usual chaos.

"Good for you. She's such a sweetheart, but her heart is vulnerable. Tread lightly."

He understood the hidden meaning, which only added to the pressure he already put on himself. Not only was he sick with nerves about being around strangers in a crowded, confined space, but the wheelchair would be a hassle, and he was embarrassed by the dependency it created. On top of that, he had Avery to think about. He knew exactly what she sought from him—her eyes told him everything. Although she deserved answers, he didn't have any.

———

Avery arrived early that evening and helped Jackson to the car. After months of physical therapy, he could rise from the wheelchair independently and lower himself into the passenger seat using the door frame for support.

She stowed the chair in the trunk, then joined him, flashing a smile over her shoulder from the driver's side. Hope and anticipation danced in her eyes, and he wished to feel the same.

For first time since the dinner party, she had on something other than shorts and a t-shirt, giving more meaning to the casual outing. The thin sundress exposed her shoulders, and the light brown dots in the fabric matched her eyes. Dangerously short, it showcased miles of her long tan legs.

This was a date, no matter how much he denied it.

"You look nice," he said awkwardly, still unsure if he should be there.

"Thank you. You do too. Is that a new shirt?"

"It is. Eleanor went shopping this morning."

She laughed when he rolled his eyes, and the carefree sound helped him relax.

"Want to know about the people you'll be meeting tonight?"

"Sure."

"Okay. I work with Henry, and he's bringing his newish girlfriend, Nicole—an elementary school teacher. She's a lot of fun and hilarious when she's tipsy. I think summertime is when she gets all the rowdy out of her system before going back to teaching our country's future leaders. Sometimes I worry about the future." She laughed again.

"I can't wait to meet her."

"Brett and Molly were high school sweethearts," she continued, "and haven't spent a day apart since freshman year. Their PDA makes me want to puke, but somehow, they aren't married with a horde of babies yet."

She paused to take a deep breath. "And then there's Ben, the eternal bachelor. He has a hard time keeping his hands and lips to himself. Keep an eye out for him. His lips have no prejudices or boundaries." She raised her eyebrows and gave him a look that told him she wasn't joking.

"I'll remember that. If his lips come anywhere near me, I'll run over his toes with my wheel."

"Ha! Good luck. He's very sneaky and obnoxious when he drinks, but he's harmless. I'll apologize for him in advance."

"Why?"

"He has a nasty habit of speaking before he thinks." She cringed, and Jackson dismissed it with a hand.

"After eight years in the military, there's not much I haven't heard. It takes a lot to offend me."

"Good. That will come in handy."

She turned her eyes to him, but he pretended to be taking in the view of the city outside his window. It was a cowardly move, and he despised himself for it. She had many wonderful qualities—beautiful, kind, strong, electric. They'd spent plenty of time together over the last several months to get to know each other as more than childhood friends. With everything he'd learned about her, he should be jumping at the chance to be hers. So, why wasn't he?

"We're here," she announced with a smile. "I know it's been a while since you've done this, but I've got your back. Okay?"

Once inside, Avery looked through the restaurant for her friends and spotted Brett and Molly sitting close and kissing in the bar. With a quick eye roll, she headed that way. She introduced Jackson and ordered their drinks as Henry and Nicole joined them.

The friends chatted about things Jackson knew nothing about, making him feel like an outsider. He'd been completely cut off from the outside world at the estate and knew nothing about movies, local bands, sports, or new events in Richmond.

He didn't care about being out of the loop, preferring it to the alternative, but it made contributing to their conversations nearly impossible. Plus, the group skirted around the uncomfortable alteration to their usual gathering—the awkward stranger in a wheelchair with a ticking time bomb masquerading as his life. He was the equivalent to a pile of dog shit on the sidewalk everyone avoided. No one wanted to look at it, much less address the unsightly mess in the way.

As he sat there, wishing to disappear, the walls of the crowded bar seemed to sway. They closed in on him more with every passing minute and threatened to cave. At least the loud music and nearby conversations helped drown out the thoughts he desperately wanted to escape and kept the smothering nature of his surroundings at a controllable level.

———

Avery

"Where's Ben?" she asked after they were seated, and the waitress left with their drink orders.

"You know him," Molly answered. "Gotta make an entrance."

"Hey, Jackson," Brett began. "Avery tells us that you're making great progress. How is it working with our girl?"

He tipped his head toward her with a curious smile. "She's a tough coach."

Sensing his struggle with the undivided attention, Avery filled in. "I've never had a patient that works as hard as him. I could say that's from his military training, but he's always been like that." She glanced over and held his gaze, hoping he read her signals. He had full access. All he had to do was take the next step.

"How long did you serve?" Nicole asked.

"Eight years."

"Wow, that's amazing."

Looking ready for a new topic, he grabbed the beer the waitress set in front of him and took a drink, unaware of her lingering eyes.

Nicole snorted out a laugh. "Geez, take a picture."

The others snickered, amused by the waitress's reaction, but Avery had witnessed it often enough when they were younger for it not to get to her. She'd also heard hundreds of Will's elaborate stories about women melting at Jackson's feet all over the world. Hell, she had been one of them. The man was a rare specimen, and the fact that he had no idea made him irresistible.

While they read the menu and decided on dinner, the friends continued to chat. The men talked about sports, excited for the start of the football season, and the women compared movies they had seen or books they were reading. Jackson remained quiet, she noticed, but he seemed to have settled into the rhythmic commotion her friends created together. She even caught him grinning at times.

The waitress soon returned with Ben's long arm draped over her shoulders. Not surprisingly, she appeared content to be the center of his attention.

"Look who I found causing trouble at the bar," the perky waitress announced, swatting Ben in the belly with the back of her hand. He didn't flinch. Instead, he planted his lips on hers, bending her backward before releasing her with a loud smack. As he strutted to his seat, he held up his hand for a high-five for anyone who'd reward him. Brett was the only one to oblige.

"Told you," Avery confirmed, leaning closer to Jackson with an all-knowing smirk.

"It's about time you showed up," Henry told Ben.

"Dude, I had something to do."

"What was her name?"

A loud belly laugh erupted out of Ben as he slapped the table. "I can't remember."

The evening progressed as it started with the group's conversations growing louder and more animated now that Ben added himself to the mix.

"Everything okay?" she asked Jackson, resting her chin on her hand, but before he could answer, Ben interrupted by calling for her from the other end of the table.

"Avery, you didn't introduce me to your date."

He was six beers in, Avery observed, and that was only since he joined the group.

"Maybe there's a reason for that," she responded without turning around, her eyes still on Jackson and wide with amusement.

"Oh. Wait a minute." Ben dropped an elbow on the table and pointed at Jackson. "You're the guy who was in that awful accident over in…" He snapped, trying to remember what he'd heard.

Henry kicked him under the table, and Ben shot dagger eyes at him.

"Were you in a tank when it happened? That would be so cool. What were you hit with? I bet it was a bomb or one of those landmines?" Henry kicked him again, harder this time. "Fuck! What the hell, man?"

"Maybe he doesn't want to talk about that, asshole."

"Oh, right. Sorry, man," Ben said to Jackson.

The group grew quiet and uncomfortable. Before Avery could end the awkward silence, Jackson spoke up. "There were two missiles."

"I knew it! Damn, I have so much respect for you." He raised his beer. "Thank you for your service."

Surprised by Ben's tribute, the others awkwardly raised their glasses.

"Thank you for defending our country, and…" He paused to beam at Henry. "Our freedom to fuck whomever and whenever the hell we please. God bless the land of the brave." Ben slammed down the bottle, then chugged the remaining.

Worried, Avery lifted her eyes to Jackson, relieved to see he wasn't angry.

"Well, I'm glad our service brings him so much pleasure," he whispered with the most adorable sideways grin.

She laughed, enjoying the rare playfulness. Maybe this was the spark that would ignite his heart. God, she hoped so. She was already burning for him. All he had to do was catch up.

Chapter Nine

☆ ☆ ☆

Jackson

W ant to get out of here?" Avery asked him, letting the thin strap of her dress slide loosely off her shoulder—another loud and clear signal he ignored.

On impulse, he agreed because he'd been ready to go for a while, but he didn't like how desire darkened her eyes with the invitation. She could have no secrets from him with those expressive eyes of hers. Even though he needed a break from socializing, he wasn't prepared for what she had in mind either.

She motioned for the waitress to bring the check, and before her friends could question her, she signed the receipt and rushed him out the door.

"Hope that wasn't too excruciating," she said, backing the car out of the parking lot.

"I enjoyed how they interacted and played off each other. Reminds me of…" He couldn't speak their names.

"I know you miss them." She reached over and took his hand. "How about a stroll? It's a beautiful night and still early. I know a place near here."

"Sure."

On the way, Avery fidgeted in her seat, excitement radiating off her like a sparkler. He could relate, but it wasn't thrilling anticipation that had his blood gushing at a reckless pace. It was not knowing her expectations and the changes a romantic moment under the stars might ignite between them that made him unsteady.

"This is my favorite spot," she told him when she parked near Gamble's Hill Park. "It's quiet, and the city becomes a light show at night."

Along the path, they claimed an empty bench overlooking the James River. Despite the air being cooler than a typical August evening, a thin layer of sweat gathered on his back. He shouldn't have allowed the evening to continue, but the hope in her eyes when she asked sent his resolve crumbling.

While they sat, they chatted about the events from dinner, her friends, and his upcoming sessions. She told him about the new exercises she wanted to try and how she could modify them for outdoor workouts. When she ran out of conversation starters, they sat in silence and watched the lights.

She reached into her purse, giving Jackson a moment to tamp down his nerves. This detour to the park hadn't been dramatic as he expected, and their easy conversation allowed his sizzling nerves to fizzle out. The fresh air and calming view did wonders for his—Jackson's head whipped around at the unexpected start of the song playing through her phone.

After a deep breath, she stood before him and held out her hand to help him up. His gaze followed, and it struck him how beautiful she looked in the soft glow of night. Highlighted by the nearby lamplight, stars, and moonbeams, all signs seemed to point to her, lighting the way. To what he couldn't be sure, but the target had to be better than what he could find on his own.

Mesmerized, he reached out without realizing he'd done it. As he stood, his body pressed against hers, and his other arm wrapped around her back.

———

Avery

"Jackson, you're dancing." Happy for him and to finally be where she belonged, she rested her head on his chest. He was getting healthier and stronger, and she took pride in knowing she had something to do with that. Listening to the steady rhythm of his heart, she shivered, knowing it would soon beat for her.

She soaked in the feel of him and envisioned the life they could have together after he healed. They'd travel and cook dinner together. Coming home after work, he'd greet her at the door and kiss her, thrilled to have her back in his arms. She'd stare into the bright pools of his eyes after making love, and her world would finally make sense. All the waiting and wishing would have been worth it, and she'd be content for the rest of her life.

With their future in mind, she couldn't wait another minute for that dream to begin. All her previous relationships had been stand-ins, mere stepping stones preparing her for this moment. Whatever she had to do, she would kick start their relationship that night.

Sliding her hand from his shoulder to the back of his neck, she leaned back and gently pulled him to her. The instant their lips connected her mind went blank. Rays of sunshine, stakes of fire, and shooting stars of varying intensity blazed through twenty years of waiting and wishing, unraveling her in his arms.

Free of all doubts and hesitations, she gave herself to him. The cars zooming by on the nearby bridge and the soft music playing faded away while she floated in a daze. Happily lost in his warmth, she hoped never to be found. His kiss was everything she imagined it would be, and when he released her, super-charged tingles continued to riot through her body.

She reveled in the passion his touch ignited until her lashes slid open and her gaze met his. The gentle beat of a ballad—ironically about long-lost love—rang in her ears, and the hope she once felt left her body, slicing her heart into pieces on the way out.

He felt nothing.

"I need to sit down," he said, shuffling toward the wheelchair and interrupting her downward spiral.

She sat beside him on the bench and stared over the river while her vision blurred with tears. How could their first kiss leave him feeling…empty? This can't be what she'd waited for, fantasized about. She wouldn't accept it.

"Avery, I just need more time."

Picking at her fingernails, she focused on keeping the tears where they belonged. "I've loved you since we were kids. When you showed up at the office, I thought it was fate bringing us together. If you can see potential with us, I'm willing to wait."

"I don't have any answers right now. Every day is a new challenge." He twisted in his chair and took her hand in his.

At his tender touch, her eyes shot to his and held. It was the first time he'd reached for her, and it meant everything.

"All I know is that I enjoy your company and am grateful to have you in my life. You're more than my physical therapist. You and Eleanor are all I have, and I don't want to lose you."

The fear in his voice was more than her fragile heart could take. She ached to comfort and give him whatever he needed, but this moment could happen over and over if she let it. A painful cycle of her begging him to open his heart, while the life she'd always wanted remained just out of reach.

"I'm not going anywhere," she said to soothe him. "One day, I hope to be more than the person you call when life get rough."

"I know, and I want to get there."

"Then, that's enough for me. But at any point, if you determine that you can't love me the way I deserve, please tell me. It will hurt like hell." She closed her eyes, not wanting to think of how crushed she would be. "But you'll have to let me go."

Holding his hand to her cheek, she prayed for God to give her the strength to let him.

———

They rode in silence back to the estate. On autopilot, she parked and removed the wheelchair from the trunk. By the time she pushed it to the passenger side door, Jackson had already climbed out and was waiting for her.

Despite herself, she smiled, proud of how far he'd come. He reached out, and her eyes flew to his as he took her hand and tugged her into his arms. She'd been begging for this from him—intention, romance, raw emotion, accepting her as his.

Leaning back, he trailed the back of his fingers over her cheek. "Thank you for telling me how you feel and for not giving up."

"I could never give up on you, Jackson. You're the only man I've ever loved." *Or ever will.*

Encouraged, she rose to her toes and kissed him, letting her emotions and desire have their way. She wanted him to want her and know he could have all of her.

His mouth responded as she leaned into him, his strong hands moving up her back and tangling in a fistful of her hair. The feel of his body through the thin dress fabric made her desperate for more. She knew all too well how it felt to crave him, and his hands, equally greedy and demanding, were forcing her over the edge.

When she offered, he took more, and soon, her own hands found their way inside his shirt. With the workouts they'd been doing, his body had evolved into that work of art she remembered. If only she could see more of him to lock this moment into memory. But his tongue brushed against hers as his head tilted to take the kiss deeper, snapping the last shred of control she clung to.

She pressed hard against him to offer more, hoping he'd take it. His knees trembled from the added pressure, but he didn't stop. Instead, he surrendered a little more, drinking her in both with his lips and hands. She wondered what changed since their kiss in the park. Maybe her confession of love helped him see her more clearly. Maybe he'd been holding back, his first moment of passion since overcoming tragedy too much to handle at first. Whatever caused this change in him, she would be on her knees later that night, thanking the heavens for it.

His lips trailed down her jawline to her neck and exposed a sensitive spot. Then again, every inch of her was acutely aware of his presence, his touch. Her body tuned in and reacted as if his fingers were electric currents set to the maximum voltage. With one kiss, he'd shocked her back to life—a life that would forever be changed.

His name floated out on a sigh as her head fell back. She needed more of this sensual, gorgeous man. More of his hands and lips on her skin. More time in his arms. All she got was a sudden gush of cool air across her face and chest. Her eyes flew open to discover he'd disconnected from her to grip the door frame instead of her waist like he'd done since they'd arrived.

"I should go," he breathed out. "It's getting late."

"Oh. Okay. Need help getting inside?"

"No. I've got it." He hid behind a smile and said nothing as he lowered into the chair.

"See you tomorrow, then."

"See you."

She watched him roll up the driveway and into the house, then let out the breath she'd held while waiting for one last gesture. Something to tell her she'd misread his eyes again. He gave her nothing.

Rounding the car, she kicked the tire. The trip to her apartment would be an emotional one. She was brokenhearted over their first kiss but hopeful after the second. Something held him back, but he said he wanted to try. She just needed to stay positive and patient. And with a little persistence and plenty of seduction, she should be able to knock down his walls.

It was finally happening. Maybe not how she expected or wanted, but that was okay. Putting the car in drive, she couldn't wait for the next day—the official start of their love story.

———

Jackson

A bullet to the head disguised as a migraine began to rattle inside his skull the moment he entered the house. It had to be a punishment for what he'd done. He shouldn't have kissed her that way. He was a weak excuse for a gentleman, allowing his loneliness to take over his better judgment. She wanted more than he could give, but damn, it sure would be nice to feel something again. Something other than pain and an infinite void where his heart used to be.

Somehow, he managed to get himself to his room and out of the wheelchair before the agony, nausea, and dizziness incapacitated him. He laid on the bed, his arms splayed across the mattress and accepted the merciless torture. After all, he deserved it.

Chapter Ten

✯ ✯ ✯

Jackson

O ver the next two months, the lake became
Jackson's refuge from the storm. It had the power
to calm his nerves, if only temporarily, and reset
his thoughts. But that warm October afternoon, as he
looked out over the smooth water, the storm raged around
him.

Although battered and weak from fighting against his
inner turmoil without a reprieve, he still couldn't bear to go
inside. One look at him in his current mood, and Eleanor
would see right through him. He couldn't lie to her, and
since he didn't care to talk about his predicament, he simply
stayed where she'd never venture.

Eleanor's dramatic detest of weather and bugs usually
lightened his mood. Whenever she began a rant,
complaining about the heat or gnats that congregated near

the water or her precious garden, he'd grab a drink, park his wheelchair somewhere with a clear view of the show, and bask in the glory that was Eleanor Brown.

But even that entertainment couldn't bring him to face her that day.

Nearly two months had passed since he and Avery officially started dating. While her presence and bubbly personality helped ease his loneliness, his feelings for her hadn't developed as he'd hoped. He'd give anything to take her in his arms and feel…something.

How could her love be so strong already and seemingly infinite?

It would help if he could look at her and not see Will. The more time they spent together, the more her expressions, laugh, energy, and phrases reminded him of what he lost. Sometimes, the pain was too much to ignore. He also struggled to separate the woman from the girl he remembered in middle and high school. He hadn't been attracted to her then—she'd seemed immature and naïve, even though she was only three years younger.

Almost a decade later, she'd grown up—a fact she made strikingly clear every time she tried to spark some intimacy between them. He could have her whenever, and however, he wanted. If his heart would soften just a bit, he might be able to enter her world, satisfy her cravings, and drown out the distractions.

The only thing stopping him…it wouldn't just be sex to her. Allowing their relationship to go there would make promises he wasn't sure he could keep, further complicating their already delicate relationship.

They could take that leap when their relationship was stronger—when *he* was stronger. Thankfully, she'd been patient, satisfied with his efforts, and more forgiving than he deserved, but time was running out. Her flirting and affection had advanced beyond his comfort level, and he didn't know how to handle it without hurting her.

Frustrated, he snatched the fishing rod off the dock with a sigh, jammed the hook into the lure, and tossed the line into the water. He didn't care to fish that day but needed a distraction, and there was nothing else to do. He'd finished the book he opened the day before and had already completed an upper-body workout. Now, he waited for Avery to arrive for their regular Tuesday session and provide the company he needed to pass the time.

God, he hated boredom.

"Hi, handsome," he heard Avery say and soon felt her soft hands on his shoulders.

She kissed him quickly on the cheek, then straddled the wheelchair's footrest. To see her, he had to shield his eyes from the late-afternoon sun.

"You're here early. What's that?" He nodded toward the large basket she carried.

"Guess."

"Snakes?"

"Eww. Why in the world would I bring you snakes? Try again, silly."

Jackson pretended to contemplate the basket, then squinted when he returned his eyes to her. "Fireworks."

"Interesting idea, but you cause enough of those when you kiss me." She leaned down to press her lips to his. "Boom," she whispered, then stood. "Give up?"

"I never quit."

"True, but it may take all day. How about I tell you?"

"Sure."

She removed the towel on top to reveal food containers, glasses, a bottle of wine, and china.

"You made dinner?"

"Well, Eleanor made it." She rolled her eyes with the confession. "It's so we can enjoy a little private celebration."

"Oh, yeah? What are we celebrating?"

"You don't remember?" She poked out her bottom lip and tilted her head in a dramatic pout.

"Of course, I remember. Not only do I never quit, I don't forget either." That was the trouble, wasn't it? He remembered everything in vividly gruesome detail. Setting down the fishing rod, he reached into the tackle box and retrieved a long-stem pink rose. "Happy birthday."

Gasping, she set down the basket to take the flower and sit on his lap. "You remembered."

"And," he leaned over the arm of his wheelchair, "this is also for you." Holding up a tiny gold gift bag, he laughed when she squealed and clapped her hands together, causing the rose to wiggle in his face.

She reached inside the bag, removed two small pieces of stiff paper, and studied the fine print through her sunglasses. "Oh, Jackson. I wanted to go to this so badly. They sold out in the first week. How did you get tickets?"

"A magician never reveals his secrets."

"Thank you so much." She circled her arms around his neck and squeezed before pushing the glasses onto her head to kiss him. "Wait." Leaning back, she studied him. "There are two tickets here. Does that mean you're going with me?"

"You know I'm not a fan of stuffy dinner parties," he said flatly, looking down his nose at her.

"It's not a party. It's a gala fundraiser. That's totally different, and all the money raised goes to the Warrior Angels Foundation." Tears filled her eyes, surely thinking of Will, and she blinked fast to clear them. "Jackson, it's this weekend. On your birthday."

"Yeah." He fiddled with the hem of her shorts, unsure if he was ready to face the rest of the world a second time.

Placing a finger under his chin, she lifted his face. "When I was little, I believed we were destined to be together since our birthdays were so close. It was my wish every time I blew out the candles."

"Avery, I…"

"I know you don't feel the same, and it's okay. Really," she added when he frowned. "It's not your fault that I have drooled over you since we were kids." She kissed him and lingered, urging him to offer more. When he didn't, she sat up and hid her disappointment. "Thank you for going through whatever trouble it took to get these."

"Actually, it wasn't too hard. I texted Harrison, and he got them for me."

Avery smacked Jackson on the chest and returned the sunglasses to her face. "Either way, I'm excited and can't wait to see you all dressed up."

He groaned, making her giggle.

"Will Harrison be there, too?" she asked.

"Yeah."

"You're not excited to see him?"

"No, I am. It's just…we haven't talked much since losing Billy."

She noticed his spike in heart rate and laced her fingers with his. "I bet you'll pick up right where you left off. You always said he was like a father to you."

A smile emerged despite his gloomy mood. "Billy used to joke about how generous he was to share Harrison with me. I should have been jealous of how close they were."

"But you loved them both."

He nodded and looked out over the water. Emotions he wasn't prepared to face came bubbling back to the surface.

Recognizing the trigger, Avery slapped her leg and stood. "Why don't we get started on your workout? I have a fun game for us to play today."

"Can we eat first? I'm starving, and I smell chicken."

"Jackson! Did you skip lunch again?"

She stomped her foot, her fists resting on her hips, and he tried not to remember the little girl she'd always been to him before they reconnected. "Guilty."

"How are you supposed to build muscle if you don't eat?" She let out an extended breath when he shrugged, then checked her watch. "Fine. Let's eat."

———

"Alright. No more stalling," she demanded, jumping up from her spot on the dock. "We have a lot to do, but don't worry. You're going to love today's exercise. I promise."

He pointed at her. "I'm holding you to that. If I don't, you'll have to up your game plan."

"Oh, I'm ready. But it's the fourth quarter, and you're down by six points. Are you going to step up, Mr. Running Back, or will you fall short of the goal line?"

"I always get the touchdown."

"We'll see about that." Leaning on his thighs, she pressed her lips to his and let a soft moan escape, surely hoping to get his blood moving. It would take more than that.

"I don't think the defense kisses the offense before the game-winning touchdown."

"This team does, and you're not even in the red zone yet."

"I'm impressed with your football knowledge."

"I watched you and Will play my entire life. Picked up a thing or two." She winked before resetting her face. "Now, stand up," she demanded, impressing him with her take-no-shit coaching voice.

"Yes, ma'am."

She waited while he moved the chair's footrests aside, took off his shirt, and gripped the arms of the wheelchair. With a grunt, he pushed up, and she stepped closer to help. His hand flew up to stop her.

"Okay, big shot," she teased. Now that he was standing sturdy in front of her with a cane and ridiculous smile, she matched it with pride. "Been practicing that, have you?"

"What else do I have to do around here?"

Twisting, she checked the dock behind her. "Let's see if you can make it to the edge."

"Seriously?" He'd rarely taken more than a few steps during their workouts, and now she wanted him to walk halfway down the dock.

"What's the matter? Scared?"

Another grunt escaped. "Never."

Without waiting for further insults, he strained to lift his leg an inch or two off the wood planks and set it down in front of him. The angle made the back leg harder to lift, so he dragged it across the rigid surface.

"Good. This time, start with the other leg."

He did as she instructed, and after a few minutes, he'd moved forward several planks.

"I'm so proud of you, but we have a long way to go."

When he swayed, he reached for the railing to steady himself, but not before catching a glimpse of her grinning. She was enjoying his suffering way too much.

"Man, watching you work is making me sweat."

"What?" He looked up in time to see her pull her T-shirt over her head, revealing a lavender and white striped bikini top and her tight torso.

"Going swimming today?"

"Maybe. Keep moving. We don't have all day."

After he'd crossed several more planks, he watched her wiggle slowly out of her shorts, paying him no mind. "What are you doing?"

"It's weird how the temperature out here keeps getting hotter and hotter."

"Right. I know what you're doing."

Closing the distance between them, she tossed the shorts behind him with a flip of her elbow. "Is it working?" She kissed his bare shoulder before moving up his neck to nibble his ear.

"Alright, alright. Damn it." The nibble worked, he had to admit, and angled his head to see her grinning at him. So damned proud of herself. "Are we walking or not?"

"You're flustered, Jackson."

"No. I'm just ready to get this exercise over with. It's not exactly a walk in the park, you know."

"I do know. At your speed, you'll have plenty of time to take in the view." She spun around and strutted slowly to his next destination. "Three more planks."

It took more effort than he expected to complete the challenge. Along the way, his blood pressure surged, causing him to sweat like he'd run a marathon. Yet, none of that mattered. He was finally strong enough to move. Marveling at himself, he picked up a leg to continue only to have the world around him blur. He blinked hard to focus on the scenery beyond the dock and reset his foundation, but instead of sunshine, trees, and water, he saw hazy swirls of light, like drunk fireflies on a windy night.

Then, the lights scattered and dimmed as a storm darkened the skies. Thunder echoed in his ears before cold rain splashed off his bare back.

"Shit!" He shivered as his mind awakened, and he leaned on the cane. The first thing to come into focus was Avery standing inches away with the wheelchair, ready to catch him. Her bottom lip was tucked sheepishly between her teeth as she stifled her amusement. "Did you just throw water on me?"

"You were about to pass out."

"Oh," he managed as his eyes wandered downward, noticing her missing bikini top. "Avery."

"Don't stop now," she instructed, her tone relaxed and sensual. "There are only a few more seconds left on the clock, and you haven't scored yet. I'm still winning."

"Since when is stripping part of your lesson plan?"

"Since you became my boyfriend. Plus, boyfriend or not, I'm in charge of your therapy and get to call all the plays."

"Oh, really?" Damn, she did look sexy with her hair tied up loosely off her neck and her cheeks pink from the heat.

"Yep." She stepped back to the edge of the dock and planted her feet. "There are only a few steps standing between you and your game-winning touchdown. What are you going to do?"

He never backed down from a challenge, even though he knew what she planned to do next. Shuffling toward her, he wrestled with how to respond. Could touching her nude body end his hesitation and numbness? He wanted their relationship to work. Shouldn't that be enough to make it so?

With every inch he moved toward her, his heart raced faster. Her eyes never left his face, daring him to follow through on his desires.

"Touchdown," she sang softly when his toes reached the edge of the dock next to her. She hadn't moved from her spot, turning her head to him, and he did the same. With eyes locked, shoulders touching, they stood motionless in the silence and breathed.

———

Avery

Needing a distraction, she gripped the bikini strings on her hips and pushed. With that one motion, she stood before him bare, vulnerable, and impatient for his next move. Time dragged by while she waited, wondering if he would take what she offered. Then, he shifted, his hands cupping her waist and crippling her already straining system on contact.

"Jackson." His name sounded more like a plea. She wanted to touch him, pull him close, and feel his body against hers, but she was frozen in the moment. Everything she'd ever dreamed of, wished for, prayed over stood before her.

He slid a hand slowly up her side, his eyes following. The turmoil clouding his mind creased the skin bracketing his eyes and mouth.

"Sweetheart." She lifted his gaze to hers with a hand on his cheek. The more he explored, the stiffer he became. "Shut out the noise and listen to your heart. What is it saying?"

"It's torn."

Those two little words packed a powerful punch, and her heart cracked once more. "Why?"

"I haven't been with anyone in so long. I don't know if I can. And—"

"Is that what's bothering you?" Relieved, she rose to her toes and pressed her lips to his.

His parted instantly, and it was all the surrender she needed. With her body begging for more, she could no longer deny it. Leaning into him, her arms circled his neck, but the added pressure made his already weak legs buckle. For support, he dropped the cane and grabbed her shoulders. She wanted to be his foundation, the person he could rely on to hold him up—metaphorically and physically—when he struggled. But his crashing weight was more than she could handle, and they fell over the edge of the dock into the cool water.

Springing to the surface, she let out a giggle, amused by the joke her attempt at seduction turned into. One day, they could tell their friends about it over dinner and share a good laugh. He would take her hand to soothe her embarrassment and—speaking of Jackson, he'd yet to emerge. She paddled hard and twisted around in a desperate search before screaming his name and diving under the water.

Panic quickly erased everything she'd ever learned about swimming, breathing techniques, and water rescue during her lifeguarding classes in high school. The water was murky from their splashing around, and her lungs and limbs burned from a lack of oxygen. If he needed her, she would be near useless.

Rising above the surface, she gulped in air and swam toward the dock for a better view and her phone to call in reinforcements. As she approached, he emerged and grabbed hold of the post beneath the dock to catch his breath.

"Oh, thank God. That was scary." Swimming to him, she reached for the hand he held out for her. "I'm so sorry, Jackson. I wasn't thinking. This is all my fault."

"No, it's not," he huffed, still recovering. "If my legs worked, it wouldn't be so awkward."

"Well, this is better, right?" Gliding closer, she wrapped an arm around the pole between them. "Swimming is a great way to build muscle without the impact. We could try skinny dipping instead of walking next time."

"But the view was so beautiful."

Feeling validated and giddy from the rare compliment, her legs wound around his waist. She shifted, bringing their bodies together. "Take me, Jackson. Here, the grass, your bed, I don't care," she managed before reclaiming his mouth. "Eleanor will be gone for a while. We have the entire place to ourselves."

"Avery, I—"

"You're safe with me, sweetheart. Whatever you want, I'll give it." She pressed her lips to his neck. "Whatever you can give in return will always be enough."

She kissed his jaw, then straightened to read his eyes. There was something new in the crystal shades of his irises. Something she didn't recognize.

He nodded with resolution. "Not here."

"Okay. How do you want me, Jackson?"

"Inside."

In his bedroom, enough sunset remained to light the room in a subtle golden glow. Perfect for the romance she envisioned their first time would have, and as she closed the door, she could feel his eyes on her.

Crossing to him where he sat shirtless on the bed, her breathing was shallow, her heartbeat erratic, and her face undoubtedly registered her excitement, but she didn't care. He was giving himself to her and nothing else mattered. She combed her fingers through his wet hair and trembled when his hands found the back of her thighs.

"I want you to touch me everywhere," she whispered, holding his gaze. He seemed more confident now, confirming he was ready for her. "I've dreamed of having you like this for years. You are my weakness, Jackson."

Her head dropped back with a sigh when he took hold of her hips. His strong hands moved up her sides under the shirt she'd slipped back on at the dock in preparation for this moment. Fingertips brushed under her bare breast, flaring a desire already burning hot within her. She lifted her arms and freed herself of the fabric, while his hands continued to trail over her skin, smooth and airy. The touch may have been gentle, but it weakened her just the same, and she couldn't move. While he took his time, tracing every curve of her torso, she basked in the pleasures only Jackson could provide.

Then, his hands cupped her breasts and impatience pierced through her core with the force of a flaming arrow.

"My turn." Climbing onto his lap, she straddled his hips and ran her hands over ridges of sculpted muscle. He took her breath away, and the eyes she wanted to see hazy with desire wandered over her body, taking in every detail. "I feel beautiful when you look at me like that."

That roaming gaze lifted to her face. "You are beautiful."

Chapter Eleven

☆ ☆ ☆

Jackson

For two hours, Jackson attempted to sweat out his frustration by increasing the weight he normally used during a workout. The house was deserted and quiet at that early hour—characteristics he normally loathed— but that morning, it was better than facing what he'd done.

He awoke in the middle of the night in a nervous fit— angry at his weakness, frightened of what Avery may say and do next, lost at how to respond. Her scent coated his skin and filled his room. The sounds that had oozed out of her throat rang in his ears, and the look of sheer happiness on her face still rolled in his thoughts like pinecones. When guilt compounded with the rest of the chaos and became too heavy to bear, he slipped out of bed and circled the living room in the wheelchair. Since his brand of pacing began to wear a track in the rug, he retreated to the gym and had been there ever since.

Why had he allowed her to seduce him? He'd like to think he'd begun to fall for her. That she'd discovered the code to unlock his heart, but he blamed her damn eyes. When they'd met his in the water, he saw something new that tugged at his conscience. Then, she uttered the words every man loved to hear with a sexy, irresistible rasp. If her usual fire or playfulness had accompanied the words, he could have ignored it, but he'd come to realize he had no power against her plea.

For that one moment in his bedroom, letting go and allowing primal need and passion to take control seemed like what he needed. But in the light of day, after he'd had time to think about the consequences, their first night together felt more like a mistake than a profound moment between new lovers. He hated himself for that.

Dropping the fifty-pound dumbbells to the floor he yanked the wheelchair around to find Avery leaning on the door frame, watching him. She wore a relaxed smile and his wrinkled T-shirt from the day before. Her nipples pushed through the thin fabric, and the hem stopped at the top of her bare thighs. Based on the seductive look on her face, he'd bet she was nude underneath. Shouldn't that knowledge make his blood simmer with something other than irritation?

"What are you doing in here?" she said, crossing the room with the same satisfied smile he saw on her evening before.

"Following my therapist's orders."

Her arms folded against the chill of his cool tone. "Do you always get up at the crack of dawn to work out?"

He wiped his face with a towel before coiling his fingers around a dumbbell and lifting it off the floor. "Usually." As he slowly lowered the weight behind his head, he evaded her gaze like a coward.

"Okay. Well," she began, fidgeting with her fingernails. "If I can't entice you to come back to bed…" She paused for his reaction, continuing after a few moments when he remained silent. "I guess I'll leave you be. See you later?"

He cut his eyes to her and forced a smile. "Yeah."

Between reps, she bent to kiss his forehead before rushing out. He listened to her retreating footsteps, pumping the weight harder and faster until his muscles burned. When his arms trembled and he couldn't lower the weight with a firm grip, he dropped it beside the wheelchair as the front door opened and closed.

Shit. Resting his elbows on his knees, he let his head fall into his hands. There had been so much joy on her face when she entered the room, and he managed to squash it like a heartless jerk. He didn't mean to hurt her. He just didn't have the words she wanted to hear.

"Was that Avery I heard leaving?" Eleanor asked from the doorway, surprising him.

"Yes." Straightening, he reached for the weight on the floor and set it in his lap. "She has to work today."

"I see." She didn't bother hiding her amusement at discovering Avery had spent the night, fueling his already heightened agitation. Now, he'd have her questions and opinions to deal with.

"Seems things are going well between you," she continued, stepping closer. When he didn't respond, she knew him well enough to read the meaning behind the silence. "Sweetie, what is it?"

"Nothing."

"Don't you dare fib to me, boy. There's—"

His hands flew up in protest, stopping her lecture. "Eleanor, I know you're trying to help, but can I please finish my workout in peace."

"If that's what you want. You know where to find me if you change your mind." She patted his shoulder and turned to leave. Before closing the door, she looked back over her shoulder. "Time can fix more than just muscles, sweet boy. Give yourself that, and your heart will follow."

When the door clicked shut behind her, he tossed the weight onto the nearby rack and sunk back into the chair. "Fuck me."

After taking a monumental leap in their relationship, she expected to be welcomed into his open arms that morning. And what did he do? The exact opposite because he'd been terrified she would ask if he felt differently. The truth would have hurt them both, and he didn't know what to do.

But if Eleanor was right, his feelings could change with patience and healing. Hell, if he would stop analyzing every fucking detail of every emotion, action, and thought, he may enjoy himself more, allowing his heart to follow.

He had the company of a beautiful woman that loved and adored him. She'd even managed to shock his lower half back to life. The least he could do was show her gratitude and affection. After all, she hadn't asked for much more than that, and he'd yet to give their relationship a good, honest try.

He'd been so consumed with all that was missing in his life that he hadn't appreciated what he'd gained. Well, no more, he decided. Their relationship would officially start over that day. He would give her the best of himself, whoever the hell he was now.

———

"Thank you for the flowers," she said shyly when he called that evening after work.

"I wanted to apologize for my sour mood this morning. I'm still learning how to deal with myself."

"I understand."

He could tell from her tone that she did, but disappointment lingered. "Will you be coming over tomorrow for our session?"

"Oh, I can't. Molly and Brett broke up yesterday, and she asked the girls and me to keep her company. Thursday was their usual date night."

"I'm sorry to hear that." He remembered the couple from his outing with Avery and her friends. She'd described them as high school sweethearts who couldn't keep their hands off each other. "They seemed happy together."

"Yeah. No one saw it coming, especially Molly. Out of nowhere, he decided her unconditional love and devotion all these years wasn't enough for him."

She sighed through the phone, and he caught the double meaning and the hint. "Well, I'm sure he'll come to his senses soon and realize his mistake."

"Maybe. If she'll take him back by then." She took another audible breath. "I better get going. I have a lot of work to do."

"Avery," he began before she could hang up.

"Yeah?"

"I ordered my tux today."

"That's awesome." No matter how upset she'd been that morning, at least excitement about their night out remained. He hadn't pushed her too far yet.

"I need to know what color you'll be wearing."

"Oh, yeah? Why?"

"That's none of your concern. What color is your dress?"

"Dark purple."

"Nice. I'll pick you up at six," he said and didn't wait for a response before disconnecting.

Over lunch earlier that day, he and Eleanor planned out the perfect evening—from the tux to the limousine and everything in between. He needed to make amends for his behavior that morning and finally give their relationship a real chance to develop. But if a night of romance didn't make him feel connected to Avery on a deeper level, then nothing would.

Chapter Twelve

☆ ☆ ☆

Jackson

O n Saturday, the limo arrived as scheduled with the flowers Jackson ordered from a downtown florist. He insisted on paying extra for the personal errand, but the limo company wouldn't waver.

"There's no extra charge for the son of our best customer," they said proudly, and Jackson had to make a considerable effort not to say what he was thinking. *Do you know how many marriages that great customer has ruined with your flowers? Or how many different women those flowers charmed into his bed? Probably never the same woman twice.*

The last thing Jackson wanted was special treatment, and certainly not because of his father. But since he couldn't convince them otherwise, he resigned to doubling the driver's tip instead.

"Don't you look handsome?" Eleanor crooned, dabbing at the new moisture pooling in her eyes.

"Thank you for your help this week and literally every day." Reaching into the back pocket of his wheelchair, he removed a corsage of tiny white and pink flowers and slipped it onto her wrist.

"Jackson, you know I would do anything for you, but this was so sweet. Thank you."

"I couldn't forget my favorite girl tonight."

"I love you." She bent down and laid a big kiss on his cheek. "Now, go get your other girl. Oh, I bet she's stunning in purple. Make sure you tell her how beautiful she looks."

"Yes, ma'am," he called over his shoulder and rolled through the side door the driver held open for him.

At Avery's apartment building, he had the driver park in front so the limo would be the first thing she saw when she stepped outside. After climbing out, he leaned against it with the flower bouquet in hand and waited for the driver to retrieve her.

The moment she saw Jackson, she stopped mid-stride and covered her face with her hands.

Goal number one: Move her to tears.

Check.

Despite the thin, strappy heels she wore, she jogged to him, threw her arms around his neck, and kissed him hard.

"You look stunning," he said when she released him, and he wasn't just following Eleanor's orders. The purple satin fabric flowed seamlessly from around her neck to her toes, except for the wide gap down the middle, exposing her tight abdomen and the soft inner curve of her breasts. Holding up her hand, he spun her around to find her back was also void of material, and he had no idea how she kept it in place.

"These are for you," he said, handing her the bouquet.

"Oh, Jackson." She held the buds to her nose before meeting his gaze over them. "And this is for you." Reaching behind her back, she revealed a small package like a magician. "Happy birthday."

"Where did you— You didn't have to get me anything."

"I wanted to." She leaned in for another kiss.

Pulling off the thin ribbon circling the tiny package, he tucked it in his pocket before unwrapping the tissue paper. As he processed what he held, his jaw dropped open. "Is this what I think it is?"

"Yes, but replicas."

"Doesn't matter." There was nothing in the world he'd rather have. The small metal tags could burst into flames, and he wouldn't let go. "Wait. There are four tags here."

"I couldn't leave you out. The four of you must always be together." Setting the flowers on the trunk, she fanned the dog tags out on his palm. "This one is a copy of Will's. This one," she pointed to the second tag and raised her eyes to his, "is yours, and these two are copies of—"

"Josh and Billy's." He didn't have the words to tell her how much the gift meant to him. "Thank you."

"Can I put it on you?" When he nodded, she slipped the metal chain over his head and pressed the tags to his chest. "Now, they can be with you everywhere you go."

"Avery." Overcome with emotion, he took her face and kissed her until he could be confident he wouldn't succumb to the ache clutching his heart. "I'll treasure them always. Ready to go?"

"So ready."

Arriving at the gala being held in one of Richmond's historic hotels, they checked in and admired at the beauty of the two-story grand ballroom. There were at least ten vintage crystal chandeliers, ornate flower centerpieces decorating every table, three walls of windows, and dual curved staircases leading to a wrap-around balcony overlooking the large dance floor and sea of white linen-covered tables below.

"How about a drink?" he asked her, then led the way to the bar at the back of the large room.

To his relief, they were some of the first to arrive, and he could easily maneuver the wheelchair around without causing too many disruptions. Following a quick search for their assigned table, he shifted into a chair while Avery stored the wheelchair a short distance away. Then, they sat close, sipping wine and watching the room and the rest of their table fill with guests, activity, and excitement.

"There's the birthday boy," Harrison said when he found them.

Jackson rose from his seat with Avery following for support and accepted Harrison's hug. "God, it's great to see you." They'd spoken on the phone several times, but that was nothing compared to feeling Harrison's loving and fatherly embrace.

"My goodness." He patted Jackson's cheek. "Look at you. So healthy, and you're out of the chair."

"Thanks to Eleanor's cooking and Avery's therapy. You remember Avery, don't you?" He motioned for her.

She shifted to proudly stand beside him, her hand resting on his back. "Nice to see you again, Mr. Barnes."

"Wow. I haven't seen you since you were probably fourteen or fifteen." Harrison took the hand she offered, laughing. "Now, I feel old."

"Where's Sophia?" Jackson asked, sitting down as Harrison did.

"She had a PTO meeting tonight, and as the President, she couldn't miss it. She planned to come afterward, but Taylor's volleyball game was rescheduled to tonight. So, it's only me here."

"That's too bad. I was hoping to see her, too. How are they?"

"As good as can be expected. We spend as much time together as work and school allows. Taylor still struggles to fully accept that he's gone."

"I know how she feels." Absently, Jackson touched the dog tags.

"The moments I forget and go to call him are when it hits the hardest." He let out a shaky laugh. "Sophia is unbelievable, though. I don't know how she does it. Since we got the news, she's faced it all with grace. She keeps us positive and focused on what's important."

"She is a special woman. I've always admired her."

"And she you." He patted Jackson on the arm, then sat back in his chair. "We both love you and think of you as our son."

"I know, and I'm grateful. I sometimes wonder where I'd be today without you two and Eleanor."

"Well, there's no need to dwell on that now. We're here for you always. Thank God for those European doctors who took such good care of you so you could come home to us."

Appreciation for the family he'd found over the years filled Jackson's heart.

"Oh, I love this part," Avery said when the presentation of the colors was announced.

Every attendee remained standing and silent as a Color Guard, representing each military branch, gracefully marched down the center aisle. Jackson stood at attention until the flags were set at the front of the room. Tears burned his eyes as the band played the National Anthem, and a familiar warmth washed over him.

The flags, the uniforms, Harrison. He was in awe of it all, and somehow, he wasn't overwhelmed by the thick crowd. Nothing had a hold of his lungs, threatening his sanity. For once, he felt at ease and content, helping him breathe freely. He'd almost forgotten how that felt.

After an Army chaplain led the convocation, dinner was served.

"I'll be right back," Avery announced after they finished eating.

He watched her cross the room and stop at a table full of people who looked to be around her age. She greeted some, hugged others, and shook hands with a man whose eyes never left her face. Even after her attention returned to the woman sitting next to her, the man watched Avery's every move, smiled when she did, and watched her walk to the bar with her friend. It didn't take long, maybe a minute or two, before the man joined them and stood close, salivating like a dog in heat. *Smooth*, Jackson mused.

"What are you looking at?" Harrison asked when his conversation with a local business owner ended.

"Nothing," he answered too quickly to be believable, but he also didn't care. "You want another drink?" He waved to the waiter.

It had been a while since he had more than one glass of wine or a beer, but he was enjoying himself. He hadn't expected to. He assumed he'd be drowning in this environment, despite coaching himself to make the most of it. What he wouldn't give to feel this free and happy every day and not trapped on a raging battlefield all hours of the day and night.

He also had high hopes for a lot to change between him and Avery that night, especially on his side. With her sexy dress and the thoughtful gift for his birthday, how could that not spark something inside him? As they traveled there in the limo, he thought it had. He adored the way she glowed when he reached for her hand and the love she poured into their kiss. The intimate moment they shared on had him feeling sparks of *something* igniting in his heart.

Then, another man showed her interest, and nothing happened. No poke of jealousy. No irritation or urge to stop it. The jerk undressed her with his eyes and clearly pursued her. His flirting was off the charts as he touched her arm or back while they talked in line at the bar. Maybe Jackson was overconfident in their relationship, knowing how deep her feelings went for him or maybe his heart was still numb.

He watched her say goodbye, hugging her friend and the man, before sauntering back with a smile and a drink in hand.

"Who were they?" Jackson asked when she rejoined him at the table.

"A friend from college. We've kept in touch through social media, and I saw her post not too long ago that she would be here tonight with her boyfriend. He's in the National Guard." She took a sip of her drink.

"Was he the guy that joined you at the bar?"

Pinching her lips, she fought back a smile. "Jackson Vane, were you watching me? Are you jealous?"

"Curious."

Disappointed, she raised the glass to her lips again and studied him over the rim. "His name is Michael, and he's a friend of theirs."

"He's interested in you."

"Oh, yeah? How do you know?"

He shrugged. "I can read people, but he was anything but subtle."

"Well, I didn't notice anything. Probably because my eyes only see you." With her hands on his thighs, she leaned over and kissed him with a little more fire than before. "How are you reading me right now?"

"That would be inappropriate to say around all these people."

"Mmm. You really *are* good at this." After a quick peck and a wink, she returned to her seat. "Where's Harrison?"

"Mingling. It's what he does best," he got out before the band started playing again.

Her face lit up. "How about a dance?"

"That's not a good idea."

"Why?"

"I'm already feeling a little woozy from drinking more than usual. Add that to my weak legs, and you've got a recipe for disaster." He cringed.

She smiled again. "Woozy, huh? I would love to see you get sloppy drunk."

Spinning around in her seat, she looked for a waiter, locating one nearby with a tray of shots. After selecting two and paying, she handed a tiny glass to Jackson, then shifted to his lap. "Now, it's a party."

"I don't think you can carry me if I pass out."

"Not necessary. I have control of the wheelchair, remember? I can toss you in it and take you anywhere I want when I want. Like…" She tapped her chin with a finger, pretending to think. "The limo where I can take advantage of you in private." She smiled until he reached out and tucked her hair behind her ear. "I want you so bad."

"I thought you wanted a shot."

"I want both." After plucking the slice of lime off the cocktail glass she brought from the bar, she held up her shot. "To you, to me, to us." She clicked the top of her shot with his before tossing it back.

He did the same but didn't notice that she'd slipped the lime into her mouth until she'd taken his. The juice mingled with her kiss, making it tart, sweet, and undeniably sensual.

With her eyes on him, she removed the lime, lingering a little longer between her lips than necessary. "What would you say if I asked you to take me to the limo?"

"I'd say, where's my chair?"

"Really?" When he nodded, she hopped up to retrieve the wheelchair, and after he was seated, she leaned over his shoulder. "You make me so happy."

Goal number two: Make her happy.

Check.

———

"Where have you been?" Harrison asked after he and Avery returned to the table. "You missed the main speaker."

"Darn." Jackson winked at her before ordering them both another drink. He was well on his way to getting drunk and feeling too good to care about the consequences.

She set aside the wheelchair, and as he pulled a chair out her chair, her friend showed up to invite her to dance.

She introduced her to Harrison and Jackson before bending down to give him a kiss that promised more to come later. "Try not to miss me while I'm gone."

"You two are chummy," Harrison joked when she strolled away, her arm linked with her friend's. "How long has this been going on?"

"A few months."

"I'm happy for you."

"Thanks."

"Are you happy for you?"

Jackson looked over at him and considered. "Yeah. Why?"

"You seemed happy until I asked." Harrison studied him. "I know you better than you know yourself, Jackson. What's up?"

"She's amazing."

"No doubt. She's a Mason."

With a sigh, Jackson gulped his wine. "She loves me."

"But you don't love her?"

"No."

"It's early. Not everyone falls quickly."

"I know, and I'm apparently not that type. She wants this to work so badly, but there are times, many times," he reconsidered, "that it's hard to look past certain things and be the person she needs me to be to—"

"Why do you have to be someone else? Jackson." Harrison demanded his attention. "You're just as amazing as she is, and your happiness is also important."

"What if I'm not capable of being happy?"

"Of course, you are, and I'll repeat, it's early. Your relationship is new, and you're still recovering. Why are you putting unnecessary pressure on yourself?"

Another sigh released the contentment he felt a few minutes before, replacing it with the usual trepidation and fear. "I don't want to hurt her."

"You won't unless you worry so much about the things you can't control that you miss out on the good stuff."

"She deserves better."

"Than you?" Harrison scoffed, disregarding the comment. "Did something happen tonight?"

"What?"

"You two were relaxed and having a great time earlier. What happened?"

Not sure if he should be talking about this, Jackson stared into his wine and contemplated how to answer. *What the hell?* "We had sex. In the limo."

Surprised by the admission, Harrison finished his drink and cleared his throat. "And that's a bad thing?"

"I didn't feel anything."

"You mean… You're not…"

"Emotionally. I mean emotionally. Down there is golden." He flashed a sheepish grin.

"Oh. So, your heart's not in it."

Jackson nodded.

"Does she know you feel this way?"

"No. At least, she doesn't seem to." This conversation was pure agony. "That makes it worse."

"You enjoy her company, right?" Harrison asked and set his empty glass on the table with resolve.

"Yes."

"And she helps you feel better?"

"Yes. Well, maybe." She gave him something other than pain to think about when they were together, but was that helping him heal? He wasn't sure that ignoring it and burying it for a few hours here or there would truly help him move forward. Then, he had the added pressure of her fragile heart in his hands.

Harrison's eyes narrowed, unsure of how to take Jackson's answer. "Let's think about this." He holds up two fingers. "One, she's obviously beautiful and gets your motor running." He smiled, his face registering his amusement, and unfurls another finger. "Three, you enjoy spending time with her. No one said you have to love or marry her."

"It's what she wants."

"But it's your life, too. Date for a while and see what happens. If you don't fall in love, or the time comes when you no longer enjoy her company, end it. You've made no promises to her, right?"

Jackson shook his head to confirm. He knew better than to make promises he didn't know if he could keep. "But I don't want to hurt her," he repeated. "She's Will's family."

"So what? Do you think Will would want you wasting your time or hers if you're not happy?" Harrison leaned an elbow on the table. "What would he say to you if he was here instead of me?"

He could hear Will so clearly. "Life is short, and there are millions of women in the sea. Try them all."

"Exactly. That's what he did…probably a little too literally," Harrison added with a laugh. "He didn't settle and soon caught one his heart didn't want to throw back."

"Nice analogy."

"Thanks. It just came to me, but…"

"You're right."

"Of course, I'm right. Now, what are you going to do tonight?"

"Have fun, live in the moment, and stop overthinking everything." *More easily said than done*, he thought with frustration.

"Right again. Now, where's that waiter." Harrison searched the room. "We're going to seal that promise with a strong drink."

Chapter Thirteen

✫ ✫ ✫

Jackson

Avery spent most of the next hour on the dance floor, enjoying being young and carefree. Although he tried not to, Jackson envied her. He'd been the same once and watching her bounce and laugh with her friends ripped open a few old wounds.

The longer she danced, the more he drank, and when Michael tugged her close for a slow dance, running a hand over her bare back, he felt nothing. She giggled when he spun her around and leaned back when he dipped her, allowing him a long glimpse of her exposed abdomen.

He detested how Michael salivated over every curve of her body. Not because of jealousy, but because he didn't want the sleaze taking advantage of her. If she ever came to him and said she wanted to be with someone else, he would let her go. Her happiness was more important than anything he needed… As long as it wasn't for Michael.

The song soon ended, and Michael escorted her back to the table, his hand lingering on her back. He continued watching her every move while she talked with the others and later when she walked away alone. But instead of returning to Jackson, she crossed the room and entered a hallway. Assuming she was heading toward the restrooms, Jackson reached for his drink to reclaim the buzz he'd managed to gain earlier. But he froze as Michael rose from his seat and followed Avery, a hungry look darkening in his eyes.

Jackson's stomach tangled into knots. The sleaze was on a mission, and Avery was his prize. Or had they made plans to secretly meet somewhere private while their bodies were pressed together? Either way, it made him uneasy.

"Would you mind grabbing the wheelchair?" he asked Harrison, who had recently concluded another animated conversation about the latest museum art show, Jackson had gathered from the few phrases he heard.

Harrison held the chair steady while Jackson heaved himself into it. "Where are you going?"

"To check on something." He rolled away without further explanation toward the hallway where Avery and Michael disappeared. Along the way and as he moved down the hall, he looked for her. Then, he heard her voice coming from the lobby ahead and stopped to listen.

"I should get going," her voice carried down the hall.

"Don't go. We were having such a good time," a man, undoubtedly Michael, urged. "You are so beautiful."

"Thank you, but Jackson's probably wondering where I am."

True, he thought, but he was more curious about Michael and his intentions.

"Why do you want to be with him? He couldn't or wouldn't even dance with you tonight."

No answer from Avery. Interesting.

"I have an idea," Michael said. "Have a drink with me, and if you don't have a good time, I'll leave you alone."

"I need to get back."

"Wait."

Avery's heels clicked against the marble floor, and soon, their reflections appeared in the window. Although his vision was slightly blurred from too much alcohol, he could make out Michael grabbing her arm as she tried to walk away. She whipped around, her hair flowing wildly around her face from the movement.

His muscles on alert, Jackson inched closer.

"Stay. I like you."

She let out a long sigh. "I'm dating someone."

"I don't care." Michael's hand cupped her face, and his head lowered, but Jackson couldn't see if their lips came together.

"Tell me you don't feel it," the asshole pressed, and Jackson's stomach rolled with fire.

"Feel what?"

"This connection and incredible passion between us."

"Michael, I barely know you."

"But you feel it, don't you? Let me kiss you and see if you can deny it then."

"No. Let go of me."

"It's only one kiss. You won't regret it."

Having heard enough, Jackson pushed the chair into motion, prepared to intervene, as Avery's reflection took off.

"Jackson," she said, stopping short when she saw him in the hallway.

"Are you okay?" he asked, noticing her shallow breaths and flushed cheeks.

"Avery. Don't—" Michael appeared behind her, pausing mid-stride when he noticed they were no longer alone.

"Can we help you… Michael, is it?"

"You must be Jackson."

Michael slid his hands into his pockets and planted his feet, the same way Grayson would when he wanted to fight. Jackson's blood bubbled with fresh and familiar resentments, but he squashed them back. Years of practice with Grayson making the feat easier than it should be.

"I was telling Avery how beautiful she looked tonight and how she deserved a real man in her life."

"Do you know me? Because I don't believe we've met."

"I haven't had the distinct pleasure, but I know your father," Michael tossed out without bothering to hide his disgust. "In my experience, the apple usually doesn't fall far from the tree."

She placed a hand on Jackson's shoulder. "Michael, that's enough."

"It's okay, Avery," Jackson said. "Apparently, your new friend has a poor opinion of my father. Welcome to the club, asshole, but don't presume to know who I am because of that."

"Well, you've spent little time with your stunning girlfriend tonight, treating her like your father would. Like another one of his sluts."

Avery's hand squeezed his shoulder as her temper flared. "How dare you say—"

He touched her hand to interrupt but kept his eyes on Michael. "I'm sure you've enjoyed drooling over her and chasing her around like a needy puppy, but she's had enough of you. So, tuck your tail and take your leave."

"And what are you going to do if I don't?" A sneaky grin sent Jackson a challenge. "Go ahead. Stand up, and let's handle this man to man."

"Please, Jackson. Can we go?" she pleaded.

"No." He pushed the chair's footrests to the side, set his feet on the floor, and stood all too quickly. The room swayed, and the asshole's face blurred. Why did he have to drink so much that night? He could make very short work of this situation if he were sober. He might be unsteady on his feet, but he could not let Michael paint him the fool.

He lifted his foot to take a step—or thought he had—before realizing he was toppling over and completely helpless to stop it. Visions of Michael's smug face flashed through the blinding pain now radiating through his legs and hips from hitting the floor.

Avery gasped and lunged for him, only to be intercepted by Michael stepping between them.

"Give me a call when you want a real man, Avery. You know where to find me."

As he left, he took the route requiring him to step over Jackson—a subtle message that felt the same as ramming the cold, metal pole of a victory flag through his back.

"Oh, my God. Are you okay?" She rushed to his side and helped him sit up. "Did you hit your head?" She touched his cheek and ran her fingers through his hair before he jerked away. "Come on. Into the chair with you."

With her help, he lifted himself off the floor and plopped down into the chair. After retrieving her purse from the ballroom, she rushed him to the limo. Neither spoke the entire way to her apartment, and she didn't move when the driver parked out front.

"What happened back there?" she asked.

"What were you doing with him?"

"I asked you first."

Images of Michael's arrogant smirk, his hands on Avery, and his possessive pleas were beating their maddening little fists against the back of his skull. "I was drunk, and I lost it."

"Why?"

"You didn't answer when he asked why you were with me." He couldn't look at her and chance seeing any pity in her eyes. The shame would be crushing, and he already felt as though he'd hit rock bottom.

"You were listening to our conversation?"

"I was worried about you."

"Again, why?"

"All night, he looked at you like you were dessert. Why couldn't you answer?"

"I don't know. I guess I was caught off guard. Jackson," she whispered and took his hand. "I love you."

"Are you sure?"

"What?" On the defensive, her back straightened. "I can't believe you'd ask me that."

"I have nothing to offer you. I don't go out or do the things people our age do. I couldn't even if I wanted to. My life is limited to that damn chair, and if he'd tried to hurt you, there was nothing I could do."

He slipped his hand from hers and looked out the window through the darkness beyond. His stomach kicked into motion, adding nausea to the drumming in his head. Another debilitating migraine would soon erupt. The pattern never failed.

"Jackson, all I have ever wanted is you and your love."

He turned to face her. "I'm not sure I can give you that."

"Can't or don't want to?"

"I'm damaged, Avery. I have no idea who I am. I don't even know if I can love anymore."

Scooting closer, she placed a hand on his thigh. "I can help you get that back."

"How?" He'd give anything to believe she could mend him and his heart, and his eyes begged her to convince him.

"Well, I'll love you more every day. We'll work on your therapy until you're moving on your own again. I'll make you laugh and lay with you when you're hurting. We'll travel the world and make new memories. I'll be your number-one cheerleader and never leave your side. All you have to do is let me."

"Is that enough for you? What if I can't match your effort?"

"It's enough."

"It's not fair to you, Avery."

"I'll decide what's fair. Our relationship is new, and I'm not ready to give up on you or us. Plus," she ran a hand up his inner thigh, "we're so good together."

"Avery."

"Stay with me tonight. I can make you forget it all."

She kissed his neck, moving up his jawline, but her touch felt like ice on his skin, helping to solidify his decision. He tilted his head away. "Not tonight."

"Okay. Then, I'll grab my things and come with you. You shouldn't be alone tonight."

"Avery, I can feel a migraine coming, and I'm exhausted." *And embarrassed, ashamed, disappointed, aggravated, hurt.* Taking her hand, he held it to his lips. "Thank you for tonight. I had a great time, especially here," he added with a forced grin.

"Yes, it was amazing, and I wouldn't mind doing that again soon. Maybe in the steam room after our next workout?" She raised a hand to his cheek, bringing his gaze to hers. "Please know that you will always be enough for me no matter what."

"See you on Sunday?"

"Wouldn't miss it for anything. I love you, Jackson."

He watched the limo driver walk her to the door and thought about all the simple things a partner should be able to do. Walking his girlfriend to her door after a date was the fucking baseline, and he couldn't even do that.

Michael had been right. *Jackass.*

But no matter how frustrating and irritating and rude and ridiculous Michael had been, Jackson shouldn't have lost control. His temper got the better of him, something he never allowed, and despite his best efforts, he'd made a fool of himself without Michael's help.

He could blame it on the alcohol, but that was a weak excuse. How he acted wasn't him or who he wanted to be. He should have ignored the guy's arrogant challenge and focused more on accomplishing his third goal for the night: falling in love. Then again, it shouldn't be this hard to check that one off the shortlist.

As the limo took off, he laid back in the seat and welcomed the retribution now pounding at a deafening level in his head.

Chapter Fourteen

✫ ✫ ✫

Jackson

W hat happened? I heard a scream," Eleanor asked, dashing into the hallway to find Jackson on his knees near the front door with Avery standing over him.

"Tell her, sweetie," Avery urged him, her eyes bright with excitement.

He waved off the demand, too winded to speak, and dropped down to rest his back against the door.

"I'll do it, then. He just walked the entire length of the hallway, twice, without the cane." She held up two fingers for emphasis.

"That's great. I'm so happy for you." Eleanor patted him on the head like an obedient dog before reaching for Avery.

While he suffered, he watched them celebrate and knew they rooted for him. He worked hard for them as much as he worked for himself.

"Ready to do it again?" Avery asked, but he could only growl in answer. "Come on, you big grump. Up you go." She grabbed his hands and helped him to his feet.

As instructed, he walked down the hallway and back to his cheerleaders, but it took every bit of energy he had left. On his last step, he collapsed into Avery's arms, pinning her against the door. But his body weight became too much for her to support, and they slid into a heap on the floor.

"Great job, Jackson." Eleanor clapped her hands. "I'm so proud of you. I'll go get you some water to help cool you down." As she spun to head back to the kitchen, she sent Avery a wink over her shoulder.

"If I had known you would get frisky, I'd have made you do this exercise weeks ago," Avery teased before looking him over. He was lying on the floor, his head in her lap, while she ran her hand over his bare chest, outlining each defined ab with her finger. "You're hot like this."

"You like the tired, sweaty, I-want-to-kill-you look?"

"Yeah, apparently, I do. Although, I like you best shirtless and touching me." She leaned down for a kiss as Eleanor returned.

"Whoops, sorry to interrupt. Dinner will be ready in about thirty minutes if you want to wash up first."

Sitting up, Jackson ran a hand over his hair before accepting and draining the glass of water. For the last hour, a throbbing pain had been pulsing at his temples, and it only intensified with every sound, movement, and blinding ray of mid-day sun streaming in through the windows. He grabbed his head with both hands, his elbows resting on his thighs.

Avery's arm draped across his back, and she tilted her head to see his face. "Another migraine?"

"Not yet, just more of the same." He rubbed the base of his palms against his forehead and temples, cursing the day and the struggles that came with it.

"Maybe a hot bath will help. I can help you to your room."

When he managed a nod, she stood and pulled him up, balancing with his arm around her shoulders, too weak to hold himself up. They shuffled down the hall at a pace he could stay in control, and while he sat on the bed, she ran the bathwater and set out a towel where he could reach it. She helped with the task often after his workouts, and he wished to find it endearing. Instead, it made him feel incompetent and weak, and that day, the edge he carried had him seething through every second.

On her way out, she softly kissed each shoulder blade, trailing a hand along his lower back before exiting the room. It was a message—the same one she repeatedly sent, and he'd ignored for the past month.

Leaning on the sink for support, he couldn't bring himself to look in the mirror. Since the gala, their physical intimacy hadn't progressed, despite her frequent attempts, and guilt churned in his belly. If anything, their relationship reverted to how it had been before sex entered the relationship, and he took full responsibility for that.

He didn't mean to, but after all the progress he'd made the night of the gala, the humiliating incident with Michael set him back two-fold. Determination, energy, drive, reasons to push forward—all of it had dissipated, and the effort he gave their relationship suffered as a result.

She was there for him and happy to be, yet he was lonely beyond measure. Could he really be this terrible at relationships? Or was the guilt he felt for his dependency on her to fill the void suffocating the love out of him? Whatever the reason, he better snap out of the rut, or he would soon drive himself insane and her out the door.

"Fuck." His boiling blood pressure had him in a chokehold, and he didn't need any more stress. What he needed was a solution to his dilemma and a good, long soak to wash away the nagging headache.

In the tub, he immersed himself under the water and held there until his lungs tightened. With his training, he should have been able to stay submerged for twice that long, but visions of Avery's expressive eyes kept flashing through his mind. Hope, love, disappointment, hurt. He'd seen them all in her since they started dating, and he had only one reaction to them all.

Guilt.

The hot water may be soothing his aching joints and muscles, but as usual, his mind was another story. He didn't hear Avery slip into the room until the creaky hinges announced her presence as she closed the old door.

He sat up quickly, spilling water over the tub's edge, and saw her leaning against the door in one of his shirts. Her breasts pushed against the soft fabric, and she had the look of a woman on a mission. How could he let this happen again?

"Avery," he managed before she strolled forward and released the button between her breasts, exposing more of her smooth skin. She took another step while he continued to wrestle with competing feelings. Part of him wanted to give her what she wanted to take the pressure off. But the other more persistent part knew it would solve nothing.

Holding his gaze, she loosened another button, then knelt beside the tub. "I want to be with you, Jackson. I miss how you feel inside me—how good we are together."

She leaned on the side of the tub and kissed him.

"Will you take me here? Now?" she begged and kissed him harder this time, trying to reignite the spark they found in the limo. It was the last time he let himself go, and she'd brought it up often. She wanted that urgent, raw sexuality he had that night, but it had fizzled out as quickly as it ignited. Impatient, she ran her hand up his inner thigh until he caught her wrist.

Her eyes widened, and her face turned stone white. She didn't want to accept that he'd stopped her seduction. Then, fire and pain flashed in her eyes, piercing him to the core.

"Avery," he whispered and released her arm. "I can't."

She sat back on her heels and clutched at the shirt to close it. "Why not?"

"I've been trying to give you what you need—" he attempted before she cut him off.

"No, you haven't. You've just been going through the motions, tiptoeing around, trying not to hurt me. You just don't want me to leave. It's not the same."

"I know."

"Do you? Why haven't you tried to kiss me like you did at the gala? Why don't you talk to me, hold me, or try to get close to me? I need you to let me in."

It hurt her when he had no response, but her eyes remained dry. "Avery, I'm sorry. I thought I was making progress."

"What changed?"

"I'm not sure."

"Well, something happened. You haven't been the same since that stupid incident with Michael. Are you still mad at me for talking to him?"

"I wasn't mad."

"No. I'm sure you didn't care that I was with another man. Did you?" His silence told her everything. "What's so wrong with me that you can't love me?"

"There's nothing wrong with you," he began, treading lightly. He'd never seen her angry and didn't know her cues and potential triggers. "You're beautiful, smart, funny, loyal."

"You could say all those things about a dog."

"Avery, I've been in a funk lately, and—"

"*It's not you. It's me.* Is that what you were going to say?"

"Not exactly." The words he needed to say were jumbling in his brain along with his throbbing headache and waning patience. He ran his hands over his face. "Can you give me a few minutes to finish up here? Then, we can talk more in my room." *Like adults*, he thought against his will.

"Fine. But it's not like I haven't seen you naked before." She spun around and left the room, slamming the door behind her.

He lingered in the tub, hoping to calm his nerves and dilute his frustration before facing her again. He wasn't looking forward to it, not with their current moods, but he climbed out and dried off anyway.

He ran a brush through his wet hair, only because it allowed him another moment to think, but his reflection caused another distraction. Staring back at him was someone he despised—a filtered version of himself or who he thought he'd been before. The person in the mirror was weak, dependent, empty, and so unbearably sick and tired of being weak, dependent, and empty.

He needed a change and to take charge of his life. He'd start with his relationship. Resolved, he entered the bedroom to discover Avery hadn't waited for him. After getting dressed, he shuffled to the wheelchair but didn't sit. He stood over it and decided with finality that he never again wanted to be the fragile and frightened person he became in that chair.

Deciding to forego the chair, he carefully stepped around it and headed toward the dining room without the cane—yet another reminder that he wasn't the person he wanted to be. For safety, he walked near the wall in case he needed to brace himself along the way. He wasn't stupid. Setbacks caused by stubborn pride wouldn't get his life back.

It took a while, and he was out of breath when he arrived, but he'd done it. He was finally walking on his terms.

"Jackson, what are you doing?" Eleanor found him leaning on the door frame when she entered the dining room and rushed to his side.

Ignoring the question, he looked over her shoulder into the empty room. "Where's Avery?"

"She said something came up, and she left."

Out of patience, Jackson shuffled to the table. Every muscle groaned with the same exasperation he felt as he lowered into a chair. "What's for dinner?"

"I'll go get it, and then you'll tell me what you did to upset that sweet girl." Tossing him a stern look, she sighed at the guilty look on his face before disappearing into the kitchen.

Annoyed to now have two disappointed women to deal with, he shoved his hands through his wet hair and dropped them hard on the table.

"Is there a problem?" his father asked flatly, crossing the room to stand before Jackson.

Fantastic. Why not add another fight with his father to his shitty day. "Not in the least."

"Where's the wheelchair?"

"Don't need it." To his surprise, Grayson took a seat at the table but remained silent. Narrowing his eyes, Jackson studied him and wondered when the condescending comments and insults would be hurled his way.

"Mr. Vane." Shocked to find Grayson had snuck in, she froze, a steaming casserole dish in her hands. "I didn't hear you come in. Will you be joining us for dinner?"

The invite seemed to cause Grayson discomfort before he reluctantly agreed and sent Eleanor into a frenzy. While she hustled about the room and kitchen, arranging the new setting on the table and lighting candles, Jackson watched his father with suspicion.

He checked his watch and readjusted his position in the chair over and over. Was he in a hurry to escape? Late for a party? Counting down the minutes because it was so unbearable to be with his son? His took rapid shallow breaths, and his eyes skipped from Jackson to Eleanor to his watch as he rubbed his hands together under the table.

He'd never seen the Great Grayson Vane anxious before. Always overconfident, he rarely showed any emotion that might be considered weak.

"You know what? I can't. I have to go." Jumping up, Grayson rushed through the kitchen and out the side door. A few moments later, his car could be heard racing down the driveway.

Stunned, Eleanor and Jackson stared at each other. "What just happened?" she finally asked.

"I have no idea."

"Well, whatever is bothering him, he'll come clean soon enough, but I don't feel good about it."

"Why is that?"

"I can't explain it. Something with him has been off lately, and I know what you're thinking." She waved her finger at him before taking a seat at the table. "It's not you, deary. He acted strangely since before you came home."

Jackson didn't know what to say. He hadn't noticed anything unusual with Grayson's behavior, but then, again, he barely knew the man.

"We should eat before it gets cold." Eleanor offered her hand to Jackson and blessed the food. She asked God to soften Jackson and Grayson's hearts toward one another and to watch over her daughter and grandchildren. All the people she loved were going through difficult times, so she prayed for their safety and healing.

After passing Jackson the bowl of roasted brussels sprouts, she picked up the potatoes.

"So, why's Avery mad at you?"

Damn. He'd hoped Grayson's unexpected appearance and swift exit would have made her forget. "Eleanor, I love you, but that's none of your business."

"Maybe not but talking it out might help." She smiled and served herself some potatoes. Although Jackson didn't eat gravy, she made some anyway and poured it on thick.

He grunted in response and accepted the bowl of potatoes she handed him. When his plate was full, he grabbed his fork but couldn't eat.

"I'm afraid I'm doing exactly what I tried to avoid," he confessed, dropping his fork in frustration.

Eleanor took a sip of water and waited for him to say his peace. She'd done that since he was young, always knowing when to wait him out and when to prod him along.

"I'm leading her on by trying to make the relationship work, and I'm hurting her because I can't give her what she needs."

"What is it, do you think, that's holding you back?" she asked casually before cutting a bite of pork.

He sat back in his chair and contemplated the question. "I don't know. What's wrong with me?"

"There's nothing wrong with you, sweetie." She patted his hand resting on the table. "You're dealing with a lot right now, and just because she's a wonderful person and has blindly and unconditionally loved you her entire life," she paused when he scolded her with his eyes, "doesn't mean she's the one for you."

That option had never occurred to him. Although it explained why he struggled to return her feelings, it didn't make breaking her heart any less agonizing.

"Tonight might have been her breaking point."

He remembered the look on her face before she ran out of the bathroom. He'd rejected her, and getting past the embarrassment on both sides might be difficult. The worst part was knowing she didn't deserve it. She gave everything to their relationship. All he'd given her was a merry-go-round of hope and disappointment.

"Reach out to her and tell her how you feel. I'm sure she's sitting around waiting for you to call."

He shrugged, doubting Avery would want to speak with him anytime soon. All he knew for sure was that he'd lost his appetite and wanted to brood in private.

"I'm sorry, Eleanor. The food smells amazing, but—"

"No problem, sweetie. I'll save your plate in case you get hungry later."

"Thanks." Standing slowly, careful to set his feet under him, he shuffled into the hallway in time to hear the front door shut.

"Who's there?" he called down the hall, surprised to see his father step into view.

The light streaming through the large window above the door fell on his back, casting his face in shadows and depriving Jackson of the opportunity to read his face and gain the upper hand.

"We need to talk."

Chapter Fifteen

☆ ☆ ☆

Jackson

I'm not in the mood." Jackson turned his back on his father, something he learned from the man himself, and shifted toward his room.

"I'm not here to argue, and this can't wait."

Grayson kept his eyes on Jackson until he disappeared into his office. What could possibly be this important? He'd barely seen his father in the seven months since he'd returned, and whenever Grayson came around, they did very little talking. Only flung insults at each other until someone stalked away. Now, late in the evening and unannounced, he wanted to have a conversation. *Ridiculous*, Jackson puffed.

It took him a while to reach the office at the end of the hallway, but it was enough time to get his blood boiling. He didn't have the patience to deal with his father's constant need to tear him down. He'd done that enough to himself already. Then again, his mood couldn't possibly get any worse. So, bring it on.

Stepping into the doorway, he located Grayson by the bookcases, holding a small black box. Since his father called this urgent meeting, Jackson waited by the door for an explanation before deciding if he would stay.

"This was your mother's," he said, opening the box.

Jackson stepped forward, his breath catching in his chest when he saw the large diamond ring sitting up in the felt, and mentally kicked himself for the gut reaction.

"I remember the day I gave this to her. We were walking on the beach at Hilton Head Island before dinner. The sunset had cast the most stunning view across the sky behind her, but it was no comparison to her. She looked so beautiful that night, as she always did." He smiled and closed the lid before taking a deep, audible breath. "She'd been so happy."

Crossing the room to a small table by the dual picture windows, Grayson set down the box and filled two glasses with brandy from the crystal decanter.

As he held one out, Jackson fought the urge to tell him to *fuck off*, curiosity getting the better of him. He stepped into the room and accepted the glass. Always suspicious, he watched his father as they both lowered into a red leather chair on either side of the serving table.

The way Grayson stared put him on alert, but he held his ground, daring his father to say the wrong thing. Maybe a good screaming match would release the tension that had been building since his therapy session with Avery earlier that afternoon.

"I'm proud of you, son."

Choking on the drink he'd been sipping, Jackson coughed to clear his throat. The absurdity of those words coming out of his father's mouth had a smoldering fury rising from the pit of his stomach. He threw back what was left in his glass, expecting it to calm the rage, but it only sparked a blazing fire. What in the hell was Grayson trying to start by saying something like that?

"Let me get this straight," he finally said, skepticism and irritation evident in his voice. "After all the years of your absence in my life and the horrible things you've said to me, you're suddenly proud? What the fuck are you doing?"

If he could, he'd pace the room to keep his hands off his father's throat.

"Jackson—"

"Don't you know my head is messed up enough right now?" His father opened his mouth to respond, but Jackson cut him off. "No, of course, you don't because you have no idea what I've been through or who I am."

He slammed the empty glass on the small table and stood anyway, ignoring the pain. After a few wobbly steps, he leaned on the back of the chair.

"I've been to war, nearly died, and lost my career and three best friends. Now, I'm living day by day on a shred of sanity, all while having to learn to fucking walk again." His raised voice and raging blood pressure drummed in his ears.

"You're right. I haven't been there for you lately."

"Lately? Don't give me that bullshit. You've never been there."

"Jackson, please sit down." When he didn't move, Grayson sighed. "You've always been headstrong, like your mother. Here." He picked up the tiny box and held it up. "I want you to have this. *She* wanted you to have it."

Confused, Jackson reached over the chair and took it. He thought about throwing it across the room, a little exercise in tension relief, but opened it instead. The pang in his chest when he saw the familiar square-cut diamond engagement ring was enough to put out the fire raging inside him. He could still picture it on his mother's delicate finger and hated how much he still missed her.

"Why are you giving this to me?" he managed, suddenly unsteady.

"Before she died, she took it off and asked me to keep it for you."

"Why?"

"She hoped you'd give it to the woman you plan to marry."

"Why would she care?" The longer he held the ring, his anger resurfaced and compounded, consuming the unexpected sadness he felt.

"What?"

"Why would she care if I kept her ring? You proudly told me that she never wanted anything to do with me. Explain why I should not toss it in the lake."

"Son—"

"I told you never to call me that."

"Jackson," he corrected. "I never should have said those things about your mother. I'm sorry."

Taken by surprise, he tightened his grip on the back of the chair and braced for the next bomb to drop.

"Is it true? Or were you trying to hurt me?"

"Both," Grayson answered honestly. "She didn't want children but fell in love with you the moment you were born. It was me she hated and resented. Me and that boy toy of…" He closed his eyes and reset his face. "I was the reason she was never around."

"You didn't feel the need to tell me that before?"

"I wasn't in the mood then."

"You're an asshole."

"I know."

Unable to look at him, Jackson turned his gaze to the window. The darkness outside only provided a somber reflection of them in the room, and it did nothing to calm him. "What changed?"

"Two things. I heard you're dating."

At the mention of Avery, the little jewelry box weighed heavy like a brick in his hand. He couldn't give her that ring. Not now, not one day in the future, not ever. At that moment, when he least expected it, he was done trying. Finished torturing them both while he attempted and repeatedly failed to be the man from her dreams. With the unfathomable idea of marriage on his mind, he knew what he had to do. It wouldn't be easy, but he had to let her go.

Jackson's attention was wrenched back to the room when Grayson started hacking, violent and loud. Stunned, he watched his father grab a handkerchief from his pocket and hold it against his mouth. In between coughing fits, Grayson reached for the decanter, poured a double shot of brandy, and drank. It seemed to soothe his throat enough to catch his breath, but he labored over every inhale. He closed his eyes, leaning back against the chair, and Jackson took the seat across from him.

"I'm dying."

Jackson scoffed. "Right."

Using the armrests, Grayson pulled himself up and set his eyes on Jackson. "I'm dying," he repeated and let out a long, ragged breath. "It's stage four lung cancer. I have six months, maybe less. Now you know reason number two."

Jackson could only stare. What was he supposed to do with that information? He'd despised his father for years. They'd argued, said miserable things, and disregarded each other.

"What about radiation or other treatments?"

"They weren't working, and when it spread to my liver, stomach, and who the hell knows where else, I stopped going." He finished off the drink and tossed the glass onto the table. The glass clinking against the metal tray on top echoed through the stale room.

"What are you going to do?"

"Live my life as I want for as long as possible. Then, I guess, I'll have to go into a care facility until…"

He trailed off, his expression telling. He didn't want to think about the end or living his final days in a sterile facility at the mercy of strangers. Jackson could relate.

"This is your home. Why not move back here? Eleanor and I can help with whatever you need."

Grayson nodded, then stood. "Well, that's all I came to say." On his way to the door, he stopped beside Jackson and placed a hand on his shoulder. "This is your home, too, and I meant what I said. I am proud of you. You're a good man, Jackson, despite having me as a father. Fill Eleanor in, will you?"

And then he was gone, leaving Jackson alone, shocked, and downright confused. He sat motionless, replaying the short conversation in his mind. He'd rarely felt anything other than anger or indifference when it came to his father, but empathy and pity over the fate he'd been dealt came easier than expected.

With one quick motion, he returned his glass to the table and pushed to his feet. He was beaten down by Avery's expectations, his conflicting emotions about his mother, Grayson's news and change of heart, and the usual chaos. He'd love to have just one moment of peace and headed to his room to find it.

———

Entering the kitchen after his morning workout, he found Eleanor humming and cooking at the stove, her back to the door. He sat on a stool at the island and enjoyed the happy scene. Her hip bounced to the song in her head as she transferred sausage to a serving dish.

"Jackson!" she screeched when she turned around and waited for her heart to drop out of her throat. "You scared me." Setting down the dish, she looked behind him. "Did you walk here again?"

He nodded with a grin and sampled a piece of sausage. "Haven't used the wheelchair since yesterday morning." The possibilities of what that could mean were exhilarating.

"Good for you." She grabbed the carton of eggs, cracked several into a mixing bowl, and whisked. "Did you talk to Avery last night?"

"I meant to, but something came up."

The hot pan on the stove sizzled when she emptied the eggs into it. "What could be more important than—"

"Grayson came back."

"Oh. I didn't hear him come in. When he left so abruptly at dinner, I didn't expect him to return."

"Me either, but he had some news that couldn't wait. I guess he wanted to tell us at dinner but chickened out."

"That doesn't sound like him. What was worrying him so?" She tossed the eggs one last time, then scooped them into a serving dish.

"Maybe you should sit down." He patted the stool next to him.

"That doesn't sound good."

He told her what he knew about Grayson's condition and plans. But when she sucked in a breath, tears filling her eyes, he pulled her into his arms and fought his own. He could handle most anything, except seeing Eleanor cry.

Chapter Sixteen

☆ ☆ ☆

Jackson

After breakfast, Jackson went for a walk to clear his head. It took a while, but he circled the house to the backyard, then sat on a porch step to catch his breath. Days like these were growing on him, and he was learning to appreciate the mild Virginia seasons.

Breathing in the cool November air, he stood again and headed toward the water. As he moved carefully on the wet ground, he stopped often to gather his balance or pick up a rock to skip across the water. The peaceful scenery, the birds singing their joyful morning songs, the sweet, gentle breeze should help him process yesterday's shocking events if he could reclaim enough head space for it.

He'd love to compartmentalize each pivotal moment and think through what he learned, how he felt about it, and what he should do next. Treat each one like a military mission—every detail and potential solution explored while solidifying an efficient and safe plan of action.

And he'd start with Avery. Mentally setting his father's news aside—the next suitcase to unpack—he tossed a rock into the lake and relived the tub discussion with Avery. Every nervous, confident, and angry movement of her hands and eyes. Her spoken and withheld words. The way her voice rose with frustration. The pain that softened it. And his role in it all.

The unexpected sound of footsteps on the brittle ground behind him sent his organized thoughts swirling out of control again. He shuffled his feet to turn around, surprised to see Avery approaching with an oversized bag. He'd love a chance to read her eyes behind dark sunglasses, but her pronounced frown told him all he needed to know.

"Hi," was all he could say as he waited for her to join him. After their argument the night before and Grayson's news, he'd yet to figure out what to say, knowing nothing he came up with would be sufficient enough to ease the blow.

"Ready for your workout?"

Her professional, frigid tone doused the sliver of hope that their conversation would be any less excruciating than expected.

"Avery, it's good—"

"I'll get set up over there." She pointed a thumb over her shoulder and walked away from him.

"Avery," he called, but she continued unrolling the yoga mat as if he'd said nothing. "I wasn't sure if I'd see you today."

"Me either," she answered but kept her back to him.

"Avery, I didn't mean to hurt you."

"I know."

"Will you look at me?" He waited while she fidgeted with the equipment, ignoring his request. "Avery." Taking her hand, he gently spun her around and removed her sunglasses. He needed that window into her emotions to carefully guide his next words.

Although he knew it would be there, the pain in her eyes still rocked him. Not wanting to face what he'd done and had yet to do, he pulled her close and pressed a kiss to her forehead. She leaned into him, still trusting, loving, and supporting him.

Avery broke the silence first, saying the one thing he never thought would grace her tongue after what happened between them. "I'm sorry for pushing you."

She leaned back and looked up at him with more compassion and forgiveness than he'd earned. It tore his heart apart to know he was about to shatter hers.

"Can we sit?" he asked, and she helped him lower to the mat before joining him. "The wheelchair is now in storage, and this morning, I walked the full distance around the house." Her eyes widened in surprise, bringing a smile to his lips. "I was able to do that because of you."

Her head fell to his shoulder. "I'm so happy for you. You put in the work, and after all you've been through, you deserve for things to finally go right."

He thought of the news he received from his father and the decision he'd yet to give Avery. Neither relationship was going right, and he would soon lose them both.

Resting against him, she placed a hand on his chest when she felt the tension return to his muscles. His heart beat faster than normal, giving away his unease. When tears pooled on his eyelids, she moved to wrap her legs and arms around him.

"Is everything okay? What can I do?"

He blew out an extended breath. "You've done enough, don't you think? For me, for our relationship. I don't deserve you."

"This is about us, isn't it?" She sat up with a new realization. "You're breaking it off."

His silence told her more than words ever could.

"I want you to know," he began, taking her hand. "What happened between us last night did not sway my decision. Grayson said some things after you left and brought forward feelings that I had been ignoring. Selfishly, I don't want to lose you." He paused when her head snapped up, her cheeks now soaked with fresh tears.

"Then don't."

"Avery, it's not fair to you." He trailed the back of his hand over her cheek. "You said it yourself, life is short. I won't allow you to waste any more of yours on me. You want and deserve something I can't give, and one day, you'll find someone who will make you happier than I—"

She shook her head. "Impossible. Jackson, I love you."

Those three words came at him like daggers instead of soothing him as they should.

"I've always loved you," she whispered.

"I know." Closing his eyes because he couldn't bring himself to look into hers, he brought her hand to his lips.

He couldn't wait for the torture to end for them both. "You've been my rock all these months, but I won't continue to take advantage."

"So, that's it? I don't get a say?" Scooting back from him, she stood on shaky legs and swatted at the stream of tears streaking her cheeks.

He followed, and she flung herself into his embrace. Emotion flowed through her body, making it infinitely harder to let go, and a familiar pang of guilt balled in his gut. "Please, Avery. Live your life and forget about me. Please. If not for me, do it for yourself."

Reality setting in, she stumbled backward—her big brown eyes giving him a glimpse into her thoughts. She'd missed out on other relationships and wasted years waiting for him to come to her. And when he finally did, he couldn't love her. Her heart wasn't the only thing he broke…he also shattered her dreams.

She should be screaming about the unfairness or whaling her fists on him in anger. Instead, she gathered her things and left the jagged pieces of her heart at his feet.

"Goodbye, Jackson."

He watched her jog away, and when she disappeared around the house, he doubled over. The usual twist in his stomach tightened, the ache spreading like wildfire with every minute ticking by in her absence.

What had he done?

With his hands resting on his thighs, he gulped in air while his world spun out of control. Every devoted gesture she'd shown him over the last six months flashed through his mind at a nauseating pace. The way her face lit up at the sight of him. Her playful smile when he was grumpy. The sweet words she'd whisper when they were alone. The soft caress of her hand on his skin. Her unconditional patience, forgiveness, love.

He'd appreciated it all but couldn't help that he didn't feel the same. Breaking off their relationship had been the right decision. One day, she would be grateful he'd given her back her life.

Taking a deep breath, he stood and looked around the yard. He needed to let off some steam, think, and forget like he would when he had legs that worked. He needed to run.

About twenty yards away sat an old tree stump. It was a short distance, but if he could jog to it now, maybe he could increase his endurance to run longer distances soon. He wanted that more than anything—to run again. And he had no reason to delay starting. However much it hurt or however long it took, he wouldn't stop until he reached that damn stump.

Resolved, he lifted his right foot, but his left knee gave out on the push-off, and he fell face-first onto the hard ground. *Fitting*, he puffed with sarcasm, yet undeterred. Rising to his feet, he tried again, taking off in a limping run toward his goal. This time, he made it several steps before tumbling. With every new attempt, he traveled farther and farther, until collapsing at the base of the stump.

Short, labored breaths burned in his lungs as he dragged himself up to sit on the flat surface. While he recovered, he rested his elbows on his thighs and watched the sweat drip off his forehead, darkening the dirt below, careful to keep his mind clear.

"Are you *trying* to beat yourself up?" Eleanor called from the back porch.

Ignoring her, he tossed his hair out of his face to search for a new destination. His eyes locked on a tree, and he took off as best he could, making it halfway before falling hard on his hands and knees. The scrapes on his legs and palms stung with the mixture of blood, dirt, and sweat, but he couldn't stop now. It was working.

He practiced until dark, stumbling and flopping across the yard. With each lap, he set a new goal and labored until reaching it. He was out of breath and bleeding, but he was alive.

Several times, Eleanor brought out water and begged him to take a break. But the challenge took his mind off all that haunted him—Avery, Will, his father, too many regrets to count—and he couldn't stop. Not when he'd made such rapid progress. And even though the war in his head still raged, he could suppress it while he worked.

An hour later when he could barely see the yard in front of him through the darkness, he dragged himself back to the house. Eleanor met him at the door and helped him up the porch steps. Fumbling with every step, he leaned on her to walk. She never muttered a complaint about his sweaty skin dampening her shirt or how heavy his tired body felt on hers, and he loved her for it. She supported him long enough to reach the kitchen and deposited him on a stool at the island.

"Drink." She placed a tall glass of red liquid on the counter within reach. "You're probably dehydrated."

She'd used that tone plenty of times during his youth, and hearing it now made him smile. He knew when he could test her and when it was best to heed the warning, so he raised the glass and drained it.

"Why are you punishing yourself?" she demanded, refilling his glass.

"Not punishment. Practice."

"Bull. Practice is not what I saw out there."

"What did you see?"

"I saw a man, broken and suffering, torturing himself for hurting someone he cares about. I saw someone who is vulnerable, lonely, and afraid. Someone who wants to forget." She paused to let her words sink in. "But I also saw a man who doesn't give up and always does the right thing, no matter the pain it might cause him. He has a beautiful heart, and I'm incredibly proud of him."

"You think I was right in breaking it off with Avery?" he asked. "You adore her."

"I do."

"She was so hurt. Like I rammed a knife into her back when she wasn't looking." His empty stomach churned thinking of the agony he saw on her face. He'd blindsided her and wished he'd been more articulate in relaying his feelings. But regrettably, he'd never been good at that.

"It will hurt for a good while, but she's young and will bounce back stronger." She grabbed a plate from the cabinet and several containers of leftovers from the refrigerator. "You're going to eat something whether you like it or not. Got it?"

"Yes, ma'am," he said with a grin.

She filled a plate with vegetables and pork loin and tossed it into the microwave. When the timer chimed, she set the food in front of him and demanded he eat. "Your muscles will thank me later."

Not willing to fight her, and because he was famished, he ate until the plate was empty.

"Good boy. Now, go wash up. You stink."

He laughed for the first time that day, and a heaviness lifted off his chest.

While he soaked in the tub, he tried music for the first time to drown out the noise while attempting to relax. Needing to crank up the volume to accomplish the task, he used earbuds so not to disturb Eleanor. It helped, but it didn't erase Avery's face and her crushed hopes from his thoughts.

At least he could say he gave their relationship a chance. It just wasn't meant to be, and now, after years of putting her life on hold, she could finally move on. Maybe with time, as Eleanor suggested, the heartache and disappointment would start to heal for them both.

Chapter Seventeen

☆ ☆ ☆

Jackson

After a long walk in the frigid December weather, he took a shower and headed to the kitchen, pausing in the doorway to watch Eleanor.

She moved about the room with intention, cooking multiple dishes at once while preparing for her signature dinner presentation. It would have been an entertaining way to pass the time had it not been for the frantic look on her face.

Before he could speak, she noticed him and tipped her head toward the dining room.

He knew what that meant. Leaving Eleanor to her controlled chaos, he entered the dining room and found his father seated at the head of the table, reading the newspaper. Although bright mid-day sun streamed through the windows, the crystal chandelier scattering the rays in brilliant rainbow patterns on the walls, the stately room seemed muted with gloom. The air thick, stagnant, tainted.

It was the first time he'd ever seen his father look out of place anywhere. Something wasn't right, and dread sat like cement in his stomach.

"Can I get you a drink?" Jackson asked to announce his arrival.

"No. Thanks."

Grayson folded the newspaper, exposing his face, and Jackson blinked twice, unsure the stranger filling a seat at their table was the Great Grayson Vane. This man was frail, his sunken cheeks dull and pale. The skin under his eyes looked bruised, matching his grayish-purple shirt and what remained of his hair. Gone were the thick locks Grayson once had, now cut short and thinning.

So much had changed since Jackson last saw him—the cancer undoubtedly taking a toll on his body. But the one change Jackson couldn't comprehend was the inconspicuous, solid-colored T-shirt and jeans. Strange attire for someone who wore a tailored suit seven days a week and for every occasion.

Setting the paper aside, Grayson motioned for him to take a seat at the table. "You seem to be moving around a little better."

He claimed a nearby chair, not knowing what to say. Years of distance and hurtful arguments hindered his ability to make small talk with the person he supposedly owed his life to. Grayson was wildly mistaken on that egotistical view of himself, and he'd be waiting longer than he had for Jackson to ever succumb to the notion. The title of lifesaver went to Eleanor years ago and more recently, Will. If he was being honest with himself, Avery deserved the recognition as well. Without her, he might not have ever gotten out of bed after Will's funeral. At the time, he'd been content to waste away until he joined his brothers.

With those memories resurfacing unexpectedly and grinding away at his good mood, the awkward silence in the room threatened to ignite more until Eleanor arrived. Her beacon of light and positivity brought back the sun and distraction, and Jackson loved her even more for it. As if that were possible.

After eating, Eleanor returned to the kitchen, leaving Grayson and Jackson alone.

"I didn't stop by only for lunch," Grayson said. His smoky eyes were veiled and expressionless, giving Jackson no information about his intentions or emotional state.

He reached over the arm of his chair to retrieve a leather bag and pulled out a long, blue folder. It was neatly organized, with several tags of varying colors sticking out of a stack of paper. He set the folder on the table, crossed his hands on top, and turned his gaze to Jackson.

"I'm working on cleaning up a few things with my will. As my only child, I need you to sign some forms. Since tomorrow is the anniversary of your accident, I thought it would be best to stop by today."

Blood drained from Jackson's face and pooled in his chest. He couldn't think, feel, breathe. "I didn't realize it was…"

The memories came rushing back while Grayson continued. He read nothing when Grayson put the forms in front of him. His limbs, fingers, and mind numb as he sunk deeper into darkness.

Visions he worked so hard to suppress tore through his mind, transporting him back to the edge of the explosion. Flashes of blinding light. Warm gritty blood on his skin. Bones being crushed by a two-ton vehicle being wadded up and discarded like a piece of paper. Cries of his brothers as they writhed in pain before succumbing to their injuries.

An object was thrust into his hand, and he recoiled, shocked by the feel of cold metal in his hand. His heart raced. His blood pressure spiked, and shallow, rusty breaths scratched his dry throat.

Sand. It was everywhere. Rubbing his eyes, he startled at a hand resting on his shoulder. Will? Eleanor? If the person said anything, he couldn't process it, and he was soon tugged to his feet by his arms.

Mechanically, he walked where his guide led him, but the hallway seemed to tilt left and right. Between each step, flashes pulsed like strobe lights timed to multiple songs at once. The brightest hit on his supercharged heartbeat as if he were connected to the power source. It radiated through him until one final surge went off inside his skull, stealing his strength.

He couldn't see. Couldn't move. Paralyzed again, he drowned in agony, grasping for support as he collapsed.

————

When he awoke stiff and weary, the only light in the room was a faint moonbeam shining through the sheer curtains. Why did he feel like an old, battered punching bag instead of someone who'd slept through the afternoon? Pushing up to his elbows, he looked around, but the room and his stomach spiraled out of control. Deciding to wait it out rather than lose his lunch on the rug, he laid back down and covered his face with a pillow.

The next time his eyes opened, the sun and Eleanor humming a happy tune—two of his favorite things—greeted him. Laying back to enjoy them, he realized his both his mind and stomach were empty.

Shooting out of bed, he got dressed and hurried to the kitchen, ready for one of Eleanor's hearty breakfast creations. But her humming hadn't come from there and the room wasn't filled with the delicious aroma of bacon frying.

"Oh, my heavens." Eleanor slapped her hand on her chest when she saw him in the hallway. "You have to stop doing that."

"I don't smell breakfast. Is it early?"

"Honey, it's two o'clock in the afternoon. You've been out cold for twenty-four hours."

"What?" How could he sleep that long and not know it? Especially when it had been so difficult for him to get just a few hours of sleep most nights.

Going to him, she placed her hand on his forehead as she did when he was a kid and frowned. "You don't have a fever. Are you sick? I was worried about you but didn't want to disturb your sleep."

"I feel fine."

"Come. I'll fix you something to eat." She led him into the kitchen and removed a large bowl from the refrigerator. "How did it go with your father yesterday?"

"Okay, I think. I don't remember most of it."

"How can you not remember it?"

His shoulders popped up. "I don't know. He mentioned something about his will, and the rest is a blur. Did you hear anything?"

"No." She scooped a spoonful of vegetable soup into a bowl. "But I saw he'd brought his briefcase. Does that jar any memories?"

With his mouth watering, he watched her place the overflowing bowl in the microwave. "I think I signed something now that you mention it. Hey, what's today's date?"

"December twentieth. Why?"

"He mentioned something about today's date being why he stopped by yesterday. Does today have any—" His stomach rumbled as the conversation came back to him.

"Oh, honey," she rested a hand on his. "Today is the day Josh and Billy died. I'm so sorry."

He slumped back in the chair, realizing now what happened.

"Is that what got you so upset yesterday?" As she often did, she wrapped an arm around his shoulders and squeezed. He clung to her for balance. "I know it's been a hard road, but if you can focus on the good things in your life, it will help put the rest in perspective."

She kissed his hair when he didn't respond and leaned on the counter to see his face. "Jackson, look at me." Her empathetic grin greeted him. "Tell me one thing you're grateful for. Go."

He recognized that all-business tone. "You. I'm grateful for you."

With a tilt of her head, she looked him over, reading him and his intentions. "Are you buttering me up so I'll leave you alone?"

"No. You're all I have. Without you, I wouldn't be here."

Fresh tears soon replaced her teasing smile. "I love you too, sweetie, but I disagree. You are stronger than you give yourself credit for." She kissed his forehead before moving on. "Give me something else that makes you grateful."

"My progress so far and being able to walk again."

"See? All part of His plan. Thank you, Jesus."

He smiled, admiring her faith. Sometimes, he wished he had a touch to get him through each day. His belief in a higher power had waned since coming back, and he often wondered why God, if he existed, was constantly testing him.

"One more," she demanded.

He thought for a moment. "I'm grateful for this second chance." Although the journey so far had been grueling, and he still had a long way to go, he meant it. "It's something my friends didn't get. For them, I won't waste this opportunity."

"That's my boy." She touched his cheek, admiring the man he'd become. "Hey. I have an idea," she said, taking his hand. Excitement lighting her pretty gray-blue eyes. "Why don't you go visit their parents?"

The thought of seeing his friends' parents, after all they'd been through and on this day, had his chest tightening again.

"Jackson, you can do it," she insisted when she felt the tension return to his body. "After you finish your soup, of course. You'll need your strength."

———

Less than an hour later, Eleanor and Jackson arrived at Billy's childhood home to visit his parents, Harrison and Sophia.

"Go on. They're expecting you," she said, putting the car in park.

"I don't know about this, Eleanor. What if seeing me today is too painful? I can't do that to them."

"Maybe seeing you will help ease the pain, at least for a little while. Did you think of that? They love you, and you need this. Now, go."

Exiting the car, he noticed Sophia waiting for him on the front porch. He had so many fond memories of her growing up. She was witty, kind, and always made him feel safe and welcome in her home.

She stepped off the porch of their elegant two-story brick home and jogged to meet him halfway. With his legs unsteady on the sloped driveway, she nearly knocked him over, her arms wrapping around him with force. She buried her face in the hollow between his neck and shoulder and sobbed. Holding her and feeling the bond they've always shared pour into him, he was suddenly glad he'd come.

Catching her breath, she pulled back and framed his face in her hands. "Jackson, I can't believe you're walking." She held him at arms-length and pushed at the hair that had blown into his face. "You look incredible. So handsome, as always." Draping her arm around his, she escorted him toward the house. "Harrison is going to be so excited to see you. We've missed you."

"I've missed you, too." More than he realized.

Once inside, Harrison appeared in the doorway of his home office and took Jackson in his arms. "My boy. It's so great to see you again and without the wheelchair. I can't believe it. How are you?"

"It's been a tough couple of months," he answered honestly.

"No doubt. Come on, let's sit."

Sitting on the soft, plaid settee next to Sophia, Jackson looked around. "It feels so strange being in here."

"That's because you all were forbidden from coming in here for many years. You boys couldn't be trusted." Sophia squeezed his hand and nudged his shoulder, flashing a weary grin.

"We were fine with that. We claimed it was too girly for us, but we were more terrified of what you might do to us if we broke something."

"Smart boys, you all were."

"I still can't believe you're walking already," Harrison chimed in. "Avery must be good at her job."

"She is. How are things with you?" he asked to change the subject and avoid having to explain his many failings in their short relationship.

"Pretty good," Harrison answered. "Your father's keeping me busy, and I've been thankful for that. It's given me something to focus on."

Since the company's inception, Harrison had been his father's right-hand man and provided well for his family. Grayson affectionately called him the company janitor since he cleaned up the failing companies they purchased. Then, Grayson would do his part and sell them for a hefty profit, which they both shared. Harrison had a special way with people and was a trustworthy business partner—the perfect complement to Jackson's reckless and ruthless father.

Sophia had also been close friends with his mother, Jacqueline, and knew firsthand how they treated their son. Both she and Harrison had gone out of their way to include him in their family. They took time to attend his cross-country races in high school, and he often stayed at their house for dinner or overnight when returning to the estate was too much to bear.

But Jackson hadn't gone there to talk about Grayson. He came to talk about Billy and feel the warmth and healing power of two people he adored and hadn't realized he desperately needed in his life.

Before anyone could inquire about Grayson or his illness, Jackson diverted the conversation back to Billy and their childhood together. As the group's chief instigator, Billy suffered the most injuries due to his lack of respect for the body's limitations. Most of the trouble they got into came because of Billy's fearlessness and grand schemes.

Always at the ready with a joke or prank, usually inappropriate for the situation, he competed with Will for the biggest personality in the room. He was electric like Will, but also unpredictable, earning him the nickname of Firefly from Eleanor.

"Please don't be a stranger," Harrison said to Jackson when Eleanor returned to pick him up. "We're here for you, always."

He took them both in his arms and wished he hadn't waited so long to visit. "Thank you. I'll see you soon."

"Good visit?" Eleanor asked when Jackson was back in the car with a smile.

"I love them almost as much as I love you." He turned to face her. "Thank you. I might not have done this if you hadn't pushed me."

"Strongly encouraged," she corrected and patted his leg with the love and wisdom of the mother she'd always been to him. "And yes, you would have. Eventually." She put the car in motion. "Next stop, the Wilsons. I called Josh's parents, and we got lucky. They both took off today for—well, you know."

He nodded in response, knowing this day would also be hard for them.

"Where are we going?" he asked when Eleanor missed the turn toward their neighborhood.

"We're not meeting them at their house."

He was about to ask where they were going when he saw it. His heartbeat quickened, and a new instinct to retreat had him sweating. He couldn't fight it, no matter how much he detested the feeling, making him question who he was now.

Chapter Eighteen

✩ ✩ ✩

Eleanor

Eleanor drove under the black iron archway and
through the cemetery until locating the Wilson's car
parked in the shade of a large Oak tree. Jackson
wrung his hands together, his nerves returning.

"Look at me, Jackson." His eyes glistened, and she knew
where his thoughts had taken him. "What happened to Josh
was not your fault. His path was his own. They understand
that."

He turned his attention to the cemetery beyond as Claire
and Thomas exited the car. Running his hands through his
hair, he took a deep breath and opened the door.

Eleanor watched him stagger down the drive, his
emotions stealing his strength, and collapse into their open
arms. For several minutes, they held him while a year's
worth of regret and sadness poured out. His body

shuddered, and she quickly prayed, asking God to help him understand how lucky he was to have so many people in his life who loved him.

Soon, the trio walked to Josh's grave a few paces away and sat on the grass around his headstone. She tried not to watch, but seeing the three of them sitting together in the dappled shade of the tree was heartbreakingly touching. It took some time, but sobs finally gave way to laughter, and the good mood continued after Jackson returned to the car.

"One more to go," Eleanor announced as she took off, waving goodbye to Josh's parents. "I didn't get ahold of Will's parents, but we'll drive by to see if they're home."

––––––

Jackson

On a high from the previous two visits, Jackson tapped edgy knuckles on the Mason's front door, anticipation eating at his insides. Will's parents held a special place in his heart, and too much time had passed since he last saw them. Caroline and Jonathan were as kind as Eleanor, and like Harrison and Sophia, had long ago accepted him into their family.

Footsteps could soon be heard approaching from the other side. He couldn't wait to be swallowed into their embrace and feel the familiar comforts of another home that held fond childhood memories. The door opened, and he braced for impact.

"Can I help you?" A woman he didn't recognize asked when he didn't speak. She had short, white-blonde hair and a baby on her hip. A red sauce streaked across the child's chubby cheeks and matted in the woman's hair. She seemed frazzled but offered him a friendly smile.

"I'm sorry, I thought…" He trailed off, leaning back to see the house number affixed to the brick beside the door. He'd spent countless hours there but seeing the stranger in the doorway had him second-guessing his memory.

"Are you looking for the Masons?"

"Yes. Do you know them?"

"They were the previous owners of this house. We purchased it from them in August at a steal."

"Do you know where they moved to?" he interrupted, losing patience.

She shifted the toddler to her other hip. "They moved to North Carolina. Murf, Murphy-something or other," she attempted, seemingly unaware of his growing frustration.

"Murfreesboro?"

"Yes, that sounds right. Such wonderful people. How do you know them?"

Ignoring her question, he apologized for the interruption before returning to the SUV, devastated and confused.

"That was quick. Were they not home?" Eleanor asked.

"No. Did you know they moved?"

"I had no idea."

"The new homeowner said they sold the house a few months ago and moved to North Carolina." How could he not know they left, and why hadn't Avery told him? It didn't make any sense.

"Well, I guess we'll just have to track them down, and maybe, when you're fully mended, you can go for a visit." She shrugged like he worried for nothing and started the engine.

But Jackson couldn't put it out of his mind. Something must have happened for them to up and move without a word so soon after losing their son. For the first time since their breakup, he wished he could talk to Avery.

On the way home, the emotional rollercoaster ride he'd endured during his visits finally hit him. A dull throbbing pulsed around his temples. His back and legs ached more than his chest. He needed air but couldn't force enough in to fill his lungs completely.

"We're almost home, sweetie," Eleanor soothed before switching to a tone she knew he couldn't ignore. "I want you to lie down while I prepare dinner. Got it?"

"Yeah."

As he dragged his weak body through the house, he decided to follow Eleanor's advice. Maybe it would keep the migraine and memories from hanging out and starting trouble. He collapsed onto his bed, his eyes drifting shut, and listed things to be grateful for.

He enjoyed seeing his friends' parents. In addition to Eleanor, they were his family in every sense of the word that mattered. He was thankful he could show them the progress he'd made so they didn't have to see him broken and bound to a wheelchair again. Of course, they didn't know all he'd been through to get there, but he knew and being on his feet again meant everything.

His thoughts soon returned to Eleanor and her love and devotion to him. It had been her idea to make the visits. She called ahead, encouraged him when he got anxious, and spent her afternoon transporting him around town. She kept him grounded and moving forward.

She'd always been his foundation, but over the last eight months, she'd been his lifeline. He wanted to do something to thank her, but no idea seemed enough or suitable for his Eleanor.

When she called him for dinner, he resigned to brainstorming later. For now, his empty stomach took priority.

Chapter Nineteen

★ ★ ★

Jackson

April brought yet another anniversary Jackson would rather forget. The month of his forced homecoming. He'd been a shell of himself when he returned to Richmond twelve months ago—hollow, fragile, vulnerable, drowning.

Since then, his body and mobility had drastically improved, and so had his outlook on life. He still had a long way to go, but he'd accepted that recovery was a process. Nothing would happen overnight, and it certainly wouldn't happen without goals, hard work, and patience. He was getting better at forgiving himself for setbacks and pushing aside thoughts of surrender whenever the finish line seemed to creep further away.

Through winter, he spent hours walking, jogging, and building muscle, resulting in a new chiseled physique.

Physically, he felt more like the athlete he used to be. He could only jog a mile before needing to rest his legs, but it was farther than he could run a month ago. Given the circumstances and his doctors' predictions, he'd take it.

Every day, he ran with purpose, blurring the line between determined and obsessed. Some might call him addicted. Whichever label was used, he would happily admit to being obsessed with, addicted to, and consumed by the euphoria brought on by moving again, rebuilding what he'd lost, and finally being set free. Each mile he accumulated inched him closer to his goal of running twelve to fifteen miles in a single outing. He'd get there one day. There could be no stopping him now.

Rounding the corner of the estate after his morning outing, he was surprised to find two vehicles parked in the driveway. The red sports car and white van could only mean one thing—the cancer had taken over, and his father was moving in. Heading inside, the tension Jackson released during his walk knotted again in his neck and shoulders.

"Oh, Jackson. I'm so glad you're home," Eleanor greeted when he found her in the front parlor. She turned to the tall man in blue scrubs standing behind her. "This is Grayson's son."

The man reached out a hand. "Nice to meet you. I'm Reese with Hospice of Virginia. Will you join us?"

With a nod, he followed them to the coffee table covered in pamphlets, forms, and folders, and sat next to Eleanor. He could sense her unease and didn't like how her eyelids were already red and swollen. He should have been there to receive them and shield her permeable heart from absorbing the pain his father's presence would bring her.

"Where is he?" Jackson asked her.

"In his room." She blotted the corner of her eyes using the worn tissue she'd been clutching. "He looked so fragile."

Not knowing what to say, he accepted the hand she offered as the three of them went through a mountain of paperwork and explanations of what both parties would be responsible for.

"How was he? His mood and energy, I mean," Jackson asked when Reese went upstairs to talk with Grayson.

"Not good. They brought him in the van and had to wheel him in on a gurney."

When she began to cry again, he wrapped an arm around her and held her close.

"Someone else brought his car and dropped it off. I didn't see who." Sitting up, she tapped the tissue under her nose. "We'll need to pack up his apartment and bring his belongings here."

"Don't worry about that. I'll take care of it."

While Eleanor distracted herself with organizing documents into piles and folders, his thoughts wandered to Grayson's will. Who would he leave the apartment, the estate, and his business to—Harrison, a friend, a woman he'd slept with? Shaking his head, he dismissed the question to refocus on helping Eleanor. After all, assuming or speculating about his father's wishes was a pointless waste of time since he barely knew the man, his life, or the people in it. But he worried about Eleanor and hoped Grayson would take care of her even after he was gone.

He looked through the information Reese provided with her before tucking each document into a color-coded folder. The contraption hospice set up in Grayson's room, and their staff would provide most of the treatments someone in his condition required, but they wouldn't be tending to him around the clock. Jackson and Eleanor would have to fill in the gaps.

As she slid the last document into the folder, the doorbell rang.

"Were you expecting someone?" he asked.

"No. Would you mind getting it, dear? I need to gather myself."

With a pat on her arm, he hurried to the door, and opened it to a bald, stocky man in a navy suit, holding a briefcase.

"Can I help you?"

"You must be Jackson. I'm Adam Dufrene." When he wasn't invited in, he explained further. "Your father's attorney. He asked me to stop by."

"Oh. Sorry. Please, come in." Stepping aside, Jackson shut the door behind him.

"Call me Adam," he said slowly, distracted by the awe and wonder of his surroundings.

"First time?"

"Yes." Adam cleared his throat and straightened his tie. "You have a beautiful home."

"Thank you, but it's not mine. Follow me." He led Adam to his father's suite upstairs and knocked before turning the knob. He motioned Adam in, but before he could escape, Grayson called for him.

"Yes, sir?"

"Come here, son."

Reluctantly, Jackson entered the large room. He hadn't been in his parents' bedroom since before his mother died, and seeing it brought back memories he wasn't prepared to receive.

His favorite hide-and-seek spot as a kid, the four-poster antique bed, centered the room. To the left was the bathroom where he sat at the vanity with his mother while she curled her hair or applied makeup. He often told her she didn't need any of it, and he could still hear her light, airy laugh in response. She'd smile and look at him through the mirror with eyes that matched his own. He treasured those rare moments with his mother and would have liked more of them.

He glanced out the double windows facing the backyard, instantly regretting it. Every detail of the day he found his mother lying on the hardwood floor underneath came rushing back. How agonizingly delicate she looked. His father sweeping her into his arms. The endless void that remained after he rushed out the door, leaving Jackson behind.

Turning his attention away from the vision, he stopped at the foot of the bed. His father sat propped up with several pillows against the ornate wood headboard. An IV bag hung from a silver pole on wheels beside him, and an oxygen tube circled his protruding cheekbones. He'd lost more weight, his skin more lavender in color now.

"We have some things to go over with you," his father announced, but not in the commanding tone he'd heard all his life. This time, he sounded weathered, weak, and nothing like the man who went out of his way to intimidate and torment.

Adam pulled a folder from his briefcase. "Jackson, your father is designating you his power of attorney. If he becomes incapacitated, you will be responsible for all decisions regarding his care." He pulled a pen out of his jacket pocket. "I'll need your signature on these forms."

A refusal shaped on Jackson's tongue as his hand reached for the pen without permission. The form appeared before him, and his body went numb. He stared at it, not wanting the responsibility.

"Jackson," Grayson's rasp broke into his thoughts. "I trust you."

A nagging headache pulsated behind his eyes. With no other option, he scribbled his name on the line, making him the one thing that could stand between his father living or dying.

Adam tucked the folder and pen in his briefcase without further instructions, but as he turned to leave, he placed his hand on Grayson's shoulder and squeezed. A gesture of unspoken understanding and rapport established from years of enduring trials and triumphs together.

"I'll show myself out," he said to Jackson, leaving a consuming void in the room.

"I need a promise from you," Grayson began slowly. "No interventions, treatments, or resuscitations," he paused to force air into his lungs. "Promise me."

"Whatever you want." His own voice sounded hollow, the echo vibrating off walls that seemed to expand and contract with every one of Grayson's labored inhales.

He needed to get out of there and didn't wait for permission. Escaping into the hallway, the door shut as he leaned against it. His heartbeat pounded like fists on metal in his ears as he breathed deep.

Instead of returning to the kitchen where Eleanor and Reese still huddled over more paperwork, he headed to his father's office for a drink—preferably a strong one. With everything that had evolved over the last two hours, he teetered dangerously between either punching something or curling into a ball on the floor. Neither would have a healthy ending, so he poured two fingers of Scotch and tossed it back.

He waited while the warm liquid coated his dry throat before pouring another. In one swig, he drained the glass a second time and hoped he found the courage to face whatever test came next.

———

Every day for the next two weeks, Grayson slept. Rarely did he acknowledge the hospice staff that stopped by to monitor equipment, change sheets, or check his vitals. He never acknowledged Jackson's presence or Eleanor when she fussed over his every need. The more he ignored them, the less Jackson cared. He had questions, but he'd given up after several failed attempts to talk with his father about his wishes.

Eleanor stayed in a constant state of unease, always worrying about Grayson's care and comfort. She visited him often, prayed over him while he slept, and handled him with grace and compassion, no matter how terrible or ungrateful he acted.

Jackson envied her patience, but he didn't have it in him to do the same. Maybe if he and his father had a relationship once. Maybe if he hadn't been made to feel like a nuisance all his life. Maybe if his father hadn't been a colossal asshole, he might have been able to muster the effort. But the man upstairs preferred to remain a stranger and to die alone—something Jackson could happily accommodate.

———

One afternoon after a workout, Jackson found Eleanor crouched over the island, her cell phone on the counter, and her eyes red rimmed.

"What's wrong, Eleanor?" he asked, rushing to her side. "Is it Grayson?"

She wiped her wet cheeks with a towel. "Jackson, I'm sorry," was all she could say before sobs stole her voice.

"It's okay. Whatever it is, we'll face it together." He held her, hoping his support would give her the calm she always gave him, but it only made her cry more.

Stepping back, he looked her over. "Are you hurt?" No blood or marks could be seen on her clothes and skin, but she relieved his worry with a shake of her head. "What is it, then? Please tell me, Eleanor. You're killing me." He'd gladly take any burden or pain she felt if it would stop her tears.

She took several deep breaths to gather the nerve to look into his eyes, now deep with worry. "Can we talk in the parlor?"

He'd only seen her stall like this a handful of times in his life. Always his rock, her strength never wavered until it came to delivering news she knew would hurt him. Nothing good ever followed a trip to the parlor. His chest ached with anticipation as they walked in silence to the formal sitting room at the front of the house. Cuddled on the small beige couch—the same one they sat on while talking with Reese and when she told him his mother had passed away—he breathed in some peace and cursed the clouds for casting a solemn glow through the windows.

"My daughter called while you were out. She and her husband have officially separated and are getting a divorce."

"I'm sorry to hear that."

"As you know, they've been struggling for a while." Heat painted her cheeks from trying to keep her frustration out of her voice. "He's moved out and isn't helping to support the kids. Heather's having to return to work."

Understanding she'd already made her decision, he nodded. "When do you leave?"

"I don't want to abandon you and Grayson. Especially now. My heart is being ripped in half, having to choose between my two families." Tears spilled over her dark lashes. "I love you so much."

"I know that and love you too, but you shouldn't feel bad about this. I'll miss you more than you know, but your daughter and grandkids need you."

It took everything he had not to beg her to stay. Doing so would only make the transition more painful for them both. The least he could do was support her when she needed it. After thirty years of taking care of him and his parents, she deserved to live the next stage of her life guilt-free and how she pleased.

Holding her, a gift idea to thank her for all she'd done for him finally came to mind. Unfortunately, he would need his father's help to make it happen.

"When do you leave?" he asked again.

Her eyes rose to his and pleaded for forgiveness. He braced for the answer. "Next week."

"Okay," he said on a sigh. "What do we need to do to get you ready?"

She dabbed at her eyes again and sniffed. "I need to pack, of course, so I'll have to find some boxes. I need to buy a car, something that can haul my belongings and run the kids around. There are a few things here I'd like to take care of, and I also want to visit a few friends."

"Make me a list of the things you want done around the house, and I'll take care of those while you visit and pack. I'll ask Harrison and Thomas to bring over some boxes from work. Then, we'll go shopping for that car this weekend. How's that sound?" He smiled as she jumped off the cushion to give him her signature hug, shoving him back against the couch.

"I'll take that as a yes," he said, laughing. "Now, let's get to work."

As Eleanor crafted her list, he went upstairs to talk with his father. He needed to be a part of her going away present whether he wanted to or not. She'd been his loyal and hard-working employee for many…

Employee, he scoffed. What a heartless title for someone who'd saved his life more than once, tirelessly supported Grayson's, and never once complained about any of the sacrifices she'd made over the years. No. She was family, despite his father's attempts to keep her in her *place*.

Jackson rolled his eyes as he turned the knob on his father's bedroom door and pushed it open. Finding Grayson asleep, he started to back out when violent gagging coughs consumed his father's body. Instinct and training kicking in, Jackson rushed to his side and sat him up. He snatched a small towel off the bedside table and held it to his father's mouth until the ruthless convulsions stopped. Grayson's milky blue eyes locked on Jackson's face as he strained to breathe—his hand trembling as he gripped Jackson's arm.

"I've got you. I'm not going anywhere," he soothed and set the towel, now coated with blood, aside.

Lost at seeing his father frail and dependent, he didn't know what to do next. It didn't help that Grayson seemed to be waiting on him for something. But what? He didn't exactly have experience in these types of situations, especially where his father was concerned. Besides, he could barely handle his own shit, much less all of…*this*.

After laying Grayson down, he sat in a nearby chair and began with why he'd stopped by.

"I have some sad news. Eleanor is moving in with her daughter in Stony Creek. She leaves next week."

No reaction from Grayson.

"I thought we should do something nice for her. What do you think about giving her the SUV?"

When Grayson continued to stare at him, his eyes blank and unresponsive, Jackson grabbed his hand.

"Dad, can you hear me? Squeeze my hand if you can hear me," he demanded, fear creeping in until his father's fingers dug into his palm. Although weak, the movement set him at ease.

"Good. Now, squeeze my hand if you agree to give Eleanor the car."

Fingertips pressed again.

"Thank you, she'll be so happy…after I convince her to take it." He grinned, determination taking over.

Rising, he slid his hand away and turned to leave until a last second clutch around his wrist tugged him back.

"What is it?" His father didn't answer, so he sat down again. "Do you want to see Eleanor? Are you in pain? Do you want me to get something for you?"

Shaky fingers tightened around his arm.

"Is it in this room?" Another squeeze. "Is it in the bathroom? Dresser? Closet?" *Bingo.* Although he had to play Twenty Questions, at least they were finally communicating.

As he stood, Grayson pinched his lips and opened his mouth over and over, trying to speak. Jackson leaned closer but heard only ragged breathing and beeping machines. He grabbed his father's hand when frustration twisted his face.

"It's okay. We'll get this. Pocket? Is there something in your coat or pants pocket?"

Nothing.

"Box?" *That's it.* He was getting better at the game. "Let me go look, and I'll be right back."

After searching through the built-in drawers, shelves, and cabinets in the walk-in closet, he found three boxes of varying sizes and carried them to the bed.

Grayson pointed at the medium box covered in black felt, and Jackson opened it. A silver necklace with a heart-shaped locket was pinned to the matching felt inside. Engraved flowers with tiny diamonds at the centers decorated the top.

"Was this my mother's?"

Grayson slowly rolled his head left then right.

"No? Interesting. Don't tell me you bought this for one of your mistresses." He glared down at his father, who closed his eyes and rolled his head. "Good. Who, then? Was it Grandma's?"

Grayson answered with a hard blink.

"It's beautiful. What do you want with it? Give it to Eleanor?"

Another blink.

"Thank you. What about these?" he asked, pointing to the other two boxes.

Grayson motioned toward the larger box of sturdy white cardboard and then to Jackson.

"For me?"

Curious, he lifted the lid. Piled to the top inside were newspaper clippings, photos, certificates, and programs from his time in school. But one innocent-looking article sitting on top had him in a chokehold. The large color photo of him, Will, Josh and Billy sat above the fold on the front page—a candid shot of them goofing off and laughing on the football field just before dusk. The article detailed their decision to join the military over playing college football, despite being recruited by Division I schools from across the country.

He'd forgotten about the interview and never saw the article published. It was now one of the most precious things he owned. He pressed the dog tags under his shirt to his chest and set the article on the bed to shuffle through the rest of the stack.

Articles and stat charts for football games and track races. Photos of him at games, birthday parties, or holidays. Sport banquet programs, certificates, medals. The accolades meant very little to him when he was competing. He only cared about the experience, development, and challenge. So, who would have collected all this? He couldn't imagine either of his parents taking the time, mainly because they hadn't attended any of it.

Eleanor must have done this, he decided. Despite her hatred for non-perfect weather, she was always there dressed from head to toe in school colors. She'd even paint her face with all four of their jersey numbers and bring either a cowbell, pom poms, or a homemade sign with glitter paint. The sight of her in the stands with smeared paint and glitter on her cheeks, screaming with the rest of the parents, was one he'd never forget. She had a way of making him feel special, and she knew he would want these mementos one day. As usual, she'd been right, and he was beyond grateful.

"Thank you for this," he said, turning to his father, but Grayson had already fallen asleep.

Setting the lid on top, he returned the unopened box to the closet, placed a clean towel by the bed, and dropped the stained one into the hamper. The unnatural amount of blood on that towel worried him. If someone wasn't there to sit him up when the coughing took over, his father might drown in his own fluid.

Accepting that he was that someone now, Jackson grabbed several blankets and a pillow from the hall closet and arranged them on the floor beside Grayson's bed. Soon, the two remaining people he'd had in his life since birth, good or bad, would leave him either by choice or fate.

Growing up and even while in the military, he'd been Eleanor's focus, and he couldn't imagine not having that steadfast support. On the opposite spectrum, he'd always believed he'd be better off without his father looming in the shadows of his life. But in Grayson's final days, he just couldn't hate him anymore.

After Eleanor drives away and the earth claims his father, he would officially be alone for the first time in his life.

Chapter Twenty

✫ ✫ ✫

Jackson

The next day, Jackson helped Eleanor run errands. The hardware store to get supplies for those final house repairs she wanted done. Picking up the moving boxes Harrison and Thomas saved. A trip to the bank and gift shop while she visited with a friend at a coffee shop downtown. The grocery store where she loaded up two carts with a month's worth of food—her way of caring for him in her absence.

As he placed the last of the bags on the counter, the afternoon hospice nurse paused in the doorway.

"What is it, Marc?" he asked.

"I just wanted to let you know that I increased your father's morphine dosage. He should sleep more comfortably now."

"How is he?" Eleanor asked, exiting the pantry.

"He shouldn't feel any pain, but he doesn't have much time left. If you haven't already, you should start making arrangements."

Eleanor looked to Jackson after Marc went upstairs. "Have you talked with Grayson about his wishes?"

"I tried. He doesn't want to talk to me about it."

"Me either."

Since Grayson wasn't talking or couldn't, Jackson tucked the question away as something to answer when the day arrived.

Over several days, Jackson completed Eleanor's home repair list. He enjoyed the labor and rewards of a hard day's work, but it left little time to exercise. And his stress and anxiety controls lagged as a result.

Nightmares tortured him like a domino line—every hour was one tragic event after another, crashing into each other and building toward a grand finale. Except, there never seemed to be an end in sight or a way to stop them from coming.

With the increase in medication, Grayson had fewer coughing fits. For his father's sake, that was good news. Selfishly, he was at loose ends over it. No coughing meant no distractions during his feeble attempt to soldier on through the night.

The cold, hard floor didn't bother him. He'd slept in far worse conditions before. It was the agonizing silence. Domino after relentless domino tumbled without permission in high-definition surround sound, fueling his already robust hatred for the emptiness accompanying the darkness of night.

———

On Saturday, Jackson welcomed the sun. He got up and started bustling around the house, even before Eleanor. He made breakfast and prepared the back porch table with two plates, glasses of fresh squeezed orange juice, and a small vase of early spring flowers from her garden. The same devoted care and attention he received every day from her.

"What's this?" she asked, her expression bright and animated as she stared at the small gift bag he placed on the table before joining her.

"Just a little going away present from Grayson and me."

Touched, she patted his arm. "Jackson, my dear. You shouldn't have gotten me anything."

"Yes, we should, and we did. You deserve this and more for all the times you've been there for us. I owe you my life, Eleanor. You've saved me in more ways than I can count, and I love you so much."

Fresh tears glistened in her eyes, reflecting the early morning sunbeams. "Oh, sweetheart, I love you, too, but I didn't save you. That was your doing and God's. I just had the honor of being your loyal cheerleader." With a wink, she patted his arm, then peeked inside the bag.

"Open the larger box first," he instructed. "It's from Grayson."

Surprised, she lifted a brow before slowly removing the lid to expose the delicate silver necklace. She ran a finger over the heart, and her curious smile quickly faded to unrestrained emotion.

"He said it belonged to my grandmother and wanted you to have it."

Her hand sprang to her lips. "Louise was an amazing woman. She and my mother were best friends as kids. Although they grew apart over the years, she was always kind to me. I might never have been hired here if it wasn't for her. She recommended me, and the rest is history. Oh, I'm going to treasure this."

Still smiling, she closed the lid and grabbed the second box—rattling the contents inside. She held it up to her ear like a kid on Christmas morning.

Pure joy swam through him while watching her. This feeling must have been why his mother got involved in charitable causes and why Eleanor gave so much of herself to others. Whoever said giving was better than receiving could not have been more right. It was liberating.

"Is this what I think it is?" Disbelief covered her face as she pulled out the keys and turned them over in her hand.

"Your favorite monstrosity is yours if you want it," he announced, using her nickname for the oversized SUV. "No need to go car shopping this weekend."

"Jackson, it's too much. I can't accept this."

"Yes, you can. And you will also accept what's in that envelope."

Her eyes widened before her gaze shifted to the bag. Setting the keys aside, she pulled out the envelope and ran a finger under the flap to reveal the contents inside.

"Jackson." A hand sprang to her chest. "I—"

"It will help you get set up at Heather's with enough left over for unexpected expenses." He took her hand. "I need you to take it." With a weary smile, she relented, understanding that taking care of her in this way gave him a sliver of peace.

"Okay, my sweet boy."

———

By mid-morning on the day of the dreaded move, all chores had been checked off the to-do list. Thomas provided a few more boxes upon request after Jackson insisted Eleanor pack whatever she wanted from the house. After all, it was her home too, and she loved it more than anyone.

When neither could think of another task to further delay her departure, he loaded the boxes into the monstrosity while she cried. She sobbed uncontrollably when she hugged him goodbye, and tears continued flowing as she drove away. Seeing her upset and watching her leave was as miserable and heartbreaking as he'd expected, and he was at loose ends.

He stood there, staring down the driveway and wondering what to do next. After a year of spending every day together, he had no idea how to function without her. When Marc arrived for the afternoon shift, Jackson took the opportunity to get away.

He wandered wherever the road took him for over two hours. Anything was better than roaming the estate without purpose, reminding him of the fact that his life was no different than his path that day—meandering, meaningless, lost. Other than being Grayson's caretaker, he had no purpose. He just took up space in the world. Something had to change and soon. If only he knew how.

Although he tried to think of literally anything else on his walk, his mind kept bouncing between his pointless existence and Eleanor. She should have arrived at her daughter's house by then, probably playing with the kids or fixing them lunch before unloading the SUV.

She moved only an hour away, but he doubted he'd see her much. All her spare time would be devoted to her three grandchildren, and he would be…doing what, exactly? Once his father no longer needed him, what would he do?

Going to college sounded overwhelming. A desk job unbearable. He couldn't reenlist with his recovery on-going or serve as a recruiter now that he was a civilian. He scoffed at the title and wished he didn't still hate it. Since brainstorming a future he couldn't fathom made his head ache, he turned around and headed back.

"Mr. Vane," Marc called later, locating Jackson in the kitchen, washing his empty smoothie cup and blender at the sink.

"Everything okay?"

"It's as expected at this stage, but he's having difficulty breathing on his own. I recommend a thoracentesis be done immediately to remove the—"

"No." He didn't hesitate.

"He's not getting enough oxygen. We need to extract the fluid so he can breathe."

"As his power of attorney, I can't authorize that."

"Jackson, think of your father." The use of his first name instead of the usual cold formality meant Marc was desperate.

"That's exactly what I'm doing. He made me promise not to intervene and accept whatever course the disease took."

"He's suffering."

"I understand, but if you can't do as he wishes, then maybe it's time we got someone else to take your shifts." He waited as Marc considered his options.

"All right. If that's what he wants. But you must know, at this rate, he may have only days left."

"Thank you."

With a sigh, Marc left the room.

Later that afternoon, Jackson stopped by to check on his father. He looked even more fragile than the week before, his lips and skin a light purple, and he wouldn't respond. He was dying, and Jackson was helpless to stop it.

He didn't know if Grayson could hear him, but on the off chance he could, he grabbed a book from the dresser, sat near the bed, and read aloud. A story about Theodore Roosevelt, a man his father admired, should bring Grayson comfort. Or at least he hoped it would.

After a while, the words he recited barely registered. The easy cadence of the author's writing transported him to another time, helping him forget about life-or-death decisions, missing Eleanor, the haunting past, and his mysterious future. The power of a good book provided exactly what he needed—a short memory.

———

Is today the day? The first thing to cross Jackson's mind with every sunrise. Would the fight end that day?

Whenever he wasn't exercising, he read aloud at Grayson's bedside. The hospice staff stopped trying to make small talk with him days ago, and other than Eleanor when she called to check on him, he rarely said a word of his own.

He didn't mean to be unsocial. He just couldn't bear to talk about his father's disease or how it was torturing his delicate body anymore. Watching and listening to it every night and day took a toll, and he deployed every avoidance tactic he could fathom.

One hot afternoon in late April, while Marc tended to his father, Jackson attempted to clear the overgrowth around the lake. The back-breaking work soothed his restless mind and provided another creative way to stow away where no one would bother him. As he chopped and pulled the brush from the bank, he could set his thoughts on the task and detach from the stress and hopelessness he felt cooped up in the house.

Taking hold of a large vine, he yanked the roots from the soft, wet soil and tossed it aside. As he bent down to pick up the ax for the next chore, he caught a glimpse of Marc waving at him from the back porch.

Shit.

Flipping the ax into the ground, he jogged to the house.

"You should be with your father." Marc held open the back door as Jackson hurried inside.

In Grayson's room, he first noticed all the equipment and tubes had been removed. Then, his attention shifted to Grayson's hands gently folded over his stomach. His closed sunken eyes. His purple lips. Was he too late? He placed a hand on his father's chest, relieved to feel him still breathing, even if each inhale and exhale was slow and shallow.

Unsure of what to do, he pulled a chair up to the bed and took his father's hand.

"I'm here. Eleanor would have been here, too, but you know." His gaze landed on Grayson's pale, bony hand as he tried to wade through an ocean of competing emotions. Having no other choice, he latched onto the only one he could understand. "I should have said this when you could hear me. I'm sorry for all the miserable things I said…and thought about you."

His eyes cut to his father's face. "I wish you would have been here after Mom died. I wish I would have known you didn't actually hate me. It would have been nice to forgive you long before now."

He took a deep breath. "But you were right on one account, I should thank you. All I ever wanted was for you to love me. But since your replacement was Eleanor, I thank you from the bottom of my heart for keeping your distance. You and I are oil and water, and you made the right decision."

Dropping his head on the bed, he whispered, "You were right." And when Grayson's hand tensed around his, he shot up again. "Dad? What is it? I'm here."

Frantic for something that might soothe Grayson in his final moments, Jackson fumbled for a book on the bedside table without letting go of Grayson's hand. He flipped it open, not caring which page it landed on, and immediately began reading. While the words flowed from his lips, he had no concept of time. No idea what he said. His body had activated survival mode.

"I'm here, Dad," he repeated when Grayson's started to convulse. "I'm here."

By the time he stilled again, the sun had fallen beyond the horizon. A faint glow from the sunset at Jackson's back provided the only light in the room as dread and sadness burned through to his bones. The more darkness that engulfed the room, the more control he abandoned.

With his head on the bed, he allowed himself to weep for losing the last of his blood. For the shitty hand both his parents were dealt. For avoiding so many difficult conversations over the years. For giving up another part of himself, no matter how much he despised it.

Tears he should have shed weeks ago soaked the quilt and drained him until he could take no more. Standing on wobbly legs, he wiped his cheeks with the back of his hand and took one last look at his father.

He hadn't realized how much of a burden his anger, hurt, and forced indifference had been over the last twenty years until it was gone. How many times had he wished to unload that heaviness on the source one punch, one kick, one scream at a time? Hate had ruled his life for too long.

Yet, towering over his father's lifeless body now, only three little words came to mind.

"I forgive you."

Feeling lighter, he moved to the hallway and called for Marc, his voice echoing through the big empty house.

"It's over," was all he could say when Marc entered the foyer below. He stumbled down the stairs and into the office.

Why did he feel so numb? The weight of resentment had lifted. He'd been anticipating this day and preparing for the inevitable. He knew what to expect, but thinking about it and enduring it had been two vastly different experiences.

A list of tasks to accomplish upon his father's death sat in a drawer in his room, but he couldn't think about any of it. Right then, he needed a strong drink. Maybe a shot of whiskey would deliver a jolt to his hollow soul before he tackled the first task on the list. The one he dreaded doing most of all—telling Eleanor.

After draining a shot, he poured another and carried it to the desk. Slumped over in the chair, he dialed her number. They cried together once he got the words out, and by the time he hung up, the medical transport had arrived. Jackson stood in the hallway while they placed his father on a gurney and carried him downstairs.

The sound of the door closing behind them symbolized the end of another chapter in his life. No father to tend to. No Eleanor to lift his spirits. No hospice workers and meaningless conversations to fill the silence. No one to distract him when the memories smothered him.

He dropped to the floor at the bottom of the stairs and folded his knees to his chest. Nausea churned in his belly. Blinding light pulsed with the pounding in his temples. Clutching his head with both hands, he resigned to wait however long it took for the misery to release him and a new chapter to begin.

Chapter Twenty-One

✷ ✷ ✷

Jackson

Disoriented and drenched in sweat, he listened through the darkness to regain his bearings. There was a *pop* from the back of the old house as it settled, and a breeze whistled through drafty windows, followed by eerie silence. Birds beckoned the sun to rise in the trees outside.

For the first time since returning, he wished for night. Wished he could go back twenty-four hours or skip the day ahead entirely. Nightmares seemed better than this. At least when he got lost in those intrusions, Will was alive, Eleanor still lived in Richmond, and he didn't feel so damn hollow. That morning, other than aching muscles and a roiling stomach, he felt nothing but dread—profound, dense, all-consuming dread.

He checked his watch. 4:32 a.m.

Dragging himself up and to his room, he dressed for the early morning workout he would need to get through the day's lengthy and dreaded to-do list.

The fresh air soothed him as he headed toward town instead of his usual route. It had been a while since he'd escaped the confines of the house with complete freedom—no time constraints, strangers anxiously awaiting his return, or responsibilities.

By the time he reached the city limits, the rising sun reflected in the mirror-like windows of Richmond's tallest modern buildings. Bright, cheerful shades of orange and pink lightened his mood enough to keep moving. Grateful for the boost, he took off again, traveling further away from the last place he wanted to be.

After purchasing a water at a food truck, his wandering legs stopped in front of Harrison and Sophia's house a few minutes before seven. Breathless from the spring heat, unusually stifling that early morning, and the eight-mile hike, he dropped to the curb.

"Jackson?" Harrison called from behind him. "What are you doing here, buddy?"

In standing, Jackson found the comfort he needed in Harrison's embrace. "I apologize for coming by unannounced...and for ruining your suit."

Harrison looked down at the new sweat marks on his jacket. "You're welcome anytime, and I have other suits. Did you walk here?"

"Yeah. I needed to clear my head. Do you have a minute?" He glanced at the leather briefcase Harrison carried. "If you're busy, I can come back another time."

"Don't be silly. Please, come in." He led Jackson to the small table in the kitchen, then handed him a glass of water. "What's going on?"

"I'm sure you know why my father's been absent at work over the last month."

"Yes. He worked longer than I expected. Every day he got worse, and when he said goodbye, I knew that meant he wanted to be left alone." Harrison placed his hand on Jackson's shoulder. "Does your being here mean he passed?"

Jackson nodded and soothed his dry throat with a long gulp of cold water.

"I'm so sorry. I knew he'd gone home and that Eleanor left. I should have reached out. You shouldn't have had to go through that on your own."

"It's okay. I never expected you to, and he probably didn't want you to see him like that."

"Is there anything I can do for you?"

Everything he needed to do to plan for the funeral flooded his thoughts and twisted in his chest. "I would appreciate your help making the arrangements. You knew him best, and he wouldn't tell me what he wanted."

"It will be my honor. Just tell me when and where, and I'll be there."

"Thank you. I'm heading to Adam's office now to see if he has anything in writing, and I hope to get an appointment at the funeral home today."

"All right. Can I give you a ride to Adam's office?"

"No. Thank you. I'm not finished with my workout yet, and I need it to stay sane." He forced a grin before emptying his glass.

Harrison shook his head, his lips rolling together in wonder as they stood together. "I don't know how you do it. I would have passed out halfway here." Harrison pulled him in for a hug and lingered. "Are you okay? I mean, actually okay?"

The sincere, fatherly tone made him want to give an honest answer. "Yeah. I think so."

And as Jackson headed back down the driveway, he hoped he stayed that way.

————

He continued his exercise routine the six miles to Adam's office—a modern building with corridor after corridor of steel gray walls, glass rooms, and metal accents and sculptures. Sterile like a hospital, making the hair on the back of his neck stand up and air burn stagnant in his lungs. The list of things he hated more than hospitals was a short one.

With Adam in court until later that afternoon, he made an appointment and escaped to outside where he could breathe again. He called the funeral home, scheduled a time to stop by after he met with Adam, and texted the information to Harrison.

A few blocks down the street, he came to the building where Avery worked and considered going in. Shielding his eyes from the sun, he looked up at the tall building, tormented between doing the right thing and soothing his pain and loneliness with her smile. Then again, he had no idea if she would be happy to see him. While he considered his options, the promise she demanded tugged at his conscience.

No matter how lonely he felt, reentering her life now would only confuse and hurt her all over again—something he would not do. Pivoting, he took the shortest route back to the estate.

———

After a shower and heating up leftovers he couldn't seem to force down, he arrived early for his first appointment. Adam sat behind a polished cherry wood desk that stood out among its industrial surroundings—like the last remnant of tradition preserved as a symbolic display in a museum.

Adam continued shifting through a pile of papers on the antique surface oblivious to their intrusion. His brow pinched in the middle in either concentration or frustration until the receptionist spoke up. He muttered a protest before looking up, his frown dissolving into a professional smile at the sight of Jackson standing beside her. He shot to his feet.

"Jackson." He shot to his feet and reached out a hand. "I'm so sorry to hear of Grayson's passing. He was a great man. I'm going to miss him," he added, stunning Jackson into silence with the sincerity hovering amongst the words. "Please, have a seat."

He watched Adam thumb through folders in a drawer before selecting one and joining him at the small glass table in front of a wall of windows overlooking the city below.

The lunch rush ended long ago, but the streets still hummed with activity. Pedestrians and vehicles hustled every which way, and he wished to be among them. His chest already had that airless twist in it, the same reaction he experienced when he first visited that morning.

"I'm glad you stopped by. We have a lot to go over."

"We do?"

"Of course. I figured Grayson mentioned it and that's why you're here."

"Talking wasn't our thing," he deadpanned, and Adam's confused expression had him wishing to take it back. "I just wanted to know if you had anything in writing about his funeral wishes."

"I do." He thumbed through the folder, pulled out a piece of paper, and slid it across the table. "Your father didn't want a traditional funeral. As I'm sure you are aware, he loved a good party, and that's what he wants. A celebration of life, if you will, and to be buried at the estate. In lieu of flowers, he requested donations to cancer research."

Genuinely surprised, Jackson stared at him. "That's it?" It seemed too simple, too low key for the Great Grayson Vane.

"That's all he requested. But knowing him, he'd want that party to be lavish."

Having the answers he needed, Jackson stood to leave. "Thank you for your help."

"Jackson, please." Adam motioned for him to return to his seat. "There's more."

He waited as Jackson contemplated whether he could endure another minute in the hospital-like environment. Taking a seat against his better judgment, his shaky hands folded in his lap.

"Did your father discuss his will with you?"

Jackson scoffed at the absurdity of the notion before righting himself. He didn't know if, or what, Adam knew about his lack of relationship with his father. Rarely had they ever *discussed* anything.

Then, Grayson's last visit came to mind. The one before cancer took over and his father moved back to the estate. The one before his own body revolted in response to something he didn't see coming—the one-year anniversary of the day his life changed forever.

"I'm not sure," Jackson answered honestly.

"Okay," Adam began, seemingly unaware of Jackson's internal countdown to implosion. "He owns several companies, the estate, a downtown apartment, several cars, and a mountain cabin in north Georgia. Adding that to his investments and cash, your father's net worth is more than $62 million."

His eyes stayed locked on Adam, wondering what the list had to do with him. "He's worked hard."

"Not quite the reaction I expected." Adam stared back in assessment before sitting back in his chair. "You don't know, do you?"

Annoyance pricked at the back of his eyes. A dozen more tasks needed to be checked off the to-do list that day, and the less time he spent in this glass coffin the better. He pinched the space between his eyes with two fingers, hoping to release the tension. "Know what?"

"Jackson." He waited for Jackson's gaze to meet his. "He left it all to *you*. You're his sole heir, and as of today, a very wealthy man."

"Excuse me? What about Harrison, or any of the women he was seeing?" He wouldn't have been surprised if his father divided his fortune to charities promising to carve his name on a building somewhere or designated it to those he worked with, slept with, met in passing—anyone but his one and only son.

Adam's head shook, releasing the last remaining strands of long dark hair from their shiny top perch. He pushed them off his forehead before answering. "He told me that after all you'd been through, you deserved it."

"When was that?"

"December of last year. You signed the paperwork to transfer all his accounts, companies, and properties into your name upon his death. Don't you remember?"

"Unbelievable." Jackson turned his attention to the skyscrapers and clouds beyond. "I signed something, but the meeting took a sharp turn, and I couldn't focus on what it was. He may have told me. I can't remember."

"Ahh." Adam opened the folder on the table and set a pen in front of his new client. "Well, after you sign a few more documents, you'll be able to live your life completely carefree. It's what he wanted for you."

Jackson shot up to pace, to think, to keep from bursting out of his skin. *It's what he wanted for you.* Seriously? Those few endearing words set him ablaze with fury. Where was that tender care when he was mourning the loss of his mother. Or when he'd made the official decision to join the Marines. Or when he'd lost nearly everything he ever cared about. Where was his father's compassion for him and his future then?

This support from his father beyond the grave. This out-of-the-blue trust in Jackson's ability to take a lifetime of building a legacy—an empire—and not fuck it up. Grayson's apparent desire for Jackson to take center stage and manage Vane Industries like he'd been groomed for it. It was all more than he could process, especially when his stomach had crawled back into his throat and blocked all air flow to his vital organs.

"Jackson, are you—"

"Adam, I know nothing about running his business or managing stocks or even an estate, for that matter. I'm a Marine. I don't know how to do anything else." He sounded panicky, but he didn't care. He was drowning in a sea of unknowns and strange revelations he couldn't process.

"Then sell them. That's the beauty in all this, Jackson. They're yours, and no one can tell you what to do. If needed, I'll be here to handle the legal side of whatever you decide."

He stopped pacing and turned to face Adam, his hands on his hips. "Thanks. I may take you up on that." Raking his fingers through his hair, he resumed pacing while Adam explained more documents in the folder.

Time passed slowly as long legalese meshed into run-on sentences until they faded away completely. His concentration flickered like a lightbulb connected to an unreliable source. Even after having a moment to consider the news, his brain still matched the rest of him.

Unstable.

"Wait." He interrupted an explanation of the estate's deed transfer and checked his watch. 2:30 p.m. "Shit." Without another word, Jackson rushed out the door.

Arriving at the funeral home, he located Harrison and the director deep in conversation in an office off the lobby. He informed them of Grayson's wishes and helped with decisions about displays, photos, the obituary, and the burial ceremony. Harrison suggested he hire an experienced party planner for the celebration and staff to help with the estate long-term.

"Since Eleanor is gone, I hate the idea of you living in that huge house alone, and you're going to need help with the maintenance."

"I'll think about it." *Add it to the growing list of things to figure out*, he complained to himself and wished Eleanor was there. She'd know what to do.

"Well, how about I take care of the details for the burial and obituary while you get the estate ready to receive guests," Harrison suggested, delegating and directing like the true leader he'd always been.

Harrison's support and take-charge attitude provided the reprieve Jackson desperately needed. Even if it would be temporary. He'd already made enough decisions over the last several hours to make his head pound with a new ferocity. And he'd yet to acknowledge the live grenade his father dropped in his lap via Adam's stealthy hands. With every new decision, discovery, and detail uncovered, he tilted dangerously close to his limit, and he doubted his ability to keep from crossing that line on his own.

"Perfect," the funeral director said, drawing Jackson's attention back to the discussion. "I can work with both of you along the way." He opened the overstuffed, leather-bound calendar on his desk. "Now, the only thing left to decide is the date. We can have everything ready on our end by Friday. Is this Saturday a good day for you?"

Saturday? The only-four-days-away Saturday? There were countless tasks left to start, much less finish, and his mind spun out of control. He looked to Harrison for more guidance.

"I think we can do that," he confirmed.

"Perfect," the director said again and scribbled something into the calendar.

There is nothing perfect *about any of this.*

"I'll be in touch."

"Please tell me you drove here," Harrison asked, following Jackson outside and biting back a smirk. At least he'd kept his falling apart to himself—his practiced show-no-emotion Marine face coming through to save him the embarrassment.

"Yes, I did, but can I buy you an early dinner?" The words tumbled out in a rush. To keep from alarming Harrison, he shoved his hands in his pants pockets to appear more casual. He probably looked more like a wild animal caged for the first time—confused, furious, scared—especially since that was exactly how he felt. But whether he had company for dinner or not, he had to decide what to do about his father's multi-million-dollar conglomerate, if that was what it was called, before it ate him alive. And there was no one better to talk it out with than the one person outside of Eleanor he trusted most.

The man who managed the godforsaken conglomerate.

Harrison eyed him for a bit, longer than Jackson was comfortable with, before breaking the tension. "Sure. Let me call Sophia and tell her I'll be late."

———

"I need your advice," Jackson confessed after recounting what he'd learned about his father's will and gulping the ice water the waiter brought. His throat felt like a wasteland the more he talked, the more the facts forced him to accept his new circumstances. It all felt like Grayson's last dig before bowing out forever.

His blood pressure spiked, filling him with urgency. "I know nothing about running a business, nor do I want to. And why did Grayson do this? I can't make sense of it."

"You're his flesh and blood. Despite not being able to show it, he loved you."

Jackson puffed out his disagreement at Harrison's idealistic view of the man who bore the title of his Father without ever earning it. In any other situation, he could find the sentiment endearing. In this one, it was downright laughable.

"I can teach you everything you need to know," he powered through Jackson's dismissal. "Are you sure you don't want a hand in running your family's business?

"I appreciate it, Harrison, but you know it was never that. The company was his alone—*his* obsession, *his* life, *his* legacy. Not mine. And we certainly were never a family."

"Maybe, but you might feel differently in a year when some of this stress is behind you."

Before Jackson could respond, the waiter returned to take their orders. He couldn't remember the last time he ate, and he still wasn't hungry. On a whim, he settled on a salad—the safest option for his empty and agitated stomach.

"Well, if you don't want to work with us, what will you do?" Harrison asked, his voice laced with concern.

"I don't know, and it's bothering me. I have no purpose."

"Well, what do you like to do?"

He didn't have to think long. He had only one passion. "I like to run and exercise."

"Yeah, I noticed. You're nothing but muscle, man."

"That's why I can't have a desk job. I feel alive when I'm active." And he'd had enough of the alternative for one lifetime. It was time he lived again…if only he knew how.

"What if I purchased the company from you?"

Jackson froze, surprised by the question. "You want to buy it?" he repeated, letting the idea push through the fog he'd been lost in since Eleanor left.

"I do, but you should keep a portion to maintain some ownership and share of the profits. We can work together to sell the smaller companies currently on the books when they're ready. You'll take your half of the profits and bow out of the day-to-day responsibilities after that."

"I don't know what to say, and I'm frustrated that option never occurred to me." Jackson chuckled. The most seamless and obvious solution never once poked into his thoughts. How out of touch was he? "Can you put together a proposal and send it to Adam?"

"Absolutely, buddy. I'll get it to him next week." He raised his glass, and Jackson followed. "To my friend, Grayson Vane, his ingenious mind for business, and his amazing son."

By the time their meals arrived, so had Jackson's appetite. Having a potential plan to rid himself of his father's business while helping someone he loved, snuffed out the nerves that had been sizzling under his skin since his father's health took a turn for the worse. He never wanted to stand between his father's life and death. He never asked to receive a penny, a favor, or a grand gesture. He just wanted to be left alone to find his way. To find happiness and fulfillment again, with no more tethers to this version of himself.

"What?" he asked between bites after noticing Harrison watching him.

"I'm still worried about you."

"Why?"

"You've been through a lot this past year, and I heard you and Avery broke up. Why didn't you mention it before?"

"Not a great topic of conversation."

Harrison frowned. "I don't like you being so alone all the time."

"I'm getting used to it."

"That's what I'm afraid of. Why don't you get out and meet some new people?"

"You sound like Eleanor."

"Smart woman. Friends and companionship can do wonders for spirit, mind, and body." He added a wink for good measure.

"Funny, but I need to determine who I am before I can think about dating." It was true. How could he give himself to anyone before he knew what they'd be getting?

"Who said anything about dating? I said companionship, but a beautiful woman could help you spend some of your free time."

"Now, you definitely sound like Eleanor."

"Since we agree on the matter of putting yourself out there, and you trust us both, it must be the idea of the century."

"Century?" Jackson's eyes rolled to the rusted tin ceiling before returning to his salad with a sigh.

"What do you say?"

"I say that I already tried that, and it was a disaster." Damn. He didn't mean to go there.

"Who ended it?"

"I did."

"Why?"

Frustrated by the unexpected and unwanted shift in conversation, he slumped back in his chair, dropping his fork onto the bowl with a clatter.

"Come on, man. I'm on your side," Harrison persisted. "I just want to know what's going on with you. I'm worried."

"Fine," he said on a long exhale. "After Grayson gave me Mom's engagement ring, I realized I could never reciprocate Avery's feelings for me, no matter how hard I tried. So, I ended it, as you suggested." He pushed the heel of his palm against his chest over the source of the ache. The memory sufficiently slashed a fresh wound across his heart and reopened a few more. "She deserves better."

"You're a bigger man than most, Jackson. You tried, and it didn't work out. Couples break up all the time."

Jackson looked up and found reassurance in Harrison's empathetic brown eyes. They were still bracketed with concern but lit with enough playfulness to lift the somber cloud that had fallen over the table.

"And I can promise you that Will is not mad or disappointed or cursing your jaded heart from above. You did the right thing. It's time to forgive yourself."

He nodded, trusting Harrison and his wisdom, but he'd feel better if he knew Avery had moved on and was happy.

Chapter Twenty-Two

☆ ☆ ☆

Jackson

Ms. Beasley?" Jackson called, entering the kitchen where she and her grandson Brian made small sandwiches in an assembly line on the island. "Do you have everything you need?"

She looked up from her work to give Jackson a wide smile. "We do. No need to worry."

"I wouldn't dare." He plucked a tiny sandwich from the lot and tossed it into his mouth.

The more time he spent with the duo, the more grateful he was for Harrison's advice. He hired Ms. Beasley and Brian to help with the estate several days prior, and they became fast friends.

"So, Brian, how's school going?"

"It's great. I'm learning so much now that I've settled on a major."

Jackson leaned on a stool. "What are you studying?"

"Agriculture and animal science."

"Really? What do you want to do?"

"Not sure. I just want to help farmers."

"Farmers?" He couldn't conceal his surprise.

"It took him long enough to come to that conclusion," Ms. Beasley fussed, making Brian blush with boyish pride.

"I've been having fun."

"As you should." Jackson slapped him on the back and laughed when it garnered him a disapproving glare from the new woman of the house. "The real world will always be there."

In the quiet kitchen with his new roommates, Jackson found the refuge he dreamed about for the past hour. He managed to keep his cool as curious gawkers and Richmond's elite party enthusiasts arrived in waves for his father's celebration of life. Also known as '*the event of the year*,' apparently. If Sophia hadn't been on his arm when he heard it declared, he would have made a scene. Other similar heartless comments had been sounding off around him like an untuned bell choir since the start, and it didn't take long for him to reach his limit and retreat.

Most of the guests in the sea of designer clothes, sunglasses, and hats were the so-called friends and acquaintances Grayson had forbidden him from mingling with all his life. As they gathered in groups around the backyard, colognes and perfumes overpowered the fresh air. Obnoxious sized jewelry reflected the sun and flashed in his eyes. Fake interest slanted every conversation, and his cheeks ached from having to smile through it all, as though he didn't loathe every second.

"When do you graduate?" he asked Brian, returning to the easy conversation away from the drunks and absurdity outside.

"I have about three more semesters, and then I'll need to find some real-world experience somewhere."

"Well, if I can help, please let me know."

"Thank you, Mr. Vane."

"Enough stalling," Ms. Beasley chimed in. "Brian needs to get back to work and you need to be with your guests." Something he was avoiding, and she knew it. She waved her hand in the air and rounded the island, shooing Jackson out of the kitchen.

While crossing the yard, he scanned the crowd. Too many of them seemed content, cheerfully mingling and emptying wine bottles as if they planned to stay a while. At least a cloud had blocked the sun, casting a much-needed shadow over the grounds and a break from the heat.

His suffocating suit squeezed his chest and restricted his movement like a straitjacket. Loosening the tie, he yanked it out from around his neck with one tug. He tucked it in his pocket, then released the top two buttons of his stiff white shirt. Enjoying his last few seconds of peace, he took a deep breath and realized his hot, smothering suit was the least of his worries.

————

Avery

She saw him the moment he exited the house. Every step was strong, confident, and more agile than when she last saw him. Proud of the work he must have put in, she couldn't turn away. And as always, he looked criminally good in a suit.

Despite intimately knowing her weaknesses when it came to Jackson, she couldn't look away. Every cell in her body begged her to call out to him, to touch him. She'd give her car for the opportunity to get lost in the bottomless depths of his ocean blue eyes again—to drown in the safety of his embrace and the feel of his body press against hers.

As he walked toward her, a breeze whipped across the yard, tossing his sun-streaked hair. He snapped his head back and combed his fingers through it. God, he was heartbreakingly beautiful.

His hard, tanned body was another transformation and another of her weaknesses. She could see the muscle he'd gained beneath his shirt in the motion of his strong forearms as he rolled up his sleeves. Absently, she fanned herself with her hand. No matter the weather, he had the power to heat her core to molten lava. But after he'd shattered her hopes and dreams, she would be a fool for letting it happen again. However harmless this gawking sesh may be.

It took months and even more wine for her to accept that their relationship wasn't written in the stars, but seeing him and feeling her body's reaction to him now meant she could no longer lie to herself about one thing: her heart hadn't moved on as she'd hoped. And in the spirit of being honest with herself, she only went to the celebration to lay eyes on him, and he did not disappoint.

Yet, feeling her heart flutter at the sight of him wasn't what had it breaking again. It was that nothing had changed between them. After their time together, how could he come within a few feet of her and still not see her?

Her sad, pathetic life—always in his shadow, invisible and irrelevant.

Screw that.

"Hi, Jackson," she said, stepping into his path. His eyes landed on her face, and her show-him-what-he-gave-up confidence floated away with the wind. It dissipated just as quickly as her resolve to forget him had.

"Avery, I didn't realize you were here," he said, recovering from the surprise. "How are you?"

"I'm great." Damn. Why did he have to look at her like that? Like he could see into her soul, exposing her innermost desires. She lowered her eyes, or he may learn more than he wanted to know. "You look good, and you're moving around much better now."

"Yeah, and I've been jogging too. I'm up to about two miles now. All because of you."

That last comment had her gaze springing to his again, rendering her speechless.

"You look—" He stopped when someone called for him from inside the crowd. "I'm sorry. Maybe we can talk later?"

She caught his scent as he hurried past—sweet, rustic, and undeniably Jackson, and cursed the weak excuse for a woman she'd become. There she stood, alone and in the same yard where he broke off their brief relationship, breathlessly in love again, and all it took was a glance and an airy brush of his hand on her arm. Would she forever crave his attention and touch? Was there no end to this torment?

"Avery?" She heard someone say, snapping her out of the pity party.

She spun around to see a gift from the heavens sent to save her from herself. "Eleanor! Oh, it's so great to see you. I've missed you so much."

After a tight squeeze, Eleanor studied her. "You look magnificent in this outfit, my dear. How have you been?"

"I'm good." She forced a smile, but it convinced no one, even herself. "Okay, I can't lie to you. I'm struggling, Eleanor. I talked with Jackson for the first time since…" she trailed off, incapable of saying it out loud.

Since he dumped me and shattered my heart.

"I haven't forgotten. I haven't moved on. Help me, Eleanor." Feeling desperate, she no longer understood the person she'd become.

"I know it's hard, sweetie, but think of this as a learning experience. You have a better idea of what you want in a partner and what you don't. There's someone out there for you, and don't you ever settle." She ran her hand over Avery's hair and smoothed the strands blown astray by the breeze. "You deserve to be happy and treasured by someone who loves you. *That* is what you should never forget."

Avery started to reach out for a hug but stopped when she saw Jackson approaching over Eleanor's shoulder.

"Eleanor?" he called and jogged to her, his arms wide and ready for her embrace.

Avery stepped aside to give them space and watched the reunion, her heart swelling with competing joy and jealousy. She loved them both, happy they would have this time together. But deep down, she wished Jackson could be that happy to see her. She wanted to be snug in his arms and feel his reluctance to let her go.

"I thought you couldn't make it," he said, drawing back with his hands on her shoulders.

"It took some maneuvering, and I was late, but I couldn't miss Grayson's…whatever this is." She let out a puzzled giggle.

"It's a celebration of life and, apparently, what he wanted."

"You solved the mystery. Good boy." She placed a hand on his cheek. "I've missed this handsome face."

"Have you seen Harrison yet? Come, I know he'll be excited to see you."

He led Eleanor away, leaving Avery to wallow in her misery…alone yet again.

After a while, the crowd began to disperse, and she considered following their lead. Jackson was busy, Eleanor's attention fell to others, and she knew no one else that remained. She felt out of place, hopeless, and pitiful, waiting for Jackson to notice her.

Forcing herself to accept that their brief encounter might be the last time she saw him, she waved a white flag and headed to her car parked in the front yard.

———

Jackson

"Were you going to leave without saying goodbye?" he called, jogging up to Avery beside her car. Her short, pleated skirt billowed from the sharp movement as she stared at him in shock.

"You were occupied. I didn't want to disturb you," she said weakly and swallowed hard, giving away her nerves.

Maybe he shouldn't have followed her. The hope and longing he saw in her eyes earlier should have been enough to remind him to keep his distance. But they'd been friends most of their lives, and he wanted to get back to a place where they could be again.

"Thank you for coming."

"I didn't know him that well, but I wanted to pay my respects."

Her gaze stayed on his face as an awkward silence fell between them. Neither knew what to say, even after all they'd been through.

"I'm happy to hear you're jogging now," she blurted out.

"Yeah, it's been my therapy, emotionally."

"That's wonderful."

"What about you? How's work?"

Attempting this exercise in small talk was unbearable. Her eyes kept searching his face for something—answers, feelings, more things he couldn't give her. As much as he'd like to repair their friendship, she clearly wasn't ready.

"It's busy but good. I got an offer to transfer to the Arlington office," she said, cutting her eyes to a rambunctious couple as they stumbled toward their ride idling in the driveway. She turned back to him. "It would be a promotion, but I don't know if I want to move. Then, sometimes, I think I should, you know, start over."

"A promotion is exciting. You deserve it. You're good at what you do."

"Thank you, Jackson. That means a lot."

"I passed by your building the other day. I almost stopped by to say hi," he said stupidly, making her smile and her cheeks bloom with color. Why couldn't he keep his mouth shut and end this suffering?

"You should have. It would have been nice to see you."

"It was the day after my father died. I wouldn't have been very good company," he backpedaled. The longer he stood there, the deeper he sank.

Trying to figure a way out, he looked over the grounds and remembered his duty to the guests in the backyard. He turned back to announce his exit, but her lips crushed against his before he could say a word. The unexpected force of her body pinned him against the car behind him.

For a brief moment, he considered following Harrison's advice. Wouldn't he be better equipped to get through the challenging months ahead if he had someone by his side? No, he decided when his hands found her soft, familiar skin. He wouldn't lead her on again. Wouldn't hurt either of them with his inability to meet her expectations.

Gently, he took hold of her arms and unfurled them from his neck, discharging her lips from his.

"I need you, Jackson. More than I need air to breathe. Please give me another chance."

"I can't do that, Avery. If I said yes now to satisfy our needs, I'd only break your heart again later. I won't do that to you."

"Why do you fight it? If you would give our connection more time to grow, you may feel differently. Why can't you try?"

Her pleading tone sounded as though it came from a spoiled teenager, not an ex-girlfriend, reminding him of one of the many reasons they would never work out. While their age gap totaled just a few years, it seemed greater at times. He'd seen and experienced more than she would in her lifetime, and it had changed him. Maybe if he hadn't endured so much, overcome so much despite himself. Maybe if he was still that carefree guy traveling the world with his buddies. Maybe then, he wouldn't feel like her elder, and she wouldn't feel like his best friend's little cousin.

"Avery, I don't want to hurt you."

"Please don't do this."

His anxious and increasingly annoyed fingers found their way into his hair. "I should get back to the—"

"Why, Jackson?" She stomped her foot and dug in. "If you want me to move on, I need to know why you can't or won't try."

With his frustration mounting, he caved. If speaking the truth would help her overcome this ridiculous obsession, he wouldn't hold back. "All right, if you want to know."

She stumbled backward when danger overtook his facial features, and his body went rigid. He felt it and no doubt, she noticed. There was no more hesitation or worry over hurting her feelings. Empathy and care no longer coated his voice. She'd crossed a line, and he was about to say things she would soon regret making him say.

"Jackson, I'm sorry," she managed, her voice uneven, as she took another step back.

"Too late. You wanted to know. So, here it is."

He closed the distance between them as tears sprang to her eyes and spilled over her cheeks, adding layers to his guilt. She may have started this, but he would be the one to finish it.

"I'm not attracted to you in the way you want me to be. I care about you as a friend, but I don't love you." He could almost hear the shards of her heart shattering on the ground, but he'd already gone too far to pull any punches. "And I don't think I can get there no matter how long or hard I work at it. And frankly, it shouldn't feel like work."

She sucked in a breath, devastated by his admission, but when anger replaced shock, he was proud of her. Fire burned in her eyes, and he braced for the backlash. After all, he did this to her and deserved whatever she gave him next.

"Jackson, I…" She paused, her mind and heart battling over the contrasting love, hurt, and rage she felt. Then, her posture straightened, signaling the start of her victory lap.

Her arm lifted slowly until a pink painted nail pointed at him. "I've wasted so much time waiting for you."

Lost in her memories, she launched into a pace. She had more to get off her chest before this episode between them could be put to rest. That's why it surprised him when she shook her head and reached for the car door handle.

Turning to face him, she flicked him a brittle smile. "Thank you. Thank you for helping me see that my life shouldn't revolve around you. I deserve better than this. I deserve to be loved and cherished by someone who appreciates me and can't live without me." She threw open the car door, dropped herself inside, and sped away.

"Yes, you do," he murmured when her taillights disappeared around the corner. It hurt like hell to disappoint and cause her more heartache, but he did what he had to do for her to be happy. She'd never find that if she continued to wait on him—he'd always be out of reach.

With his hands in his pockets, he strolled back to the party. The sun had fallen behind the trees, and the despicable day would soon be over. And so would this phase of his life. He felt eighteen again, facing his future with one loaded question: What now?

But finding the answer at eighteen had been much easier than at twenty-seven. His list of options seemed infinite back then, and he'd had hopes and dreams. At the time, he knew exactly what he wanted to do with his life.

Now, almost a decade later, he had no plan, no prospects, no dreams. He lived each day in survival mode, and that was okay. Harrison, Eleanor, and his father had been right. The past sixteen months had taken a toll, and he needed time to heal.

To do that, a few goals to focus on should help him continue moving forward. First, he would rebuild his body back to normal. *No*, he corrected. *Better than normal.* He'd give himself one year. By then, he should be able to check goal two off his list: craft a plan for his future. How did he want to spend the rest of his life? What was important to him? What did he want to accomplish?

Twelve months. Plenty of time to think, plan, heal, and grow.

Feeling another weight had been lifted, and with spirits high, he rejoined the few lingering guests in the backyard.

Chapter Twenty-Three

☆ ☆ ☆

Jackson

Running through the city, Jackson turned onto a path, or street, whenever the mood for a change struck. He enjoyed the freedom, pausing to work his upper body as he pleased because he had no time constraints. After the third stop, he checked his watch. Thirteen minutes before four o'clock, and he'd already gone ten miles. A far cry from where he was a year ago when he pushed the reset button on his life at the end of his father's.

His endurance had improved, and the recovery period required between long-distance runs had decreased steadily over time. Now, he exercised at least five times a week and could accumulate double-digit mileage on runs.

This one, he predicted, would be his longest—despite not knowing where he was. Eventually, as he usually did on these random routes, he'd see a landmark he recognized and choose a way home from there.

Home, he mused. Settling into a rhythm at one location had once been a foreign and unwelcomed prospect. In fact, he'd gone to great lengths to avoid it for most of his adult life. Although he appreciated the childhood Eleanor gave him, he never thought of the estate or Richmond as home. Too much of his father was in the walls, the grounds, the city.

But the estate was his responsibility now, and he'd carved a rhythm of calm there after two years of ups and downs, triumphs and challenges. At least the rollercoaster no longer moved at a pace he couldn't handle.

He'd come to realize over the last year that he had almost too much. Too much freedom, resources, and opportunities to be and do anything. The endless possibilities hadn't helped, and he was no closer to deciding his future than when he made the vow—a realization that constantly gnawed at him like a swarm of termites. Little by little, his lack of answers ate away at his resolve, pushing him closer to his breaking point. If he didn't get answers soon, he might crumble to dust under the pressure, just like the insects' meal. He could already feel himself weakening as his body grew stronger.

Taking off again, he contemplated the deadline he gave himself. It was a few weeks away in the month he despised the most. Despised might not be the right word, he considered as he stopped at an intersection and waited for a truck to pass. Loathed, dreaded, detested—all words he could use to describe how he felt about the month of April.

He also despised, loathed, and detested the fact that he still knew very little about himself. With Richmond growing on him, he hoped to find contentment there, but every passing day, he felt more misplaced than the one before—like he was supposed to be somewhere else.

Most nights, while he laid awake staring into the darkness, something tugged in the back of his mind, urging him to leave. After running around the city for over a year, maybe he had simply grown bored with his surroundings.

The adventures he experienced while traveling with his friends were defining moments. Each one provided an opportunity to learn about himself and what he was capable of handling, solving, and surviving. Maybe he needed that now—similar moments to shake up his monotonous rut. A little adventure might help him find purpose and meaning in his life.

But traveling long distances was out of the question. Busy airports, crowded airplanes, strange or sudden noises, cabs, and hordes of people in every corner. It seemed too overwhelming, too risky. Plus, he still couldn't imagine experiencing that thrill again without his friends. Without Billy to dare him into pushing beyond his limits. Without Will to entertain him with his stories and antics. And without kindhearted, level-headed Josh to talk him out of doing something stupid. No, he wasn't ready. Not yet.

What about something that involved running? After all, it was his passion and the only thing he truly enjoyed doing. Although, he ran so much now, the challenge would have to be monumental for it to be life-altering. It also had to matter. In this new adventure, he needed to push himself beyond comprehension, and the reason for doing it had to motivate him.

Did anything motivate him these days? Now that he'd restored his body, he lacked reasons to get up in the morning—motives to keep pushing forward.

Damn it. Letting his mind jump into the whirlpool of negativity only sucked him in further. A dangerous habit that rarely ended positively. Resetting the direction of his thoughts before he went under, something he'd trained himself to do over the last year, he maneuvered through the traffic on autopilot. He brainstormed ideas for activities, challenges, and adventures with a running component, but his mind remained frustratingly blank.

All his life, he'd never been short on ideas. Before completing the first quest, he had already thought of and planned out the next. That day, he could focus on nothing but the busy street ahead.

He stretched his legs and looked around while he waited for a red light to change. The area of the city seemed neglected. Some buildings were constructed with the red brick typical of 1970s design. Others donned unpainted cinder blocks or wood siding, but all showed their age.

An abandoned warehouse sat in the distance behind a leaning chain-link fence and overgrown shrubs. A group of kids played basketball with a makeshift hoop hanging from a tree in the empty front parking lot. Although the neighborhood needed repairs, it was alive with activity and had a warmth that didn't match its appearance.

When the light turned green, he stepped off the curb and noticed a new billboard advertising help for PTSD.

Instantly, he thought of Will, and a jolt of regret, sharp and unforgiving, shot through his chest. With the base of his palm, he rubbed hard against the source of the pain until his heart stopped trying to claw its way out.

Will would've given him a suggestion, or ten, but only after a long, cleverly orchestrated production. He would have insisted on taking Jackson to one of their usual hangouts for a drink. He'd ask a series of questions, most of them ridiculous and seemingly off track. A lively story or two would be tossed into the conversation, and after a while, Jackson would wonder if he'd ever give him the advice he needed. They'd laugh a lot. He'd flirt with the waitress more. And soon, he'd get to the idea he conjured up long before the merry-go-round discussion was set into motion.

But among all the theatrics, Will would have encouraged him to dream big. Otherwise, what was the point?

With a smile, Jackson continued down the block until he passed the recruitment office, where he and his friends officially committed to the Marines. He paused out front and let that unforgettable day unfold in his mind.

The way they waltzed in together, confident and fearless, would forever be etched into his memory. The day after high school graduation, their service was officially committed, and they celebrated with a week of camping and cliff diving at Crater Lake National Park in Oregon.

His lips curved at the memory, then he considered the odds of advertisement and the recruitment office being on his random route that day. It must mean something.

Resting his hands on his thighs, he watched the idea come together—one piece at a time, as if an artist drew it in sections on the sidewalk in front of him. The details had yet to be added, but the direction of his life-altering adventure had finally taken shape.

———

"You're doing what?" Ms. Beasley asked, fear shining in her dark eyes after he explained his idea. Grabbing a towel from the counter, she dried her hands and tossed it onto her shoulder.

"I'm going to run to Orlando, Florida."

"Run? Like with your legs and not on a plane or in a car?"

He laughed, his cheeks aching from smiling the entire twelve miles home. "That's right. You know how much I enjoy running. Why not run somewhere fun?"

"I could think of a million reasons why not."

"I need to do something big for myself and honor my friends, and all veterans, really."

She searched his eyes for something to calm her fears. Crossing her arms, she must not have found what she wanted. "How is running that far going to help you do that?"

"I don't know. I just can't stay here. I can't keep living this way."

"You have a beautiful life, sweetheart."

Frustrated with his inability to explain how much this means to him, he sat at the island and tried again. "I'm not used to being stationary. For two years, I've been merely going through the motions of my life. I have no life here, and it's time I did something to figure out my future. Whether it's here or someplace else."

"You want to leave and sell the estate?"

Disappointment hardened her expression, sending a sharp dagger of guilt through into his stomach. She loved the estate as much as Eleanor.

"I don't know. But something is pulling me away from Richmond, and I need to find out what and why. The only way to do that is to follow it."

"Follow what, dear?"

"I don't know."

"How will you know when you get there?"

"I don't know that either," he had to admit, wishing he had a different answer.

His ability to make sound decisions quickly served him well in the Marines, and he rose up the ranks. But with this road trip idea, the details were blurry and his purpose unclear. Either he was out of practice, or the idea was too ridiculous for his mind to process. The only thing he knew with certainty was that he had to go.

"I think the answers will come to me while I'm running. I can't explain how, but I feel it. This trip will help me find my purpose and ways to give back. It's what I need to do to hopefully feel whole again."

With a sigh, she placed her hand on his cheek. "How can anyone argue with that? What can I do to help?"

———

Over the next several weeks, Jackson prepared for what he expected to encounter along his trek south. He trained on different terrains to test his limits, gathered supplies, practiced running with a full backpack of essentials, and planned how to refuel and recuperate. Finally, he decided to leave on the first day of the godforsaken month of April to give him one good thing to balance out the weight and sorrow the month carried.

That morning after a run, he sat at the kitchen island—his favorite spot in the house—and researched a possible route, deciding on only three stops to add to the adventure. He'd visit Eleanor in Stony Creek, Virginia, Will's parents in Murfreesboro, North Carolina, and Myrtle Beach, South Carolina. The rest he'd figure out as he went.

After calling Eleanor, he leaned back in his chair and took a deep breath, satisfied with the plan. He'd thought through as much of the process as he could in advance, but there was one last thing he had to do before he could leave.

Chapter Twenty-Four

✮ ✮ ✮

Jackson

Two days before his journey began, he made plans to meet Harrison for a drink. Following Grayson's celebration, they'd spent more time together, fishing or meeting for drinks or meals.

Sophia preferred him to join them for family dinners. The get-togethers quickly became his preference too, giving him a break from his perpetual solitude and a taste of real family life.

Plus, he had to keep his win streak going. At one point, he'd racked up six in a row before getting knocked off his pedestal. Taylor had asked him to play UNO one night last summer, and they'd been squaring up ever since. Sometimes it's card games, other times board games— most of which he never played growing up. He would miss it all while he was away.

He arrived at the restaurant near Harrison's office on time and grabbed an empty table by the bar. When his beer arrived, he checked his watch. It was unlike Harrison to be late, even by a few minutes.

"Jackson Vane? Is that you?"

He looked up to find a man around his own age with dark blond hair and a broad smile towering over the table.

"Wow! You look so different," he said in wonder and far too exuberantly for Jackson's comfort level. He'd gotten better at being around people again, but he still wasn't ready for whatever level of socialization this guy had in mind.

"Do I know you?" The man's face looked vaguely familiar, but Jackson couldn't place how they knew each other.

Without an invitation, he took the empty seat at Jackson's table.

"It's me, Ben Stevens. You dated my friend, Avery."

Shit. Their first date with her friends all came back to him, including Ben's random spurts of laughter, cringe-worthy comments, and loose lips. How could he forget?

"You don't remember me, do you?" Ben leaned his elbows on the table, his hands wrapped loosely around a bottle, while he smiled accusingly.

"I remember."

"Good. Did you know we also went to high school together? It hit me later that night after you left. I think we had English together our junior year."

"Wait. You were the kid who created that movie trailer for our final project in Ms. Brady's class." He remembered Ben as a scrawny, clumsy kid—his appearance, usually unkempt, shirt untucked and wrinkled, and his thick, wavy hair was always wild, like he encountered a windstorm on the way to school every day. But he had serious artistic talent. Even back then, Jackson had been impressed.

"You look different as well," Jackson said. Ben had put on some muscle, his clothes were neat, and his hair was precisely styled.

"The ladies love muscle." He winked, the ladies' man version reemerging. "You obviously know that. Man, you're even more ripped than you were playing football. You must work out, what, every day?"

Jackson's shoulders popped up in answer.

"So, what are you doing now?" Ben asked, sitting back in the chair. "You're walking, I see."

Since he'd planned to stay until Harrison arrived, Jackson resigned to having Ben in his space for a while, but hopefully, a very little while. "I'm not doing much other than working out." He grinned. "Seriously, that's all I do now because I have too much time on my hands."

"I know what you mean. I was laid off two months ago and can't find another job. My savings account is drained, and I do not want to move back home."

He was about to commiserate with that sentiment when Ben said, "Hard to get laid when you have to take the girl back to your parents' house. Am I right?"

Ben tried to laugh it off, but Jackson could tell it was becoming a concern. He had no idea how to respond nor did he want to. He settled on a safer topic.

"What do you do?"

"My passion is photography. I did some of that with my last job but spent most of my time designing print and social media ads. Not that exciting."

"I imagine it's hard to find jobs in that field."

"Yeah." The conversation lulled for two glorious seconds before Ben was back at it. "So, why are you sitting here all alone? Want to join us? The crew is here, and there's plenty of room for one more." He waved toward his friends in the back of the restaurant. "Don't worry, Avery's not here," he added when Jackson hesitated.

"Oh. How is she?"

"She's good. Rebounded with some Michael guy."

"What? You're joking?" He had to be. Avery wouldn't turn to someone as vile and fake as that asshole.

Caught off guard, Ben frowned. "Ugh, nope. Apparently, he'd been chasing her for a while, and she finally caved."

Chasing was an accurate enough word. Stalking was probably better. "Well, I'm glad she's happy."

"I don't know about that, but at least she's moved on if that's what you're worried about."

"That obvious?"

"Yeah, but it doesn't matter. I know how she felt about you. She confided in me after your breakup."

"I'm surprised you're still talking to me."

"You didn't do anything. Relationships are tricky, one hundred percent miserable, and us guys have to stick together." With a hearty laugh, Ben snatched his beer from the table and held it up. "Here's to being single and free to do as we fuckin' please."

Still trying to figure Ben out, Jackson forced an uneasy smile and raised the bottle to his lips.

"You're sure you don't want to join us?" Ben asked, leaning back in his chair with a curious smirk. "Drink away your troubles with some awesome company?"

"Thanks, but I'm meeting a friend. He should be here soon." Irritated that Harrison hadn't saved him from this strange encounter, he checked the time.

"Something wrong?"

"No, I just really wanted to talk to him before I left," he said absently while searching for Harrison near the entrance.

"Left as in leaving Richmond? Are you going on a vacation?" He perched an elbow on the table, excited to listen.

"Not really." Not knowing how to describe it, he waved it off. "It's complicated."

Ben grinned with eager suspicion. "Hot chick?"

"No. Nothing like that."

"Come on, man. I need to live vicariously through other people right now. My life sucks. What's so important that you must talk to this dude about?"

Jackson studied him. Ben seemed genuine enough, and most importantly, harmless. "Fine." After explaining his plan, he drained the beer to calm his resurging nerves. His anxious energy to get on the road and started on each layer of his journey was back and eating at his ability to relax.

"Woah. That's deep."

Jackson motioned for the bartender to bring another beer.

"Are you going by yourself?"

"Yeah. Being alone is another thing I've had to get used to since coming back. I'm getting quite proficient at it."

"Shit, man. You shouldn't make that trip alone. It can't be safe or healthy. What if you get injured? How will you carry the things you'll need along the way? Who's going to keep you company? Although, I bet you wouldn't have any trouble with warming you—"

"I'm used to surviving in the unfamiliar on the bare minimum," he interrupted since Ben's rambling took an interesting, but not surprising, turn. "This will be nothing. All I need are clothes, shoes, and food. I'll grab a hotel when I get tired of sleeping outside."

Ben clapped his hands together and pointed at him. He obviously hadn't been listening.

"I know!" he trudged on. "I'll go too. A road trip sounds hella good, and Lord knows I need separation from this depressing town. Think about all the fun things we could do. The women we would—"

"Stop right there. I don't need a wingman."

"Not with your looks you don't." Ben chugged the rest of his beer and set aside the empty bottle, looking primed to negotiate a deal Jackson never laid on the table.

"I was talking about the trip."

"Think about it, Jax. I'll follow you in a car and carry your supplies. You'll need more clothes than you can carry. And who wants to sleep outside in the heat and bugs?" He dismissed that idea as ridiculous with a grimace.

"Actually, it's not that—"

"With my help, you can sleep in a nice hotel every night and recharge for the next day. I can make the hotel reservations while you run and keep you company when you're not." He paused to wait for Jackson's decision until another exciting idea came to mind. "Oh! And I can document your trip on social media with photos and videos. You want to honor veterans, right? This could show the world how you're doing that."

He had a point, but Jackson didn't know if he could tolerate Ben's personality for the next several months. He'd intended to make the trip alone—no distractions to get in the way of the mission, and Ben reeked of complications.

"Oh, thank goodness," Harrison said, rushing up to them. "I was worried you wouldn't still be here. I'm sorry I'm late." He squeezed Jackson's shoulder, then reached out a hand to Ben. "Hi. Harrison Barnes."

Pushing back the chair, Ben stood and shook his hand. "Ben Stevens. Nice to meet you. Hey, you're Billy's dad." He waved a finger between himself and Jackson with his other hand. "We all went to high school together."

"Guilty," Harrison confirmed, pulling his hand free.

"Cool. I'll leave you be. Jax, think about what I said. I'll be back in a few for your decision. I'm so fuckin' excited." With a pump of his fist, he strutted across the restaurant to rejoin his friends.

"He has plenty of energy." Harrison laughed when he saw Jackson's stunned expression. He motioned for the bartender before taking a seat. "What does he want you to think about, Jax?"

"Don't you start. I'll have to fill you in after I recover. Rough day?"

"No. Thrilling. I finalized the sale of the last of your father's companies. You're officially free and clear."

"That's great." And perfect timing. "Was it the offer you showed me last week?"

"Yes, and I was able to get the price up another fifty grand."

"How'd you manage that?"

"Tricks of the trade, my boy." A sly smile graced his face before he gave the bartender his order. Loosening his tie, he leaned back in his chair to release the stress from a long workday. "So, what's on your mind?"

"Well." Jackson's nervous hand rubbed the back of his neck as he braced for Harrison's reaction. "I wanted you to know that I'm taking a trip to Orlando in two days." He took a long pull from his beer to calm his growing jitters. He may be a grown ass man, but he'd still feel better with Harrison's support and approval.

"That's wonderful. How long are you staying?"

"I don't know. Depends on how tired I am, I guess."

"What?"

"I'm not just going to Orlando. I'm planning to run there."

Harrison lifted the glass of wine the bartender dropped off to his lips, paused, then set it down again. "You're running to Orlando? That's what, 700 miles?"

"It's more like 750."

"Why? Why not just go there like everyone else? Safely, in a plane?"

"You know how much the guys and I loved to push ourselves. We never played it safe. Those risks and adventures shaped us, and I miss that in my life. I miss them, and if I don't do something soon to figure out who I am without them and the military, I'll go crazy. The running and the adventure along the way…I think it will help me find myself again."

"I get that, and I want nothing more for you. But please tell me you're not going alone."

"I'd planned on it."

"Damn it, Jackson. You're alone too much as it is, but at least Ms. Beasley, Sophia, and I are nearby, if needed. Now, you're wanting to run halfway down the east coast by yourself. I'm going to worry myself sick thinking you're stranded on some deserted back road with a broken ankle or passed out somewhere." He laughed, but the worry lines were deep around his eyes.

"I'll be fine. Don't worry. I've survived worse."

When Harrison glared down his nose at him, unamused by the joke, Jackson held up his hands, his eyes sorrowful. "I wasn't talking about what happened to us. Look, I've prepared my entire adult life for this. I know how to survive in situations far more dangerous than this, and I enjoy being outdoors. Spending a few months running and pushing myself doesn't sound all that bad to me. It sounds like a dream."

"I know. I believe you can literally do anything, but I'm still uncomfortable with this. Can't you take someone with you?"

"It never occurred to me to ask someone until Ben stopped by tonight. That's what he was talking about earlier. He wants to go with me."

"Oh, really? I like him more already. He seems like a handful, but I'm sure he could be useful along the way."

"I don't know." Jackson's hand raked through his hair while he considered Ben's offer. He and Harrison both made points he couldn't ignore.

"You should say yes. If not for yourself, for me, Sophia, Eleanor, and all the people who love you." He took a sip of wine before tipping the glass toward Jackson. "Who knows, maybe he'll prove to be a great friend once you get to know him better."

"Or another headache."

———

After their drinks were emptied and Jackson's trip thoroughly explored, Harrison paid the tab before rising to wrap Jackson in a hug.

"Whatever you decide to do, I support you. But for my sanity," he paused to offer an uneasy smile, "text me often to let me know you're safe."

"I will." He hugged Harrison goodbye, then his legs moved through the crowded restaurant without full permission. As he approached Ben and his friends, several of them with disapproving eyes, Molly tapped Ben on the shoulder. Hopefully, he wouldn't regret what he was about to say.

"Hi, Jackson," Ben exclaimed when he turned around, the only one happy to see him. "Are you coming to join us?"

"Thanks, but not tonight. Can we talk? Privately?" He led Ben away from the table, that what-in-the-hell-are-you-doing jab still annoying his gut.

"Well? Did you decide?"

"I'm leaving on April first at 6 a.m. Can you be ready?"

"Absolutely. My lease runs out tomorrow, so I'm good to go. Thanks, man. I promise you won't regret this."

We'll see, Jackson thought and turned to leave. He'd invited Ben to set Harrison's mind at ease, but he had to admit, it would be nice to have a way to carry more clothes and supplies during the long trip. Regarding Ben's company, he wasn't sure he wanted it, but he'd already opened that can. No going back now.

"Oh, Jackson?" Ben called and waited for him to turn around. "My truck was repossessed. We're taking your car, right?"

Without a word, Jackson dropped his head and continued toward the exit.

"I'll take that as a yes," Ben yelled over the crowd noise at Jackson's back.

He rolled his eyes, one hundred percent regretting his decision, when he heard Ben say, "Kids, I'm going on a field trip."

Chapter Twenty-Five

⁎ ⁎ ⁎

Jackson

As the sun made an appearance on April 1ˢᵗ, Jackson checked the weather outside his bedroom window. The sky was clear and streaked with the bright warm colors of dawn.

Perfect for starting the journey of a lifetime.

That beautiful morning, he felt rested—bizarre since he hadn't slept a minute in days. Yes, he was excited and impatient to get out of Richmond, but it was more than that. After enduring two years in survival mode, damn it, he deserved this. He deserved happiness, and this trip should help him find it.

"What are you doing up at this hour," he asked when he found Ms. Beasley cooking in the kitchen. Parking his suitcase next to the garage door, he strolled to her and draped an arm over her rigid shoulders. "I'd planned to fix breakfast so you could sleep in." He kissed her hair, then picked a piece of bacon from the warming plate.

"I couldn't let you leave without cooking you one last meal," she said with a forced grin and tears in her eyes.

"Don't do that." He rested his head against hers. She'd only been taking care of the Vane estate for a year, but their friendship didn't take long to grow and fortify. "I'm not going away forever. I'll be back before you can miss me."

"Impossible." With a sniff, she wiped her cheeks with a towel.

"I'll miss you too, but I have to do this. You understand, don't you?"

She nodded and patted his chin. "Such a sweetie you are. Now, go get whatever it is out of your system and come back to us."

"Yes, ma'am." He kissed her again, this time on the cheek with a loud smack, making her giggle.

"You're in a great mood this morning."

"I'm excited to get—" The doorbell ringing cut him off. Checking his watch, he headed toward the foyer. Ben was early, a promising sign.

Opening the door and laying eyes on Ben with his forehead pressed against the doorframe, Jackson pinched his lips to stifle his amusement. Dark circles—the same purplish color of the wisteria growing behind him—framed his eyes, and his clothes looked to have been pulled from the bottom of a hamper.

"You look like shit."

"And you're too chipper at this ridiculous time of day." Ben's hands dragged down his face, but he perked up when he stepped inside. "Is that bacon I smell?"

"Yep. Come get some breakfast."

"Bless you," he said on an exhale as he followed Jackson to the kitchen.

He introduced Ben to Ms. Beasley, then handed him a plate. "Go ahead. I'm sure you could use a good meal. What'd you do? Stay up all night?"

"Yes," he answered absently, scooping a hefty spoonful of scrambled eggs onto his plate. Overcome with hunger, he didn't see Jackson and Ms. Beasley wince when he grabbed a few pieces of bacon and sausage patties from the tray with his fingers. "Yesterday was the last day on my lease, so I had to get everything packed and moved out." He took a heaping bite of eggs and groaned with pleasure. "After all that manual labor, I deserved a few drinks and the company of a female or two."

Ms. Beasley shot Jackson a disapproving glance, making Ben slump back in his seat.

While they ate, Jackson and Ben discussed the trip's logistics, such as hotel reservations, communications, and luggage transfers. Each day, they'd meet up for meals and prepare for the next task.

"Is this how you were in the military?" Ben asked, his mouth full of a second helping of eggs.

"What do you mean?"

"We just made some detailed and regimented plans for clothes and a plastic hotel key. I can only imagine what you'd come up with for transporting weapons and shit."

"You have no idea."

"But there's one small detail we haven't covered."

"What's that?" Jackson asked, setting his plate in the dishwasher.

"How should I pay for the hotels? Unemployed, remember?" He pointed the fork at himself and beamed.

Crossing the kitchen, Jackson bent to rummage through the small backpack he planned to carry while running and removed a credit card from his wallet. When Ben's eyes widened as he reached out to grab the card, but Jackson yanked it back.

"This is for hotels, food, and supplies only. Understood?"

"Got it, Boss. Or should I call you Captain? Sergeant? General?"

"Boss will do," he joked and handed over the card.

After breakfast, he led Ben to the garage. "Take your pick."

"No way?" Strolling around each sparkling new car, Ben opened and closed doors and sat in each one. "I can drive any of these?"

"Any except the one at the end." The tiny red sports car his father preferred was off-limits. It was too small for their needs, but he knew he couldn't bring himself to sit in it. Some wounds were slow to heal.

"This one," Ben decided, opening the door to the sporty silver hatchback before dropping into the driver's seat. "It looks like it's never been driven." He ran his hand over the smooth leather steering wheel.

"Probably hasn't. My dad only drove one car. I have no idea why he bought all these." Snatching the keys from the hook on the wall, he tossed them to Ben before opening the garage bay door. "Get your things packed up. We'll leave in ten."

————

Instead of starting his journey at the estate, where he had mixed emotions, mile zero, he decided, would be Will's gravesite. From there, he planned to run fifteen miles before stopping for lunch and a rest. Then, if he felt up to it, he'd try to run another ten before stopping for the night. At that pace, he would reach his first destination, his beloved Eleanor in Stony Creek, Virginia, the next day.

At the cemetery, Jackson wandered the grounds until locating Will's grave. He sat on the grass and leaned against the headstone.

"I still can't believe you're gone. I see your name carved into this cold stone, but it just doesn't seem real. We had so many plans and places to go. You wanted to kiss a girl in every country." A laugh escaped despite the pain lodged in his throat. "All those girls have probably cried themselves to sleep every night since. Damn you. Why did you do it? Why didn't you come to me? You didn't have to go through it alone."

Trembling, he wiped away escaped tears with his shirt before placing a hand on the headstone. "I miss you so much. I'll never be able to repay you for what you did for me. All I can do is honor your memory by paying it forward. I'm not sure how yet, but I promise I will. I love you, buddy."

He traced Will's name with a finger then stood to click his heels together. A hand raised to his forehead in a sharp salute.

With a deep breath and a quick goodbye, he was ready.

Ready for his life to begin.

————

Once outside city limits, Jackson stopped to rehydrate and to work his upper body under a large tree. That day was unusually sweltering for April, and the clear sky offered no reprieve from the sun. Although he was well-acquainted with heat and sweat, the shade was a welcomed break.

While he stretched and sipped on the water he brought in his backpack, he checked a few stats on his watch. He wasn't surprised to see he'd already traveled twelve miles. He felt better than he had in a very long time.

Removed from the bustling city streets, he could put in his earbuds and enjoy his regular *Ups* routine, as he'd affectionately named it—push-ups, sit-ups, and pull-ups. He loved to test his limits, to see what his body could handle with one more rep and increase his endurance. And the best part of finding that failure mark with each exercise was his mind going blank as it focused on his burning muscles. Just his body and the music working in rhythm. No distractions or visions or fears. Only fuel for the goal.

Tossing the empty water bottle into the backpack, he continued down the narrow rural road. Several more miles brought him to a small town with little more than a traffic light and a few dusty storefronts lining the street. Except for a neon sign blaring the name of a diner, the area appeared abandoned and forgotten.

With his phone, he checked the location on the map. He was several miles north of Petersburg and only twenty-five miles from Stony Creek. This would have to do. He texted Ben the address before heading inside the ancient diner to wash his hands and face.

After claiming an empty booth by the large windows that framed the front of the old building, he looked around. The old-fashioned diner hadn't changed since the 1950s. There was a wide opening in the wall between the kitchen and the tall counter at the center of the dining area, and the jukebox played a happy bebop tune quietly from the back corner. The place smelled of old cooking oil and dusty antiques. If he hadn't been so hungry, he might have snuck out and continued down the road to the next town, but an empty stomach took priority over skepticism.

"What can I get…oh, hello, sweetness." The waitress leaned on the back of the booth opposite him and batted her eyelashes. "Can I get ya a drink?"

He ordered ice water, opened the laminated menu, and paid the young waitress no mind. With his appetite, he could think of nothing but eating every entrée listed.

When she returned, she helped herself to the empty bench seat, propping her chin on her hand. She said nothing, only continued to stare at him with a smile.

She looked to be in her early twenties, he guessed. Her hair, bright blonde on the top and brown underneath, was pulled up in a thick ponytail on the top of her head, and she wore more makeup than seemed natural for her age.

"So, what brings you to our little town, handsome? You're obviously not from around here."

"I'm just passing through with a friend."

Unfortunately for him, he was her only customer, and she gave no indication that she'd be leaving soon.

"Oh, yeah? Does that friend happen to be female?"

"No."

"Lucky for me. Is he as good lookin' as you, sweetie?" she asked. Her eyes raked over him as she chewed on her lower lip.

So much for subtleties, he mused and drained half his glass of water.

"Jules, get back to work," a man yelled through the opening behind the counter.

Ignoring the command, she rolled her eyes and held out her hand. "I'm Julie," she said with a southern drawl before sliding out of the booth, her fingers trailing lightly across his palm with the motion.

"Jackson."

"Nice to meet you, sweetie," she purred. "I'll be back to take your order when your friend arrives." On a slow pivot, her eyes stayed on him until she finally strolled back to the counter.

He could feel her watching him as she pretended to wipe the counter with a rag. Unphased, he returned to reading the menu, struggling to find anything that wasn't deep-fried or smothered in gravy.

Ten minutes later, Ben dropped into the seat with a sigh. "Man, you sure know how to pick 'em. Where the hell are we?"

"No idea, but I'm starving."

Ben ordered a sweet tea when Julie returned, matching her flare as he watched her sashay across the room and back. She set the sizable plastic cup, full to the top with tea and dripping down the sides and joined Ben in the booth. "You fellas in town for long?"

"No. We just stopped by for lunch." Ben leaned back in the booth and rested an arm on the top of the seat behind her. "My buddy Jackson is running to Orlando and this fine place is his first stop."

"No kiddin'?"

"Nope. It's your lucky day."

"Hey, Earl," she yelled across the diner to the man in the kitchen and pointed her thumb at Jackson. "This guy here is runnin' to Orlando. Isn't that wild?"

Earl looked at them through the opening behind the bar, then returned to his work without a word.

"He never gets excited, except when I don't do something right, which is like every day."

"You live around here, Julie?" Ben asked before sipping his tea.

"Yep. I live on my daddy's farm about a mile from here. Got a little trailer all to myself." She twisted a lock of hair around her forefinger, her jaw working a wad of gum.

Jackson barely listened to what she and Ben were going on about, but it was apparent young Julie hadn't been outside of that small town her entire life.

"You two handsome fellas ready to order?" She removed a pencil from her apron and set a notepad on the table.

Jackson ordered the grilled chicken and vegetables, and when she turned her big brown eyes on Ben, he smiled. He hadn't stopped ogling at her long enough to read the menu.

"What's your name?" he asked and held out his hand. She slid her hand in his, but when her knuckles touched his lips, her pronounced gum smacking came to a halt.

No matter how badly he wanted this spectacle to end, Jackson couldn't look away. It was all too ridiculous to be real. Something right out of a Saturday morning cartoon where the characters said and did outrageous things for a laugh. Except no one was laughing and the Ben and Julie show was paying out in front of him in full reality.

Damn.

"Julie," she managed to answer, fanning herself with the notepad.

"What do you recommend, Julie?" Ben asked in a smooth tone.

"I…uh…I like the…uh…barbeque and fries."

Jackson's stomach growled, probably angry from having to bear witness to this exchange.

"Great. I'll have that," he decided. "How long will it take? My buddy has some more running to do, and he's hungry."

"I'll tell Earl to put a rush on it. Just for you."

"Thank you, my dear." He kissed her hand again and held on as she stood.

"I'll be back real soon."

As she bounced away, Ben shook his head before taking a long drink of tea. "Man, I love country girls."

What did I do? Jackson thought. The snap decision to blindly trust a near stranger to do an important job went against the grain. Before letting someone into a military mission, they first had to complete intensive training, conditioning, strategy discussions, exercises, and tests. His traveling companion went through none of that verification process, yet here he was, getting on Jackson's last nerve. On. Day. One.

"What's that look for?" Ben asked when he turned his attention back to Jackson.

"Nothing."

"Well, I know I've said this like ten times already, but I appreciate you letting me crash your trip. I promise you won't regret it. Look," he said as if he planned to produce proof of his worth. Reaching inside his pocket, he retrieved his phone. "While you were running, I created the social media pages." He opened an app and showed Jackson a page titled 'Jackson Vane-Memorial Run.'

The first picture posted was of Jackson kneeling by Will's grave, his head down and his hand on the headstone. With the sun rays shining through the leaves, covering him in a dappled shade, it captured exactly how Jackson felt at that moment.

"What do you think?"

"It's perfect," were the only words that came to mind. The photo explained Jackson's reasons for taking the journey without saying a word, but the image included a well-written and surprisingly accurate caption about

Jackson's service and friends. Ben had resourcefulness and a brain behind that dumb, goofy expression. Surprising.

Encouraged by the compliment, Ben pointed at the phone. "Scroll up to the next one. It symbolizes the official start of your journey."

Jackson scrolled to a photo of him in mid-stride, slightly blurred in the distance, and Will's headstone in the foreground, the focus of the shot. The post included a description of Jackson's goals for the trip in the caption.

"I don't know what to say. They're outstanding."

"Glad you like them. I'll text you the links so you can send them to your friends. If they follow along, maybe it will help them understand and set their minds at ease."

Earl soon called for Julie with impatience, his deep voice rumbling through the small diner like thunder. She responded, collected the overflowing plates, and delivered them to her only customers. Jackson's mouth watered at the first sight of his meal. Then again, with his empty stomach, he'd eat dirt if she put it in front of him.

"This looks amazing," Ben complimented, making Julie visibly swoon. "Thank you, sweetheart."

"If you fellas need anything, just holler."

As she walked away, Jackson dug into his food. He sighed when the dull knife slid through the grilled chicken breast like warm butter. With the first bite, a satisfied moan shuttered in the back of his throat. Chef Earl was a mastermind.

"Man, she's hot."

Ignoring him, Jackson took another bite.

"Seriously, man? Look at her." Ben picked up a fry and dipped it in the small container of ketchup without taking his eyes off Julie. "I suppose you've had plenty of women who are way hotter."

Jackson refused to validate Ben's ridiculous questions with a response.

"What? Don't you date?

"No."

"Jackson Vane, the guy who could have any girl in high school and looks like you do, doesn't date?"

"No."

Ben leaned over his plate and whispered. "When was the last time you got laid, man?"

Raising his gaze to Ben over a fork full of broccoli, he let his eyes do all the talking. They screamed for Ben to shut up and let him eat in peace.

"I get that you're not ready to divulge all your secrets. Me?"

"I didn't ask."

"It's been about…" Ben checked the wall clock over the old metal cash register on the counter. "Twelve hours. And you know what I'm thinking?"

"I can only imagine."

"A little taste of Julie in the cornfields out back would make a nice dessert."

"I don't need to know that."

Ben soon picked up his sandwich, a welcomed bookend to the ludicrous one-sided conversation. Jackson could now enjoy his Eleanor-like meal in peace. Julie stopped by less and less as she had other customers to tend to. By the time their plates were empty, every table had been taken, with more people waiting outside for their turn.

The surrounding town may be long forgotten, but Earl's cooking could withstand any test of time, and it was well worth a trip into the past for a taste.

With Jackson's energy restored, he couldn't wait to get back on the road. He paid the bill and tipped Julie generously. But before he could escape, Ben positioned him under the neon sign, proudly displaying the diner's name despite the sunlight. He added Julie and placed her hands on Jackson's shoulder. Something she looked all too happy to do. Like an experienced model, she leaned in until Ben was satisfied their first stop had been properly memorialized.

"Thanks, Julie," Jackson said, caught off guard by her lips on his cheek before she hurried back to the diner. "I'm leaving," he told Ben, whose gaze and attention had followed Julie. "Text me the hotel's address when you check in. Ben."

"Yeah, yeah. Text you when I get there. Got it." He secured the camera in the trunk of the car, then slapped Jackson on the back. "I'll call the hotel from inside. See you in a few."

Jackson should have left long before the spectacle reached this point. Shaking his head, he checked his watch and took off, grateful to be alone again and where he belonged.

Chapter Twenty-Six

✫ ✫ ✫

Jackson

Later, Ben knocked on the door of Jackson's hotel room.

"Want to get a beer? I saw a bar with a live band a couple blocks from here," Ben said. He was fidgety, making Jackson wonder if he was up for whatever trouble Ben had planned.

Before the interruption, Jackson had settled on the bed with a book to rest his sore muscles, but sitting in the quiet room for too long had repercussions a cold beer and a loud band could easily remedy.

"All right," he conceded. "Just keep your lips to yourself."

"What?"

"Nothing. I'll meet you in the lobby in ten minutes."

Letting the door shut behind him, Jackson opened his suitcase and changed clothes. Since he brought only a few items for activities other than running, it didn't take long to get ready. Snatching his wallet from the dresser, he walked out the door in five.

"Expecting someone?" Since they'd claimed two seats at the bar, Ben spent more time watching the entrance than he did talking. He knew very little about Ben, but one thing was painfully evident: the man loved to run his mouth.

Ben flashed a guilty grin over his shoulder before taking a quick pull from his beer. "I may be staying here while you're in Stony Creek."

"You're unbelievable. Is she coming here?"

"What do you think?"

"I think you're unbelievable."

"Thanks."

With a roll of his eyes, Jackson began his usual survey. From his stool against the wall, the one no one ever wanted in every bar because of its splendid seclusion, he could see the entrance, the stage, the expansive bar, every obnoxious drunk, and any potential threat in the room. He located each exit and item that could be used as a weapon if needed.

That can't be normal.

He shook the thought away and continued taking the area to memory. After eight years of training, that habit would be hard to break, not that he was trying, and it gave him something to do.

Around the stage where the band set up, tables were alive with animated conversation. Servers rushed this way and that, carrying trays of food and drinks. A long line of customers waited in the lobby for a table. There, he noticed a familiar face talking with the hostess.

He poked Ben with an elbow, then tipped his beer toward the door. Julie's face lit up when Ben's head whipped around and located her among the crowd. She waved before taking off toward them, her wavy hair now flowing down her back and over her bare shoulders. She wore a barely-there pink tank top and a short black skirt that clung to her petite frame.

"Hi, good lookin'," she greeted, circling her arms around Ben's neck before planting a loud kiss on his lips.

Apparently, Jackson had missed a few things during his last run, and he was grateful. Lunch with those two when they barely knew each other had been more than he wanted to witness. He assumed tonight would be worse now that they'd advanced beyond flirting. Lord, help him.

Ignoring them as best he could, Jackson waved for the bartender to bring another round. A few more of those would be needed if he were to make it through the night with his sanity. He watched the bartender grab a beer from the cooler and pop off the top with a bottle opener attached to his belt. Snatching it off the counter when it arrived, he drank deep. Although he'd enjoyed it, the first thirty miles of his journey tested him, as Ben and Julie were, and the cool liquid soothed and doused his scorched nerves.

"Hey, Jackson," he heard Ben say and turned to see both Ben and Julie smiling at him. "Julie brought a friend." He motioned to a girl, who looked to be the same age as Julie with straight brown hair standing behind them. She leaned forward and waved. "This is Beth. Beth, this is Jackson."

Giving her a nod, Jackson returned to his beer and the band starting their first song. The speakers drowned out the absurd conversations going on beside him, and to his approval, they played classic rock and played it loud.

After the first few songs, the crowd began to sing along, transporting Jackson back in time to Ireland. At a pub in Dublin surrounded by strangers, he and his friends sang songs they'd never heard and got sloppy drunk on an endless supply of Guinness.

Later that night, they never made it back to their hotel. Instead, they passed out in a field a few miles from the pub. The farmer who discovered them was kind enough to let them sleep off the booze, but when the slumber party interfered with his chores, he crept close with his tractor and laid on the horn.

His howling laugh echoed across the rolling land as the four of them scrambled into fighting mode while vomiting like the drunken idiots they were. Thanks to that prankster farmer and countless pitchers of fresh, flavorful beer, he'd awakened to a freight train in his head, a sunburn, and memories he'd never forget.

That trip was one of many they enjoyed before being deployed the first time. Dreams of going back came up often while huddled around a flimsy card table in the middle of the desert—there and countless other places they hadn't visited yet. They'd had so many dreams together. Each one a drop in the sea of regrets he carried.

When the band took a break, Julie's friend slid off her stool, the sudden motion drawing his attention. What was her name again? Irrelevant, he decided and refocused on keeping watch over the room. Without the band, the room noise degraded to a gentle roar of multiple simultaneous conversations. Way too quiet.

As he sat there, brooding in the hum of everyone else's normal, he wasn't prepared for Ben vacating the seat beside him, opening the door to intruders into his precious space should any be brave enough to approach. He was giving off distinct *I'm-not-here* and *don't-mess-with-me* vibes.

Or so he thought.

"Hi," Julie's friend said again as she pulled herself into the tall stool, exposing the pocket seams of her ripped jean shorts. "Julie told me what you're doing. My dad was in the Navy for four years before I was born. How long did you serve?"

"Eight," he responded, wondering how long she would be in his ear.

"You don't say a whole lot, but that's okay." She grabbed her drink in one hand, the straw with the other, and studied him under her lashes while she sipped. "I don't mind doin' all the talkin'."

As promised, she talked about random topics without his involvement or encouragement. Her thoughts had no purpose or pattern, and she seemed to say whatever popped into her mind. It didn't matter, he barely listened. But the final thread of his patience snapped when she tried to talk over the band.

He enjoyed the music. It was doing its job, but if he didn't escape this little ambush Ben and Julie cooked up, he might say something he shouldn't to what's-her-name. He looked over her shoulder at Ben for help, but he was too busy fondling Julie's tonsils with his tongue to notice.

With a sigh, he reached for his wallet and motioned for the bartender to bring him the tab.

"Are you leaving?" she asked, poking out her bottom lip.

One glance at her transported him back ten years. While Ben obviously didn't have a problem, her age was Jackson's second obvious issue with the evening's intended set-up. Even if what's-her-name was older or acted less like a highschooler from a teenage movie, he had no plans to entertain, date, or sleep with any woman of any age anytime soon.

Maybe all that he'd been through had matured him beyond his twenty-eight years, but that couldn't be all. Girls like her lacked something he'd want in a partner. Something he couldn't describe if he tried. Not that he'd spent any time thinking about it, and he certainly wasn't searching for her. He had goals to accomplish, a journey to fulfill, and internal demons to defeat. Not to mention finding a way out of the situation he found himself in at that moment.

Thanks a lot, Ben.

"Yes, I'm leaving," he answered over the band and handed the bartender his credit card. He'd planned to stay just long enough to finish off his beer, but that changed the second she placed her feet on the footrest of his stool and a hand on his arm. With teeth clenched, he turned his eyes on her and realized he'd already stayed too long.

"I could use some fresh air." She batted her long eyelashes and lightly ran her fingernails up his arm. The sultry look she gave him had his patience and interest in being polite shattering like a hammer on glass. "Would you like some company?"

He didn't bother answering. Instead, he scribbled an angry resemblance of his signature on the credit card receipt before pulling two bills from his wallet. She followed him off the stool without an invitation, and he snapped. His body reacted on instinct. A hand on her shoulder. A gentle push to return her to the stool. A pulse of his jaw, indicating his next words were not up for negation.

"I don't know what you've been told, but I'm not that guy." Scooting by her, he handed Ben the cash. "Enjoy the rest of your night on me. I'm heading back." He heard Ben call his name, but he didn't stop. The sooner he got out of there, the better.

"Where are you going?" Ben asked on a huff, stepping into Jackson's path down the sidewalk.

"Back to the hotel to relax."

"She could have helped you with that."

Jackson refused to dignify that comment with a response and stepped past. Solitude definitely had its perks.

"Just sayin'," Ben yelled after him.

Back in his room, Jackson texted Ben the schedule for the next several days. In response, he received a photo of Ben sandwiched between Julie and what's-her-name. They appeared to be having fun, and he was happy for them. He remembered what it was like to feel limitless and carefree. More than anything, he wanted that for himself, too, and hoped this trip would help him find it and more.

Before turning out the light to rest his aching joints, he responded to Ben's text.

Jackson: Have fun but don't get anyone pregnant.

Chapter Twenty-Seven

✫ ✫ ✫

Jackson

After having breakfast in the hotel restaurant and packing, Jackson stopped by Ben's room to slip the key under the door. As he bent down, the door swung open to reveal a sleepy, hungover, and startled Ben. He wore only boxers and a wrinkled t-shirt turned inside out.

Jackson smiled. "Rough night?"

"What the hell? Why are you lurking outside my door?"

In answer, he held up the room key between two fingers.

"Right." Ben snatched it and tossed it on the nearby dresser. "You headin' out?" he asked, his tone softer and more alert now that he was more awake. He stepped forward into the hallway.

"Whoa." Holding up both hands, Jackson mirrored him. "Where do you think you're going like that?"

Ben looked down and laughed. "I, uh, was hungry."

"Sweetie, who's there?" a female voice called from inside the room.

Jackson's eyes widened with amusement.

"It's just Jackson."

"Oh, really?" Rustling could be heard before she appeared. An oversized T-shirt, Ben's no doubt, draped over her small frame, stopping mid-thigh on her tan legs.

"Hi, there," what's-her-name said.

Ben's smile brightened. So damn proud of himself. "You remember Beth."

"Yes, of course. *Beth*. It's nice to see you again, *Beth*." Her wild dark hair framed her bare face, still puffy from sleep. The night must have taken a curious turn for Ben, and he wondered what had happened to Julie.

As if on cue, Julie bounced to the door. "Hi, Jackson. Want to come in?"

"Absolutely not," he blurted, then recovered. "Thank you. I need to get going. Tomorrow morning," he confirmed with a stern pinch of his brow at Ben.

Ben was to drop off Jackson's suitcase at Eleanor's the next day. He packed what he needed for that night in his backpack but would need a change of clothes for the rest of his stay.

"I'll be there."

Jackson looked him over, wondering if he could be trusted. "I can't take you seriously like this."

"You're just jealous," Ben bragged, wrapping an arm around the waist of each of his companions. "But don't worry. Nothing could keep me away," he added, before the girls pulled him back inside, the door slamming shut after them.

"Not convinced."

————

Almost twelve months had passed since he last saw Eleanor, and he was home the moment she burst through the front door and met him in the front yard. Her soft arms wrapping him in the embrace he'd missed so much.

"You look so amazing. Sweaty but amazing," she added, separating herself from him for only a moment before pulling him in for another hug.

"So do you—not the sweaty part, of course—and happy."

"I am. The kids give me so much joy." She leaned back to frame his face with her hands to study him more closely. Her way of sniffing out lies. Seemingly satisfied with what she'd learned, she patted him on the cheek. "Unfortunately, you just missed them."

"That's okay. Gives me some time with you first."

"Like old times." She circled an arm around his and led him toward the house. "Please come in and rest your legs."

The front door of the little brick rancher opened to the living room. Eleanor stepped around the couch to let him enter before closing the door. The house was old and cramped but clean. She ran a tight ship when it came to her household, and he would bet that she had the kids on a strict chore schedule, as she did when he was young.

A couch, recliner, toy box, and small television lined the edges of the living room. On the walls were framed photos of Eleanor's three grandkids and daughter, along with several bold crayon marks in blue and green. He assumed a misguided child committed the crime before Eleanor arrived. She would not tolerate that behavior and knew the kids would fear her as much as they loved her.

She led Jackson to a small eat-in kitchen, and he was sad to not see a dining along the way. Eleanor preferred one for family dinners. The white-painted wood cabinets were nicked and looked original to the house. Some sat slightly ajar, unable to close flush on the rusty hinges. The linoleum floor, torn in spots, was faded where the sun slanted in through the small windows. The ancient electric stove had only four burners, each perched at a different height.

He claimed a seat at the small table by the sliding glass doors, leading to the back patio. Pushed up against the adjacent wall, the table had only three chairs. He wondered where the others sat when they came together over meals as Eleanor would demand—one thing she never wavered on. Then, he noticed a bright green card table and two colorful chairs folded up against the other wall. The *kids' table*, he mused.

Eleanor strolled to the sink and blotted the sweat on her forehead with a towel. The air conditioning unit in the window worked hard to cool the room, but it couldn't keep up with the heat drafting in.

"I'll get you some ice water to help you cool off." She filled a glass with ice from the freezer and water from the tap, then sat beside him. "I'm so glad you're here. It warms my heart to see you healthy and strong." She leaned on the table and took his hand. "Tell me. How's the trip so far?"

"Interesting. Running's the easy part, and I enjoy the work. It's all the other stuff that will take some getting used to."

"Like what?" Eleanor asked, worry forming in the creases around her eyes.

"Ben, the guy I told you about who's helping with the logistics, he's a little much." He paused for a sip of water, thinking of all that transpired the day before. "He seems harmless, but I didn't fully think through my decision before I opened my mouth. I just wanted to settle Harrison's concerns, but I'm starting to think I'll have to deal with his antics more than he helps me."

She laughed, and it was music to his ears.

"What is he doing?"

"What isn't he doing? One minute, he's taking these amazing photos, and the next, he's making out with the first girl he sees."

Eleanor's eyes widened, her jaw going lax in disbelief. "No, he didn't."

"And this morning when I stopped by his room, he was with that girl and the friend they brought for me the night before."

Another laugh escaped before she could clasp a hand over her mouth. "That's a hoot. I take it you turned her down and that's why she ended up with him."

"What do you think?"

"I think you should have taken them up on it." She winked as she fanned herself with a newspaper she'd snatched off the table. "You know how I feel about young love."

"There was no possible scenario, real or imagined, where I would fall in love with that girl."

"Maybe not, but you would have loved giving her a test run."

It was Jackson's turn to feign shock. "Eleanor, you little minx."

"What? There's nothing wrong with having fun, so long as you're safe and both on the same page." Her make-shift fan jumped into action again. "She wanted to, didn't she?"

"I'm not having this conversation."

"Of course, she did. One look at you and they all do."

"Can we talk about something else? Something a lot less inappropriate...please?"

"If we must."

"Thank you. How about the kids? How are they adjusting?"

Her expression changed from sassy to delighted in a flash. "They keep me on my toes, that's for sure. Libby attends preschool three days a week to get ready for kindergarten next year. She's finally getting the instruction and social skills practice she needs. She's come a long way. Ethan is eight. I'm sure you remember his spitfire attitude." She laughed when he nodded. "Well, nothing's changed, and he's always getting into something he shouldn't. I have to watch him or—"

"He'll draw on the walls?"

"Saw that, did you? He took a crayon to the wall right after I told him not to. I swear that boy will be the end of me, but there are even more times when he's the sweetest kid you'll ever meet. Then, there's Whitney. She's thirteen going on thirty and has more sass than I know what to do with."

"Sounds like her grandma."

She smirked. "Got it honest, huh? Well, it took us a while to understand each other," Eleanor continued, ignoring the comment, "but things are much better now. I didn't tell them you were coming. They're going to be so excited to see you."

"I'm looking forward to it. It's been a while. How's Heather doing now that the divorce is final?"

"She was drowning when I arrived, but she's holding her own. Still working two jobs, but I'm so proud of her. She's a tough cookie." Eleanor glanced at the clock. "Oh, I'm sorry, sweetie. Are you hungry? I know you usually have a protein smoothie after your workouts. At least, you used to," she added with a touch of sadness. "I picked up the ingredients for you yesterday if you want to make one while I get lunch going."

Touched, he covered her hand with his. "That's very thoughtful. Thank you. But how about I take you out to lunch?"

"Such a gentleman. I'd love to." She leaned forward and kissed him on the cheek before going to the refrigerator to remove the fruits, vegetables, almond milk, and powdered protein for his shake.

"If you don't mind, I'd like to freshen up and change first," he said, snatching up the small backpack he brought off the floor.

"Sure, honey. Down the hall, first door on the right."

The tiny bathroom was just big enough for a small sink, tub, and toilet. Five toothbrushes sat in a cup on the sink, and he imagined the chaos that must ensue when they all tried to get ready at the same time.

With a chuckle, he dropped his bag on the back of the toilet and grabbed the knob in the shower to turn on the water, only to have it come off in his hand. He reinstalled it and tried again until learning the trick to turning it successfully. He washed, changed, and stuffed his dirty clothes in the bag, then rejoined Eleanor in the kitchen.

———

When ready for lunch, the pair boarded the monstrosity his father gifted her and drove to a nearby restaurant.

"They have the best chicken and dumplings," she beamed as they settled into a booth. "I know you don't eat things like that, but they're delicious."

He smiled, wondering if her cooking had changed when she moved. When they lived together, she adapted many recipes to fit his healthy lifestyle. Now, she cooked for three growing kids and their busy mother when she was home. He doubted Heather often got to enjoy family dinners while working two jobs.

Sadness always leaked into Eleanor's voice whenever her daughter's sacrifices came up in their phone conversations. She'd refused his help each time he offered, but no more. Seeing her shoulders droop and her eyes glisten with tears that day had been the last straw.

After ordering, he took her hand and resolved to do something about it whether she wanted him to or not.

"Eleanor, you know how much I love you, right?" he began.

"Of course, honey. Why in the world would you ask that?"

"Is Heather happy here?"

"I think so. It's been a tough year for her, but she's doing better."

"Are you happy?" he continued, despite knowing what she would say.

"You know me. I'm happy when the people I love are happy. Jackson, what's going on in that head of yours?"

"That's a complicated question. But right now, all I'm thinking about is how I can take care of you, Heather, and the kids. It would make *me* happy if you'd let me." He didn't wait for her protest. "I know you don't want to be a burden or take advantage of me, but Eleanor, Grayson left me more money than I'll ever need. Let me do something good with it."

"Oh, sweetie," she sighed. "What do you propose?"

"I want to buy you a house in Richmond that's big enough for the entire family, low-maintenance, and near the best schools, and I want to help Heather get a better job where she won't have to work as much to make the same money or more." He wanted to do this for Eleanor, but his plan wasn't completely selfless. If she lived in Richmond, he could spend more time with her and ensure she was cared for.

"Jackson, you have the biggest heart, and I love you so much." She squeezed his hand. "Let me talk with Heather."

———

The next morning, Jackson worked out until the kids left for school, then joined Eleanor for breakfast. Thankfully, Ben came through and dropped off his suitcase, giving him clean clothes to change into after showering.

"I talked with Heather about your offer," Eleanor finally said while she set their plates in the dishwasher. "She said you are the kindest person she's ever known, and yes, she'd love to take you up on your offer—like she could refuse." Laughing, she threw her arms around him. "I'm grateful for you and the joy you bring to my life."

"You deserve this and more. I'll make a few phone calls to get everything set up. Then, you all can go house shopping when you have time."

Over the next two days, he spent most of his time with Ethan since he rarely left Jackson's side. He showed the boy his workout routine and talked about listening to his mom and grandmother. They went on a short run together and threw the football in the backyard. Both things neither of them had done with their fathers. And each night, Eleanor had to coax Ethan away from him with promises of ice cream or more time later.

On his last morning there, he gave Eleanor the social media links and reluctantly tore himself from her and Ethan's embrace. Leaving wasn't easy, but he now had the motivation he needed to start the long journey ahead.

Chapter Twenty-Eight

☆ ☆ ☆

Jackson

Depsite the drizzly weather, Jackson's spirits remained positive. Running in the rain didn't bother him, but the thunder threatening in the distance was a cause for concern. Standing under an awning of a restaurant, he texted Ben the address. To meet his mileage goal that day, he needed a good meal and dry shoes.

"You look tired," he observed out loud, taking in Ben's red eyes and hard scowl. "Did you enjoy your stay a little too much or did something happen?"

"Shut up." Ben scrubbed both hands over his face.

"Julie keep you up all night? Or Beth?" He wasn't ready to slide this one under the rug yet.

"Neither."

"Oh, really?" He couldn't stop his curiosity from taking root. Ben looked too miserable for someone who didn't have a care in the world. "Trade them in for someone better?"

"Wouldn't you like to know?"

"Kind of why I asked."

Setting his elbow on the table, Ben propped his head up on a fist.

"Well?" he persisted. "What was her name, or do you not remember?"

Stalling, Ben chugged his water and motioned to the waiter for a refill. "I just had too much to drink last night, that's all."

"That's all? Somehow, I doubt that, but I'll let it go for now."

"So kind of you."

To Jackson's relief, their meals arrived quickly. They ate in silence while he sent emails to Harrison and Adam, seeking their help with his plan for Eleanor and her family. He promised to call that evening to discuss the details further.

"Where are we stopping tonight?" Ben asked after the waiter removed their empty plates and refilled their glasses. Now that he had eaten, his normal self had surfaced.

"I hope to get another fifteen miles in if my legs will hold up. Then, we'll cross the North Carolina border by tomorrow."

"Didn't you have someone to visit there?"

"Yes, Will's parents in Murfreesboro."

"That's right. I think I'm going to find something fun to do tomorrow." Ben posture straightened to match his excitement. "Want to join me?"

Understanding what Ben had in mind, he didn't need time to consider his response. After all, he evaluated his readiness to get back on that saddle before leaving Richmond, and the answer was a resounding: "No thank you."

"Why not? Is running the only thing you're going to do on this trip? Somehow, you turned down Beth, and let me say, you missed out, my friend." His eyebrows wiggled, making Jackson grimace. "You leave bars before they get hot and hang out with old ladies. What's up with that, man?"

A laugh escaped before he could stifle it. "Maybe one day, but I don't want to risk getting injured. It's early, and I have a long way to go." While it was an accurate enough reason, he wasn't ready to confide that his heart needed more healing before he could seek adventures like he and his friends had together.

"Suit yourself, but to show there's no hard feelings, I'll bring you a hot chick back as a souvenir."

"Please don't."

"Yep, I will." Ben leaned back and crossed his legs, resigned to follow through on his offer. "It pisses me off how you're wasting your God-given skills."

"What in the hell are you talking about now?"

"Your looks, man. Dude, you could have a chick every night if you'd stop—"

"Why is everyone I know so concerned about my sex life?"

"Because we know it's good for the soul." A grave expression cut off his laugh, and Jackson braced for the next inappropriate thought to escape his lips. "Dude, I feel for you. Has it been so long your dick has forgotten?"

And there it was.

Ignoring him and longing for some solitary peace and quiet, Jackson motioned for the check. He paid the bill and gladly set off on the next path.

The rain held off to a slow mist for the first five miles—just enough precipitation to be a nuisance. By the time he stopped to work his upper body, his shirt had soaked through.

Peeling it from his skin, he stuffed it into the backpack and stepped into the warm rays of the sun as it emerged from the clouds. He stretched his sore legs and hip flexors at the edge of a farm, taking in the beautiful view. Vast rolling fields, horses and cows dotting the terrain, and wide-planked barns that had stood the test of time. The deep red paint of the barn behind the old farmhouse had long ago faded to a muted mauve. The white door, stained brown along the bottom from years of dirt and wear, missed a few boards.

Then, to the left of the white house, he noticed a rusty tractor and the farmer working under the engine hood. The farmer, shirtless beneath his dark jean overalls, had gray hair tied back in a long ponytail. The end of his ragged beard moved with the breeze and blew into his face. He swatted it away with his hand like it was a pesky bug, making Jackson chuckle.

Bending over, he stretched out the kinks in his right hamstring and smiled when the old farmer shouted, tossing a wrench across the yard. The tool brought Jackson's attention to the thin tree limb straining to prop up the ancient hood looming over the farmer. A recipe for disaster.

The black dog, resting under the tire swing on a massive fruit tree nearby, jumped up and barked. The historic farmhouse seemed to be better maintained than the barn, but there were no other signs of a family that Jackson could see. Other than the swing—where did the dog go?

Jackson glanced over the vast yard, and in locating the dog, his heart dropped into his stomach. It sprinted back and forth beside the tractor, barking at the farmer, now trapped under the fallen hood.

He took off through the field, running faster than he knew he could and sliding to a stop beside the tractor. With both hands on the rusty hood, he heaved it up, propping it up with his shoulder.

"Sir, are you hurt? Sir!"

When the farmer didn't respond, he placed a hand on the man's back. Still breathing, thank God. Next, he attempted to check for injuries, but one wrong move could be disastrous for them both. He needed something to support the hood long enough to remove the farmer safely. Craning his neck to look around the farmer, he located a long crowbar perched against a toolbox. It would have to do.

He stretched a leg out and dragged the crowbar closer with his foot. With it lodged into place and doing its job, he lifted the farmer and carried him to a safe spot on the grass. Other than a mark on his arm and back, he seemed unharmed.

"Now, wake up, damn it."

He patted the man's flushed cheek, then dug into his back to retrieve his water bottle. Maybe a splash of water on his face would do the trick. Focused on the mission, he didn't notice the crowbar slipping. The heavy metal hood slamming closed rivaled a cannon and echoed across the farm.

The all too familiar sound made Jackson jump, his heart sputter, and his head suddenly pound with war. Grasping at his skull to silence the torment, he pushed to his feet and fumbled for balance. Fear had taken over his body and squeezed his throat. It was all he could see, feel, taste.

Desperate for cover, he took off in a blind panic until everything went silent.

Chapter Twenty-Nine

☆ ☆ ☆

Jackson

If it hadn't been for his pounding head proving blood still pumped through his veins, he might not have believed the pillowy surface propping him up wasn't a cloud. Although, anything would be better than the ditch he expected to wake up in and feel in every aching bone.

His skin didn't burn from oil and sand mixing with his wounds. Sickening vertigo hadn't claimed his focus or stomach. He felt weakened, but not at the level that came from fighting for his life. That feeling would forever be etched into memory, and this wasn't it.

Whatever happened for him to end up there, at least he didn't seem to be in danger. He was safe, warm, and beyond comfortable. He burrowed further inside the warm blanket tucked tight around him, knowing he didn't have to protect himself in his surroundings. After all, no standard military-issued blanket, sewn to withstand every possible use, felt like this. And neither did a hospital bed—his second fear.

Opening an eye, he surveyed the dark room before considering his next move. A sliver of sunlight peeking through a crack in the curtains landed on the faded red, white, and blue plaid quilt keeping him warm. Seemed harmless enough.

Disoriented, he propped himself up on an elbow and waited for his eyes to adjust. Where was he? Then, his eyes focused on a dog keeping a close eye on him from the foot of the bed, and he remembered. The farm, the trapped farmer, the hood slamming closed. He must have blacked out, but how did he get inside and into bed? To his recollection, the farmhouse sat at least a hundred yards away from where the tractor had been parked. Having no memory of what happened after the hood fell, he doubted he got to that bed on his own.

The dog barked out a warning or an alert when Jackson tossed off the quilt and swung his legs over the side of the bed. Closing his eyes, he waited for the spinning top between his ears to come to a halt. Getting his attendant to stop howling would also go a long way in the recovery department.

"Rex! Hush it, you old mutt," he heard a deep voice say from the doorway. The dog hushed on command and trotted over. "Glad to see you're right-side up."

With both hands on his thighs, propping him up, Jackson turned his heavy head to see the tall silhouette in the doorway and said, "You too."

"Ha!" The farmer crossed the room and handed him a glass of lemonade before opening the curtains to let in more light.

The blinding glow did nothing to soothe the throb behind his eyes, but at least he could see his surroundings and determine if the old farmer was a friend or a foe.

"How are ya feelin'?" he asked. "You were out like a lightning bug at daybreak."

"I've been better." Lifting the glass to his lips, Jackson gulped down the sweet liquid as a sigh of relief hummed in his throat. Either the farmer made the best damn lemonade he'd ever tasted, or he was dehydrated. "How's your head?"

"Hard as granite. Got clocked by a stallion right across the forehead once." He sat in the corner rocking chair beside the bed and pointed at a wide scar over his left eyebrow. "Devil knocked me clear off my feet, but nothing could crack this noggin'. Changed his name to Lucifer after that." A loud burst of laughter filled the room, his round belly bouncing under his overalls.

"How long was I out?" He thought of Ben and wondered where his phone and bag were.

"Long enough for me to feed the goats and chickens, cook lunch, and fix that good-for-nothin' tractor. Purrs like a kitten on Sunday for now."

Jackson's reaction must have questioned him.

"'Bout three hours," he clarified. "Did som'em happen while I was under to knock you out?"

"Memories I thought were locked away…apparently weren't."

"Ahh. Saw the tags." The farmer raised an arm to point at Jackson's chest and his hand sprang to the chain. He pulled the four dog tags from his shirt and held them tight in a fist. "Happen often?"

"Not that much lately."

"What's your name?"

"Jackson."

"Nice to meet ya. Mine's Griffin. Friends call me Griff." He grinned. "Since you seem to have saved me from being eaten by the worst tractor in the history of machinery, I reckon you can call me Griff, too."

Jackson agreed with a nod, thinking with affection that farmer Griff was no foe. "Friends call me Jackson."

Griff laughed again. "You're funny. Can I git ya some soup? Made it myself."

"No, thanks. I really should get going." He stood, only to take a seat again when his stomach shot into his throat and the string yanked the top into motion again.

"I think you jarred your head when you dropped. Pretty big welt you got there." Griff pointed to his own temple.

Jackson's hand sprang to his hairline at the mention, and a sharp jolt pulsed through his head as his careless fingers rolled over the bruise.

"Got a scrape on your elbow, too. I've got something that will fix that right up. Be right back."

"It's…" He attempted to stop him, but Griff was on his feet and out the door before Jackson could finish the thought. He was nimble, despite the Santa belly, and apparently, in great shape. He must have carried or dragged Jackson into the house like a wounded farm animal. He rolled his eyes envisioning the scene, grateful he had no memory of it.

Rex, who had been waiting patiently by the foot of the bed, jumped up and trotted closer to lean against Jackson's legs. He looked up with his dark eyes and panted.

"Is that an apology?" he asked, rubbing the dog's velvety ears and fighting the urge to lie back down.

"Got ya some bandages and my grandma's special healin' cream. Use it every day for cuts and scratches. You'll be good as new in no time."

"What's in it?"

"You don't want to know," he said with a chuckle, "but it works better than any of that modern-day crap you git at the Wal-Mart." He reached into the mason jar with two fingers and scooped. He held up the glob of slimy yellow goo and smiled. "Good as new, remember?"

Turning away from the pungent odor, Jackson surrendered his arm. The concoction smelled of turpentine and urine. I may have burned his eyes and nose, but it soothed the ache beneath the raw scrapes.

With his elbow wrapped in a crisp new bandage, Griff twisted the top back on the jar and rose from the squeaky mattress. "You should eat something. Can you walk?"

"Yeah." To prove it, he leaned forward before slowly straightening to stand upright. He was sore in more places than he could count, but at least his stomach stayed where it belonged.

"Good job."

Following Griff on unsteady knees, he often had to rebalance himself with furniture, a wall, or doorframe. And again, Rex wasn't helping. While he attempted to travel less like a drunk, the dog stayed at his feet, getting in the way of what might have otherwise been a controlled step.

"He's worried about you." Griff tilted his head toward Rex. "He has a sense about him and knows when people or animals are sufferin'. He knew when one of my pigs had a thorn in his foot and tells me when my mommas are going into labor. That happens a lot around here." With a wink over his shoulder, he plucked two bowls from the cabinet beside the sink.

In the center of a bay window beside the kitchen, Jackson sat at the large table and admired the natural wood grain—the color of a wheat field. The marks and dents, evidence it had played a part in many meals, activities, and memories over time, only added to the character.

"That there was my great-grandfather's." Griff nodded at the table as he stirred the soup in a massive silver pot on the stove. "He milled the wood, carved the legs, and built it all with two hands. No mechanical tools back in the day. Only a hammer, chisel, saw, and elbow grease."

"It must feel incredible to make something useful and beautiful like this with your bare hands." Absently, Jackson ran his fingers over the soft wood.

"Maybe you'll learn one day and find out for yourself. You just gotta start trying."

A poignant life lesson Jackson had learned recently. Although Griff was talking about learning a new skill, it also applied to finding the will to live while drowning in sorrow, grief, or self-pity. When darkness seemed infinite or when hope was fickle, motivation faltered at the slightest setbacks. At the bare minimum, *trying* to move forward and *trying* to fight back against oppressive thoughts was the only way to stay afloat. Even when giving up was easier. Even when something as innate as breathing seemed impossible.

"You okay?" Griff claimed the seat opposite him and placed a steaming bowl on each placemat. The aroma awakened Jackson from his mental spiral, warming his soul with thoughts of Eleanor. The soup smelled just like hers, and his stomach growled.

With a chuckle, Griff grabbed his spoon and waved it across the table. "I'll take that as a yes. Eat up. A hearty meal should help that angry stomach of yours." He watched Jackson scoop a spoonful of soup into his mouth and close his eyes, savoring the taste before chewing. "I have the same reaction every time I eat it. All the ingredients were grown or raised right here on this farm."

He tasted potatoes, carrots, beef, onions, and various spices. "It's delicious. Do you do everything here alone?"

He'd yet to see any sign of family or farmhands around. Then again, he'd seen only a fraction of the property and slept through the last several hours. They could be working elsewhere or had already come and gone for the day.

"My sister's son will pitch in whenever he's home. He goes to some fancy college in New York, and if I'm being honest…" Griff propped an elbow on the table and leaned over his bowl, lowering his voice as if he didn't want his secret reaching the wrong ears. "The boy's too soft to make a dent in what needs done 'round here. But he makes the prettiest cakes you'll ever see." Another roaring belly laugh erupted as he sat back. "Other than that, it's just me and Rex."

"How do you manage it all? The animals, the fields, the equipment. Seems like too much for just one person."

"Been doing it ever since my Margaret left this world. This is her recipe, by the way." Shifting his gaze to the bowl, he grinned longingly.

"How long were you together?"

"Fifty-one years. We were high school sweethearts. Her parents didn't like me none, but she never minded. And neither did I, if you know what I mean." He winked and sipped a quick spoonful of broth. "Her pretty red hair first caught my eye. It flowed in the wind like water over river rocks. I liked how she never fussed over it like some girls did. She had a natural beauty. Her eyes were the color of green moss, and her skin smooth and pure as fresh milk."

"She must have been very beautiful."

"Ahh, yes. One look at her and I was a goner. Good thing she was sweet and smart, too." He beamed. "Bought the tractor out there when we moved in because the paint reminded me of her. Bright red with light green stripes down the side and white wheels."

"The old rusty tractor that tried to eat you?"

"That's the one."

"Her parents wouldn't let her marry me, so we ran away right after graduation. Then…"

When Griff's smile faded, Jackson set down his spoon. "What happened?"

"1969 happened." His answer dripped with heavy discontent. "My birthday was the second number called in the lottery. I was nineteen, and Maggie was expecting our first child. A girl." He forced a smile and stirred the soup in his bowl but didn't eat. "I left for Vietnam six months later with the Army and didn't see my daughter until she was almost two years old."

"What's her name?"

"Dorothy. Dorothy Jane after my momma."

"Does she live nearby?"

"No. She lives in Alabama to be near her grandbabies. Seven of them, all under age ten. Can you believe that?"

"It's hard to imagine."

"They don't get up here much, and I can't leave the farm. It's been too long since I've seen them. My sons live in South Carolina. One's a nurse and the other a lawyer. I'm a proud papa, but they don't have kids. Was such a sadness for my Maggie. She wanted hordes of grandbabies." Picking up his spoon, he took a big bite, chewing as he talked. "What about you? Have any lit'l ones?"

Surprised, Jackson puffed out a breath. "No. Don't even have a girlfriend." Feeling better, he sat back in his chair and met Griff's amused gaze.

"Ha. Well, I'm sure that won't last. So, what were you doing in these parts? People don't travel this road much, and I didn't see a car. Checked out by the road after I got you into the house."

"No car. I was running and stopped at the tree by your driveway to stretch and admire your property."

"Runnin'? The farm's miles from anywhere."

"Yep. I was visiting a friend in Stony Creek on my way to Murfreesboro."

"Are you sick in the head? Who runs that far?"

"Probably, and me, apparently," Jackson answered both questions on a laugh. "Or I hope to. I started in Richmond, Virginia, and I'm planning to stop in Orlando."

"Well, I'll be damned. Why in the hell are you puttin' yourself through all that?"

"I enjoy it, and I've got a lot going on in this sick head of mine." He pointed at his sore head with his spoon with a grin before plunging it into the bowl again.

"Like what?"

Griff tilted his head in suspicion, the same way Rex eyed him earlier, and he had to stifle a grin.

"You're not gonna go all crazy on me, are you? I git enough of that from my animals on a full moon." Gathering up their empty bowls, Griff let out another Santa laugh on the way to the sink.

"No, nothing like that. Just taking some time to figure things out." Jackson looked around. "Do you know where my bag is? I need to make a phone call."

"Sure do. Left it in the bedroom on the dresser. Rex," he called, and the dog leapt out from under the table, racing to sit expectantly at Griff's feet. "Go get Jackson's bag."

Rex took off and returned seconds later, the backpack strap secured between his teeth as it dragged on the floor. Jackson stared in awe as he dropped the bag beside the table and caught the chunk of meat Griff tossed him, gobbling it down with a few slobbery chews.

"He's a smart one," Griff beamed, rewarding the dog further with a pat on his side, before shooing him away.

Now that he'd eaten, Jackson rose to test his body while Griff tended to the dirty dishes. He needed to call Ben and preferred that conversation to not have an audience. Jackson usually checked in whenever he stopped to rest or stretch, and he didn't know how Ben would react to his recent radio silence. Four hours between check-ins would surely raise a few red flags. Or perhaps Ben was having too much fun on his adventure to notice. The latter being the more likely scenario, Jackson headed outside with a four-legged escort.

He moved slowly making sure the soup he'd eaten didn't reappear, and his legs could move without support. Satisfied with his swift recovery, he leaned against the porch railing and dialed Ben's number.

The phone ringing in his ear soon faded into the background as his gaze rolled over the fields with a new perspective. Decades of hard work, sacrifices, blood, and sweat were planted in that soil. Built from nothing. Nurtured by a family together with love and steadfast devotion.

Sunrays emerged from behind the clouds, illuminating the seas of green and yellow beyond in a swatch of light. Perfect as a painting, he got lost in the serenity until Ben's obnoxious voicemail message boomed through the speaker, ruining his peace.

Realizing his patience hadn't returned with his appetite, he canceled the call without leaving a message.

"You know you can stay here tonight," Griff said as Jackson re-entered the kitchen. "Rest a little and keep an old man company."

Enjoying his stay, he considered it. "I appreciate the offer."

"Then, if you start feeling better later, you can give me a hand. Got a few things to do and could use a little muscle. You seem to have plenty for the job." He set the wet bowls he finished washing on a towel beside the sink.

"What needs to be done?"

"Just some repairs and some heavy lifting."

"I'm game."

"Are you sure?" Griff asked, his thick brow pinching in the middle and creasing his forehead.

"Yeah. I feel much better. And besides, I never let a little headache stop me."

"My kind of guy." After tossing aside the towel, Griff called for Rex and showed Jackson to the barn and feeding troughs needing repair.

For the next hour, they worked in the blazing heat. Jackson carried wood planks, bricks, painting supplies, and tools. He followed Griff's instructions and did all the lifting. Upon finishing at the barn, he loaded two dozen planks and a roll of wire into an old truck bed for the next task.

He rode in the back of the truck with the supplies and Rex until Griff pulled up beside the obvious reason for their visit—a gaping hole in the fence surrounding a separated section of the cow field. The added barbed wire, installed to reinforce the wooden fence, hadn't stopped the thousand-pound beast that had obviously barreled through it.

"That there was done by my bull. He's a frustrating character, especially when he sees his favorite female behind this useless fence. Nothing will stop him from reaching her."

Jackson's head snapped to the animals behind him, and Griff's laugh echoed across the field. Several cows stopped munching on the grass long enough to glance in his direction. "Don't worry. He's in his own field back that-a way." He tossed a thumb over his shoulder. "In a double-enforced fence. Or at least, better enforced than this one."

Jackson climbed down from the truck bed. "How many of these do you need?"

"Grab three and the wire, and we'll see if it holds."

Jackson did as he was told. Then, the pair moved to the next area needing repairs. It took two hours to fix all six holes—some small, some the size of a large bull—but he didn't mind. He basked in the work, weather, and company.

"Can I ask you something?" Jackson said as they loaded hay onto the trailer.

"Sure. Ask away."

He lifted the next bale with a grunt and dropped it on the truck bed. "If you could have anything to improve your life here, what would it be?"

"Shoot, besides ten of you?" Griff might have meant it as a joke but neither he nor Jackson laughed. It took only a handful of hours for Jackson to understand the farm's chore list never ended.

"Well, if money wasn't an issue, I'd buy a fancy tractor with all the bells and whistles. Why do you ask?"

"Just curious." He tossed the last bale onto the bed and climbed up. "I can see that you need help."

With a nod, Griff went to pull himself into the truck cab as a sporty silver hatchback barreled down the driveway without regard for the dirt or potholes. He paused and smiled at Jackson. "Seems to be my day for visitors."

"What the hell, man?" Ben yelled out the car window when he noticed Jackson walking toward him. He threw open the door and shot out, ready for a confrontation.

"What are you doing here?"

Ignoring the question, Ben stalked closer. "I've been freakin' out trying to reach you for hours."

"How did you find me?" That question stopped him in his tracks. His hands flew up defensively as if a weapon appeared and was aimed in his direction.

Depending on his next move, Jackson thought, the action might be warranted.

"Harrison made me do it," Ben blurted, nervous hands rummaging through his hair.

"Do what?"

"I put a tracker app on your phone." Something in Jackson's reaction had an explanation tumbling out of his mouth. Wise move. "He was worried that you'd get hurt and not be able to call for help. It also comes in handy when you don't tell your buddy where you are or answer your damn phone."

Jackson patted his pockets to find them empty. "I don't have my phone with me."

"No shit."

"What's goin' on over here?" Griff asked as he approached. "From the truck, you two look like my goats rearin' up for some head buttin'."

Seeing a way out, Ben dodged Jackson and his boiling temper to greet Griff. "I'm Ben. This guy didn't answer his phone, so I came looking for him."

"Well, isn't that nice? Great to meet ya, Ben. I'm Griffin. Jackson here saved me when my tractor's evil side took over. Now, he's helpin' with some chores. We could sure use some extra hands if you're willin'."

"Yes. That's a fantastic idea," Jackson slapped Ben on the back with more force than necessary. "He'd love to help."

"Great. Let's get to it then. The cows don't care for their supper being late."

Smiling, Jackson turned to follow Griff back to the truck, leaving Ben frozen in awe at his bad luck.

"He'd love to help," Ben mocked with a pronounced frown and loud enough for Jackson to hear. After letting out his frustration in a loud sigh, he yanked off his shirt and tossed it inside the car.

"Ya comin' or not?" Griff called.

"Yeah, I'm coming."

By the time they finished delivering hay to the cows and horses, Jackson and Ben were covered in sweat and dust. It was exhausting work, something Ben was not accustomed to, and he scowled silently in the bed of the truck as they traveled from one field to the next.

"What's the matter, buddy?" Jackson asked.

"Nothing except that shit-eatin' grin on your face."

"That's what you get for brooding like a spoiled kid."

"Fuck you. It's a hundred degrees out here, and I'm covered in hay and horse shit. My skin feels like it's on fire." He scratched at his abs and back, then swatted at a mosquito on his leg.

"You should have kept your shirt on."

"Easy to say now."

The sun had begun its descent, calling more insects to the sky. While nature's playlist soothed Jackson, it seemed to do the opposite for Ben. Edgier than usual, his eyes and hands never stilled. He looked ready to pounce on any insect that dared to come near and run from any animal that eyed him the wrong way.

Griff parked beside the old tractor, joining the others and Rex at the back. "Ready for dinner and a cold beer? Our reward for a hard day's work."

"Hell, yeah." Ben perked up, but his enthusiasm was met with the back of Jackson's hand slapping across his raw stomach.

"That's kind of you, but we need to get going. There's still a couple of hours of daylight left that I could use to make some progress."

"Can we at least take a shower?" Ben complained.

"Fine by me if you want." Griff looked to Jackson for approval. When he nodded, he directed Ben to the outdoor shower. "And help yourself to anything in the kitchen."

Rex plopped down at Jackson's feet. Bending down to rub the dog's ears, he noticed his own dirty clothes and shoes. "I might wash off and change clothes, too."

"No problem. Feel free to use the one inside."

Jackson jogged to the car to grab his and Ben's suitcases. The idiot, he sighed, forgot to take clean clothes with him to the shower. What was he going to do? Walk naked back to the car afterward?

Yes, he decided, rolling his eyes. *That's exactly what Ben would have done.*

———

"Thank you for taking such good care of me," Jackson said to Griff after the three of them gathered on the front porch of the farmhouse. "I'm glad that tractor tried to eat you. Otherwise, I never would have met you."

"Right back at ya. And thanks to both of you for helping with the chores. At my pace, everything we did today would have taken me a month." He shook their hands. "Now, git before I find more chores for you."

"Yes, sir."

Jackson rode with Ben in the car to the edge of the driveway to give him some strict and detailed instructions.

"You want me to buy what?" he asked with an expression that said he questioned Jackson's sanity.

"A tractor. The best one they have, and it must be red with white wheels."

"Okay," Ben said cautiously. "Are you feeling okay? I think that bump on your head is affecting your decision-making."

Ignoring the comment, he stayed on task. "If they don't have one, go somewhere else until you find it. And I want it delivered here, whatever it costs. Got it?"

"I got it. Fuck. It's not that hard."

Eyeing Ben, he climbed out of the car to start his warm-up routine. He'd love to be there to see the look on Griff's face when the trailer pulled up carrying the shiny new tractor with no pesky quirks or stutters and a hood that would stay put.

Yes. Griff deserved that new tractor, and Ben better not screw it up.

Chapter Thirty

☆ ☆ ☆

Jackson

Until he stood outside Wills' parent's house in Murfreesboro, Jackson's emotions overflowed and consumed him. He couldn't stop wondering how Caroline and Jonathan would react to his visit, keeping him up at night. Anticipation ate at him from the inside out.

Downtime between runs was the most unbearable. His thoughts flipped back and forth between worried and eager. Frightened and elated. He was exhausted, but it didn't stop him from running each day faster than the one before. One singular goal filled him with nervous energy and purpose for three days.

Now, frozen to the concrete sidewalk, he fought the urge to crumble—his strength as feeble as a sandcastle in the tide. The front door, standing between him and some of his favorite people, was only a few paces away, yet he couldn't move.

What if they didn't want to see him? What if his presence brought back too many painful memories? What if they resented him for his role in Will's trauma? And then there was Avery, their niece, and how he'd hurt her.

His chest tightened without warning. Hands resting on his thighs, he gulped for air and scrambled for his wayward courage. He muttered the reasons he'd come and waited for his legs to start working again. If Caroline or Jonathan tossed him out, he'd never forgive himself for putting them through it, but he'd understand.

Straightening, he willed himself to breathe and walk up the driveway to the small, brick ranch. Smaller than their home in Richmond, it sat on a quiet suburban street with cascading mature trees and manicured yards. With Jonathan's meticulous attention to detail and love for all things green, his yard was picture-perfect and stood out among the rest.

The sight of it and the memories that flooded his thoughts made him smile. Memories of Jonathan crawling around on his knees, tending to weeds and flowers, shaping shrubbery, or overseeding his overly lush lawn one foot at a time. Caroline sweeping the walkway or waving at him and the boys from the window as they zoomed past. God, he missed them both so much.

As he approached, the plants and trees lining the porch seemed to spin in slow motion. Looking up, he begged Will to give him the courage to take the next step, literally and figuratively. Instead, he got a young woman with long, wavy red hair and a drooling toddler on her hip.

"Why are you lurking outside our house?" she asked in a tone that said she'd had better days, and Jackson wasn't helping matters.

"Unbelievable. How can I have the wrong house again?"

"I don't know. Now, go away," she demanded and slammed the door.

Confused, Jackson compared the address to the text Harrison sent. He had the right house. But who were the strangers inside? Climbing the stairs again, he could hear the child wailing. His conscience poked at him for bothering the young mother again, but he needed answers.

He knocked on the door and the child's screams grew louder on the other side. Next came angry footsteps before the door flew open, blowing her hair off her shoulders.

"This is not a good time to try to sell me anything," she hissed and scooped up the chubby toddler, who had taken hold of her leg.

She went to close the door, but Jackson stopped it with his hand, regretting the fear that flashed over her face.

"Ma'am, please, I'm sorry to disturb you," he said, releasing his hand from the door. "I'm trying to find Jonathan and Caroline Mason. I was told they lived here."

With the mention of the Masons, her face relaxed, but her deep emerald eyes remained cautious.

"This is their house. Who are you?"

"Jackson Vane. I was a friend of their son's."

"Jackson? Oh, my God. I didn't recognize you."

She launched forward, wrapping her free arm around his neck and catching him off guard. He didn't know how to react or what to say in this awkward moment. All he could do was search through his memories for her. The more he came up empty, the more he questioned. Sensing his unease, she soon released him, tears now glistening in her eyes.

"I'm sorry. Do I know you?" he asked, more confused than ever.

Before she could answer, the child reached for Jackson with his entire body, tumbling out of her arms. Instinct kicked in and Jackson caught the boy. He adjusted his grip, pausing when the child's head rested on his chest.

Sadness consumed the mother as she watched him rub her son's back to soothe and support him. Collapsing onto the stoop, she sobbed into her hands. What should he do? She was distraught, and he had her child. Apparently, they knew each other, but he couldn't recall how. Feeling helpless, he gave her time to compose herself and waited for her to talk to him. He crossed his legs and lowered to sit on the porch across from her, resting the child on his thigh.

While he waited, Jackson studied the small human in his arms. He has his mother's red hair, only lighter like the color of a peach. The adorable line his plump skin made around his wrist looked like a bracelet. He'd never seen skin so flawless, so soft. Holding him didn't seem as foreign or terrifying as he expected it to be. The child's little heart fluttering against his chest was oddly touching. When the child reached for him again, his pale lashes slowly closing, he offered his thumb and rocked gently—another instinct he didn't know he had. The boy's hand wrapped around the base of the finger as he drifted to sleep.

The woman soon raised her head but said nothing. Only stared at them both, lost in her own thoughts. Tears still wet on her cheeks.

"What's his name?" he asked to break the silence and get her talking again.

"William Andrew Mason," she answered without breaking eye contact. "After his father."

Stunned, Jackson looked down at the sleeping baby in his arms, taking in William's features he hadn't noticed before. The gentle curve of his nose, the dimple in his chin, the arch of his eyebrows. He thought of Will and wondered if he'd known about Sydney's pregnancy before he…

He scolded himself for thinking it. Of course, he didn't know. Will was beyond loyal to those he loved, always going out of his way to care for them before anyone thought to ask, and he would have loved and cared for his son above all else. No matter what he had to face or endure, Will never would have left his child behind. Then again, Jackson never thought he'd leave his parents—or him.

"He's beautiful," he managed through his troubled thoughts. "You must be Sydney."

She sighed. "I am."

Despite himself, his next words slid out before he could stop them, slicing his heart like knives. "Did he know?"

She shook her head. "I was going to tell him the night we found him. Avery, her parents, and I were invited over for dinner. It was perfect timing, or so I thought."

Sobs burst from her throat, and she slapped a hand over her mouth to stifle them. Jackson fought against his own, lodging in his throat, as his mind took him to that day against his will. It had been torture. Every fucking bit of it. He lost his best friend. Sydney lost the man she loved. William had the most amazing father he would never know. And the most heartbreaking of all, Will succumbed to the terrors of his disease before he could learn of a new, precious reason to live.

"I'm sorry," she said, clearing her eyes and taking a deep breath. Her posture straightened, a moment of warrior strength before the weight of her grief bore down on her once again. She slumped back over her folded knees. "It still hurts. I miss him so much."

"I know. There's not a day that goes by that I don't think about him and wish he were here."

She glanced down at William. "Seeing our son so content in your arms would have made Will so happy." Her eyes met his again with grave sincerity. "I hope you know how much he loved you."

He nodded, too choked by pain and remorse to respond.

"Oh, my goodness," she said, slapping her thighs and standing. "You must be so uncomfortable. Do you want to come in?"

"That would be great." Securing William, he rose with minimal movement to keep from waking him. "I didn't think he'd ever find you, but you were the one. I saw it in his eyes."

Her chin quivered, but she returned his smile—her inner warrior winning this battle. "I loved that man and every last unruly bone in his body." She held out a hand. "I'm Sydney Norman. Nice to finally meet you, Jackson. Although, I feel like I already know you. Will talked about you and your adventures together all the time," she added, opening the door.

Once in the living room, she transferred her sleeping baby to a playpen, where he rolled onto his stomach and fell back asleep. She grabbed tissues and two water bottles from the kitchen, then joined Jackson on the couch, folding her legs under her.

"Will's parents should be home from work soon. They'll be over-the-moon excited to see you."

"I hope so."

She tilted her head, gauging him. "Why would you say that? Of course, they will be."

An anxious hand combed through his hair. "Well, they didn't tell me they were leaving, and I haven't heard from them since the funeral. I can't help but think that, maybe, a part of them blamed me for what happened."

"Never," she touched his arm. "They adore you. If anyone is to blame for their sudden move, it's me."

"Why? If you don't mind me asking."

Her eyes dropped to her lap as she began. "After we buried Will, grief took over my life. I was always sick. I don't know if it was from the pregnancy or grief or a combination of the two, but I had to quit school and my job. I couldn't pay my share of the apartment I had with my best friend. She helped for as long as she could, but I hated being a burden."

"What about your parents?"

She scoffed through a frown. "They were ashamed and practically disowned me." The sadness in her eyes flipped to disappointment and fire. "I've never been able to live up to their expectations and getting knocked up without a husband was the last straw. They're a little old-fashioned."

"I didn't think that was still a thing."

"Leave it to my parents to be different. It should be a long story, but it isn't. They turned me away, and I went to Will's parents. They never hesitated." Her face brightened at the memory. "They took me in, gave me a roof over my head, and have supported me and William ever since."

"That sounds like them, but why did they have to move?"

"You know they don't make much money, and Will's funeral wiped out what little savings they had. Add two more mouths to feed into the struggle…" She pinched her lips together at the irony and shrugged, letting him fill in the blanks.

The burden she didn't want to be on her roommate fell on Will's parents and compounded once William arrived, but Jonathan and Caroline would never think of her and William in that way. They were family and their family stuck together. He'd heard them say that so many times, even he believed it to be true…despite his own broken parental relationships at the time.

"I could work now," Sydney continued, bringing Jackson back to the conversation. "But I wouldn't make enough to pay for childcare. It isn't worth it to be away from him, and I can't ask them to watch him. So, when Jon received an offer for a promotion at the plant down here, he had to take it. Plus," she swallowed hard, "it was hard to heal in that house."

He nodded in understanding.

"I don't know what I would have done if they had turned me away."

"I guarantee it never crossed their mind."

William fussed, letting everyone know he'd awakened, and she pushed off the couch to pick him up. "He likes to eat after a nap, no matter how short it is." She sighed. "And I should get dinner started. Will you join me in the kitchen?"

"I'd love to."

After filling William's tray with crackers, chicken, and diced grapes, Sydney prepared a casserole with rice, leftover rotisserie chicken, and vegetables.

"I hope you're okay with this. It's the only thing I know how to make...successfully."

"I'm sure it will be great."

Their conversation continued, light and easy, until a car pulled into the driveway.

Her eyes widened with her smile. "They're here. Let's surprise them." She rushed Jackson into the nearby room and returned to the kitchen in time to greet Jon and Caroline as they entered.

"Welcome home. How was work?"

"Tiring," Jon answered.

Jackson heard him drop something onto the tile floor and cross the kitchen. Undoubtedly, he was greeting Sydney and William with a hug or a kiss on the cheek. The man wrote the book on how to be a loving father and husband.

"You're in a good mood this evening," Caroline said, opening the oven door. "Are you cooking?"

"Yep. I thought we could celebrate tonight."

The refrigerator door opened and closed.

"Celebrate what?" Jonathan got out before Jackson emerged from the dining room—the anticipation too much to contain.

He stood in the doorframe, waiting for their reaction, but they only stared at him. Either their blank expressions gave away nothing of what they were feeling or his anxiety blocked his brain from processing the clues. His pulse raced in the agonizing silence as tiny beads of sweat bubbled on his forehead.

"I'm sorry to stop by unannounced," he said, hoping to break the tension.

The longer they stared, the more he doubted his decision to come. *This is wrong. He shouldn't be there. He's only hurting them.* As his spiral took him under, Caroline's hands rose slowly to her mouth. He watched her step closer until she threw herself into his arms and sobbed on his shoulder like she had at Will's funeral.

He hated making her cry, but her tight embrace gave him the acceptance he'd hoped for. He slumped further into relief when Jonathan's arm draped across his back. All the emotion he'd harbored about this vital moment poured out of him with his own tears.

"I can't believe how healthy you are," Caroline said when she released him, her hands lingering on his face.

"And look at all this gorgeous hair you have." She combed her hands through the ends, resting below his ears.

"I had to let a lot of things go over the years—military grooming being one of them." He lips curved into a crooked grin. "But I'm getting better every day. Being here is part of my therapy. I've missed you both so much."

Caroline wiped the escaped tear before it could slide further down his cheek. "We're happy to see you, sweetheart and regret not reaching out before we—"

"It's okay. I understand."

"You always have." She grinned, but her dark eyes, the same as Will's, remained saddened over it. His heart squeezed as she continued. "No matter what was happening around you, you always got it. Such a tender, perceptive heart you have."

"Thank you, but nothing that's happened over the last two years has made any sense."

"It will, darling." She patted his cheek. "It will. Come. Have a seat. I want to hear all about what you've been up to." Caroline led him and Jonathan to the kitchen table and held both their hands. "Last time we saw you, you were in a wheelchair, and now look at you. You're walking."

"And running. That seemed impossible when I first came back, but it's helping me heal."

"We're happy for you and never had a doubt you'd get back on your feet. Right, Jon?"

"Not one. Where all things athletic are concerned, you are a special breed, my friend," Jonathan added with a laugh.

"And Avery filled us in occasionally on your progress."

Jackson swallowed his embarrassment. "She did?"

"Don't worry, dear. Her feelings for you weren't a secret around here."

"No, they were not," Sydney chimed in, her eyes wide with dramatic flair.

Caroline bit back a grin before continuing. "I'm sorry it didn't work out, but I can't say I'm surprised."

"Why is that?"

"You of all people should know why. The way she felt wasn't healthy or natural, Jackson. Your relationship was doomed from the start." She took his hand and leaned in. "I know you're beating yourself up over it. Stop. She's better off."

"I'm not sure how to take that." He laughed, feeling his muscles relax a little, knowing they supported his decision. "But I had no idea how she felt until we started seeing each other, and it didn't end well." *Either time*, Jackson thought— the official break up and when she threw herself at him after the funeral.

"That puts you in the same category as every other male. You're usually oblivious to our signals." She cast her husband a sly grin.

"She had to ask me out," Jonathan explained, pointing a thumb at himself. "Oblivious is my middle name."

"Sounds like you," Jackson joked, affectionately, grateful their usual banter was still alive and well. "Thank you, though. I was worried you'd be upset with me."

"Lord, no." Caroline waved a hand, dismissing the idea. "I adore Avery. She's family, but that girl had it coming to her. It's about time she moved on and got herself a life."

"She's dating someone now," Sydney informed them, and he had to tamp down his gut reaction regarding *who* that someone was. The jackass wasn't good enough for her or worthy of her time. She deserved better.

"Good," Caroline began. "Now, enough about Avery. What else is happening in your world? I want to know everything."

Jackson sighed. He was grateful for the shift in conversation, but he couldn't decide which was worse. Talking about Avery or reliving his father's passing. "I assume you know about Grayson."

"Yes," Jonathan answered softly. "We wanted to be there to support you, but we couldn't get off work so soon after starting our new jobs. And another funeral…" he trailed off.

"I know. I didn't expect you to come. It's not like you and Dad were friends."

"Dad? I've never heard you call him that before. Did you two have a chance to mend your relationship before he passed?"

"Somewhat. Believe it or not, he apologized, and I forgave him. After all, I'm not innocent in all this either. But there's no sense in dwelling on it now."

William screamed and slammed his little palms on the highchair tray, causing the group to turn in his direction. Sydney rushed to his side, embarrassment flush on her cheeks.

"Sorry about that," she said, wiggling him out of the chair. "I guess this is a good time to announce that dinner's ready."

Chapter Thirty-One

✩ ✩ ✩

Jackson

Once seated at the table and the wine poured, Jonathan held up his glass for a toast. "To our second son and his remarkable recovery. May love, strength, and happiness continue to fill your cup."

"Hear, hear. We love you, sweetheart," Caroline added.

"Love you, too."

"How long are you staying in town?" Sydney asked when there a lull had fallen over the group's conversation.

"Just until tomorrow morning. I'm trying to keep a strict schedule for a healthy rhythm and balance."

"Schedule for what? Do you have to get back to Richmond for work or something?" She lifted William into her lap when he crawled over and whimpered.

"No. I needed to get out of Richmond. I'd been cooped up there during my recovery and needed to do something for myself and Will. I owe him my life." Pausing, Jackson kicked himself for bringing up the incident—grief and frustration seeping into his bones again. But he also couldn't answer her question without pointing back to that fatal moment. After all, it was the catalyst that changed all their lives forever, making his trip necessary in the first place.

"Since I have no plan for my future, I started a long journey to help me find myself again. I'm a week in."

"What type of journey?"

He took a deep breath, expecting their reaction to be similar to Harrison's. Shocked, disbelief, concerned. "I'm running to Orlando."

"What in the world?" Jonathan set down his glass. "Why?"

Jackson laughed at the response he typically received to the statement. "It's the only thing I know how to do, and I have nothing to show for the twenty-eight years of my life. No skills, no prospects, and no idea what to do with the next twenty-eight. I thought that by making this run, I might find my future path along the way—a purpose."

"Oh, sweetheart," Caroline empathized, her eyes glossing with fresh tears.

"I hope you do, son," Jonathan said with a smile. "You're crazy, but you deserve it."

"Thank you. This trip isn't only for me. I'm doing it to honor Will and all the veterans who struggle when they come home or are no longer with us. I'm also doing this for them because they can't."

"That's beautiful, Jackson. Will would be so proud of you. As are we." Caroline reached an arm around Jackson's shoulders and squeezed before returning to her seat. Growing up, she'd always been another mother figure to him, and he never realized how lucky he was to have so many. Until now.

"Why Orlando?" Jonathan asked and wiped at the corner of his eye with a napkin.

"Not sure. All I knew at the time I decided was that I wanted to stay on the east coast for the trip. Then, I needed the distance to be substantial for it to be worthwhile. Orlando came to mind because the boys and I went to Disney a couple of times. I have great memories with them there."

"I remember when you went for spring break your senior year. I was so worried," Caroline confessed and took an unsteady sip of wine.

"You always worried. I thought you'd have been used to all the crazy things we got into by then."

She laughed. "That's why. Every time I turned around, you four were giving me another reason to worry."

"It was usually Will or Billy's fault."

"I can believe that, but you're not completely innocent, mister."

Jackson shrugged. Better to leave that one be.

"Do you have any other stops planned along the way?" Sydney asked.

"Just three. I visited Eleanor in Stony Creek and convinced her and her family to move back to Richmond. This visit is the second, and the third is Myrtle Beach, South

Carolina. After that, I plan to let the road guide me the rest of the way."

"That sounds amazing."

"I hope you find everything you're searching for on this trip, sweetheart," Caroline added before kissing Jackson on the top of his head. She gathered the empty plates from the table and headed to the kitchen, trailed by William crawling behind her.

The reminiscing didn't stop until after midnight when yawns took over, sending everyone to bed. Exhausted from a long day, Jackson expected to sleep, but as usual, all they'd discussed and the emotions he experienced turned his emotions into a freight train.

Several hours into the harrowing ride, as his last thread of control began to fray, William's whimpers echoed into the living room. When no one checked on him, Jackson snuck into his room and found him standing in the crib with fat tears on his pink cheeks. He reached out, and Jackson melted.

He lifted the chubby toddler out of the crib and paced around the room until he fell back to sleep, but when Jackson tried to put him back in the crib, he awoke and held on tight to Jackson's shirt with both fists. Not wanting to upset him, he returned the toddler to his chest.

He continued pacing until William went lax again, then lowered him to the mattress, only to have him wake up again. Since the pattern seemed to have no end, Jackson strolled to the living room to break up the monotony. He paced circles around the couch, amazed at how such a tiny human could be so heavy. With his arm muscles screaming, he carefully lowered himself to the couch, secured Willian on his torso, and shook out his arms.

At some point in the night, he must have fallen asleep, too, as pale, orange sunrays now shone on his face through the window. Opening his eyes, he lifted his head to check on William. He was still asleep with his roly-poly arms and legs draped across Jackson's body.

"Good morning," Sydney greeted over her coffee cup when his head rolled to the side and saw her. "I had a slight heart attack when I entered William's room this morning."

"Yeah. Sorry about that." He explained how he and William ended up in the living room, bringing a smile to her face.

"He's already got you wrapped around his little finger. Gets that from his father."

"I can see Will in him. He may have your hair, but he has Will's features. What?" he asked when the color drained from her cheeks, and she turned away.

"He was with me last night."

"Who was? Will?"

She nodded and faced him again, her eyes filled with fresh tears. "He was in my room and even laid next to me."

"I'm sure he's always with you and William."

"No." She shook her head, her eyes falling on William but distant as if she were looking through to another place. "I thought I would have these sensations often. I thought I would see and feel him beside me, but he's been absent. Painfully absent." Her glossy eyes lifted to Jackson. "Until you showed up."

"Sydney," he began but didn't have the words.

"I think he's with *you*, Jackson. Not me. William felt it as soon as he saw you, and I feel him now. Can you?"

Disappointed, he shook his head.

"It's probably why I slept so soundly and didn't hear William. He held me through the night, and for a short time, I was whole again."

"I envy you." He'd forgotten what it felt like not to have so many holes in his heart. "He hasn't made his presence known to me."

Although, Jackson was beginning to wonder if Will was responsible for this journey he'd started. The day the idea came to him, he thought he was running on a random route, in control of his destiny, but maybe it had been Will, directing his path and sending him clues. Had he also sent him to Sydney? *The sneaky bastard*, Jackson thought and smiled.

"Jackson," she said absently, too lost in her thoughts to notice his amusement.

Feeling better, he folded an arm and tucked a hand behind his head. "Sydney."

"I need to ask you something."

"Sure. Ask me anything."

She set down her mug to pace, often glancing at her world sleeping contently on his chest along the way. "If Will was here…physically." She flashed an unsteady grin. "I know he would have asked you this himself."

"What is it, Sydney?"

She returned to her seat and breathed deep. "William doesn't trust easily. It's my fault, I know. I'm too protective, but he's my everything and all I have left of Will."

"Understandable. But being protective of your child isn't a bad thing."

Ignoring the comment, she shot up and started pacing again, her words falling like a rainstorm—fast and unpredictable. And based on the uncertainty in her eyes, the turbulence rocked her. "Seeing you with William and how he responds to you, I know he senses what a good man you are and how much you loved his father."

He sat up to see her better and adjusted William to his lap. "Sydney, whatever it is, just ask. I can see it's bothering you."

"Fine. Will you be William's godfather?"

Stunned speechless, he looked down at William sleeping in his arms and couldn't imagine not being a part of the child's life. He loved the little guy already. And he was Will's. That fact alone made him family.

"You don't have to answer right now. I know it's a shock and a lot to—"

"I'd be honored."

"Really?" She exhaled, dropped onto the couch beside him, and wrapped her arms around his neck. "Thank you. Now, he has a guardian angel and a godfather. He's one lucky little boy."

"I think I'm the lucky one."

"Good morning," Jonathan said as he entered the room and found the three huddled together. He sat in the nearby chair and studied them.

Unwinding her arms, Sydney scooted over on the couch, her eyes down. "Good morning, Jon."

"What's going on?" he asked, curiosity alive in his voice.

"William woke up in the middle of the night as usual, but I didn't hear him," Sydney explained. "When I checked on him this morning, I found these two sleeping on the couch."

"That was nice of you," he said to Jackson.

Caroline entered the room before he could respond, she noticed Sydney's red eyes first and rushed to her side.

"I'm fine. These are happy tears." She paused while Caroline sat beside her and took her hand. "We're all together as Will would have wanted, and Jackson has agreed to be William's godfather."

"That's great news. Will is probably doing backflips in heaven." Caroline laughed. She hugged Sydney and then Jackson, but the commotion startled William awake.

Disoriented and groggy, he reached for his mother, who accepted him and held him close.

"We'd love to stay and spend more time with you, sweetheart," Caroline said to Jackson. "But we'll be late for work if we don't get out of here."

"That's okay. I hope we can get together again soon." He stood and gave them both a hug before walking them to the door.

"I need to get William changed and something to eat," Sydney said. "Can I entice you to stay and have breakfast with us?"

He checked the time. "I'd love to. Meet you in the kitchen in a few. I need to make some phone calls."

After breakfast, he and Sydney sat in the living room while William played on the floor. Occasionally, he'd crawl or wobble over to them to be held or to show off a toy car or soldier. He'd had never spent time with children—never had the urge or opportunity—and it amazed him how natural it felt spending time with Ethan and now William.

For a fleeting moment, he envisioned having a family one day, something he hadn't considered before. But he'd been forced to rethink a lot of things recently and having children of his own no longer seemed incomprehensible. It felt right.

"What?" he asked when he noticed Sydney watching him. He'd been distracted by new and confusing thoughts and William, who had crawled into his lap.

"I'm so happy he has you. You're another puzzle piece to help him know his dad one day. Oh!" she said, slapping her leg before popping out of her seat. "I have something for you."

She rushed out and returned seconds later. Just long enough for William to crawl back onto the floor and dump a small box of wooden blocks. The kind that had letters, shapes, and animals carved into each side and painted a different primary color. The same ones he had growing up—just like every other kid, he imagined. They didn't hold his attention for long, and he imagined the same outcome for William's busy little mind. Like his father, he had too much energy buzzing inside him.

"I made a few of these for Will's family before William was born. I want you to have the last one." Sydney held up a thin leather bracelet with three small silver beads secured between two knots.

He accepted the band, he rotated the square beads and realized they were toy building blocks like the ones William played with now. Each block was engraved with a letter: W.A.M. for William Andrew Mason.

"It's a memory bracelet," she told him. "The letters could be for Will or William, or both. Jonathan and Caroline wear theirs often, but mine broke, thanks to Little Man over there."

"I'll wear it every day and think of all three of you. Would you mind?" He held out his arm and tied it around his wrist. "Thanks," he said and twisted it into place. "Now, it's my turn."

"What?"

"My turn to ask you a question."

"All right."

"You mentioned yesterday that you didn't finish college. What were you studying?"

"Accounting." She laughed when his face revolted. "I know. It's not sexy, but I love numbers and math and solving formulas. Always have. It's frustrating that I had only a few semesters left."

"If you had the opportunity, would you go back?"

"That would be great, but we can't afford it, and I can't take out any student loans. I'd never be able to repay them. Why do you ask?"

She placed her hand over the corner of the table as William waddled close and pulled himself up. She waited while he shuffled down the couch, crawled up onto the open seat between them, and climbed back down again.

"I want to help you get on your feet," he said after William crawled back to his toy box. "And if you want to… move back to Richmond." He didn't know Sydney well enough to read her expressions, but it was easy to see she was shocked by his offer. "I know this is coming out of the blue, but I want to be a part of William's life and ensure both of you are cared for. Everything is being set up. All you need to do is say yes."

She opened her mouth to speak, but nothing came out. She tried several more times before finding her voice. "What's being set up?"

"I've arranged to start a trust fund for William and an account for you to use for tuition and to buy a car and a house in Richmond. I also talked with Harrison, Billy's dad, and he's willing to offer you a job. He said the position is yours after you graduate, and the finance department was one he mentioned that had an option of working from home. You wouldn't have to worry about childcare for William."

All color drained from her cheeks before she dropped her face into her trembling hands.

"Sydney?"

"Give me a minute. Please?" She picked up William when he crawled up to her and held him against her chest while she paced the room.

"Jackson, what you're offering me, it's—I don't know what to say."

"Say you'll consider it and let me know when you've decided. And take any piece of my offer or all of it. You don't have to move back to Richmond if you don't want to." His offer wasn't an all-or-nothing deal.

"No. I want to. Richmond is my home. My friends are there. You'll be there. It's just...I don't want to hurt

Caroline and Jon. They uprooted their lives for me. But on the other hand, they deserve to have their lives back, and so do I." Feeling more at ease, she set William down and returned to the couch, curling one leg under her to face him. "You're every bit as amazing as Will said you were. Yes."

"Are you sure?"

"Jackson, you're offering me a chance to make something of myself. To take care of my son and have a life. I'll never be able to properly thank you for that."

"Just be happy and give William the life he deserves. That's all I want. It's what Will would've wanted." She moved closer, and he held her while she cried.

"I'm sorry," she said, sitting up and reaching for the tissues. "All I've done since you arrived is cry my eyes out."

"It's okay." Suddenly uncomfortable, he looked down at William. "Do you really believe Will is with me?"

"With every ounce of my being."

He nodded. "Then I better make him proud."

"You already have."

He took her hand, mesmerized by the twists and turns of life. It took one visit—just twenty-four hours—to gain the family he could never fathom before he held William in his arms. One he never asked for, but now, couldn't live without.

Over the years, multiple parental figures had come to his aid and stood up for him. He had friends that had done the same while they were with him. They, too, were his family. But Sydney and William were more, and he'd do anything to protect them.

"I should get going," he announced, wishing he didn't have to.

"Are you sure?"

"Yeah. Ben will come looking for me if I don't reach my destination on time. And I promise you don't want that." He laughed and picked up William when he whimpered for him.

"Quite the character, is he?"

"You have no idea." He kissed William on the cheek and tickled his belly, making his squeal. "I'll call to confirm everything with my attorney and Harrison tonight."

"Thank you, Jackson, for what you're doing for us and for wanting to be in William's life. He loves you already." She grabbed her phone when William laid his head on Jackson's shoulder. "Mind if I take a picture?"

He nodded, and she snapped a few photos until William wiggled for freedom.

"I wish you didn't have to go," she said.

"Me either, but we'll all be together in Richmond soon."

He hugged her one last time, then ruffled William's hair when she lifted him to her hip. Pulling himself away was harder than he expected. They'd known each other for one day, yet they were a part of him now. He waved from the end of the driveway and committed to memory the image of them on the porch waving back.

Who knew a little boy and his mother could heal so many old wounds and even more he didn't know existed? Everything he dreamed this journey would do for him was coming true. The pain was beginning to dull, and hope mounted with every stop.

Hope that he could handle the challenges ahead, heal through the pain, and find happiness. Hope that the journey would work and that he could one day build a life with purpose and meaning.

After all, he wasn't alone or weak anymore. Eleanor, William, and Sydney were rooting for him. Will watched over him and guided the way. Harrison, Sophia, and Ms. Beasley were awaiting his safe return. He was stronger. He had a family he loved, and for the first time in two years, he could be cautiously optimistic about his future.

Pausing to start his usual stretching routine, he set his watch as a text arrived from Sydney. She'd sent the photos of him holding William with a message.

Sydney: He misses you already.

With a smile and his family on his mind, he stored the phone and set off again with newfound energy.

Everything was going according to plan, and achieving his goal no longer seemed like climbing a mountain with only a rope and no safety net.

Yes. He could do this.

He was going to be okay.

Leave a Review

If you enjoyed Book 1 of The Journey Series, *A Journey Spared*, please consider leaving a review on any or all of these platforms: Amazon, Goodreads, BookBub, Barnes & Noble, social media (remember to tag me), and others. Reviews are crucial to authors and help us reach more readers.

Keep reading for a sneak peek of book 2, *A Journey To Love*. And remember to read The Journey Series prequel novella, *A Journey Worth Taking*, for a look back at Will and Sydney's love story (closed-door, sweet romance with no trigger warnings, except some coarse language & casual drinking).

TRIGGER WARNING (Book 2): Open-door romance, coarse language, PTSD, mention of suicide, loss, violence, casual drinking, and sexual harassment/assault. But none of that is the focus of the story or graphic. It's mainly about Jackson's quest to find inspiration and pay it forward, how he overcomes the odds and never gives up hope. There's more sweetness, perseverance, unbreakable bonds, and unconditional love to balance it all out and tip the scales to a beautiful, memorable, and heartfelt story.

Alexandra Grace

Keep reading for an excerpt from
Book II in The Journey Series

A JOURNEY TO LOVE

by Alexandra Grace

W hat did you think would happen?" Jackson asked, standing over Ben as he sulked on the street curb outside a rowdy Greenville, North Carolina bar.

"I didn't think about anything."

"No shit."

Ben tossed him a smile, evidence of his lack of self-control and the trouble it always attracted dripping down his face onto his shirt. The streetlight reflected off the full set of perfect, white teeth he still possessed…thanks to Jackson. "But she was hot, right?"

With a shrug, he looked around. The empty street suggested they'd stayed out longer than they should have.

"You could have stopped him a little sooner." Ben pointed at his swollen cheek and the stiff paper towel plugging his bloody nose. "This is on you."

"Try again."

"He was twice my size."

"You should have thought of that before touching his *hot* girlfriend."

Ben's dark, bloodshot eyes glared at him as he yanked what sounded like sandpaper out of his nose. "She started it."

"And you sound like a sullen teenager."

He puffed out his disapproval, his fingers flying to his swollen lip with a wince.

"Come on." Jackson pulled him up by the arm.

"Where?"

"The only place you can't get into trouble."

"But things were just gettin' good in there."

"You're welcome to stay." Jackson's stride didn't hesitate as he headed toward the hotel. "But I'm off extraction duty for the rest of the night."

"Fine. I'm coming."

———

Darkness lingered the following morning when Jackson stepped outside to start his run. Hours of tossing and turning had drained him of what little energy he had left, yet he couldn't spend another day doing nothing. He needed exercise and fresh air to soothe his escalating anxiety— courtesy of Ben Stevens.

Cutting his warmup short, he took off down the street. Although he desperately wanted to think of literally anything else, he couldn't get Ben and the bar fight out of his head. It would be nice to have one night where all hell didn't break loose.

The ludicrous situations Ben created—almost always involving of a woman—and the boyish charm that leaked out of him like cheap cologne, gnawed on Jackson's nerves. Most days, he seemed to be the other side of trouble's magnet, making Jackson fantasize about sending him packing more times than he remembered.

But he never followed through. Ben didn't have malicious or deceptive bone in his body. He just didn't have an off switch or bother thinking through the consequences before acting—a skill Jackson spent eight years fine-tuning in the Marines. They balanced each other out, and in his own awkward way and sometimes without realizing it, Ben also rescued Jackson.

His impulse to cannon ball himself into chaos got Jackson out of the hotel and gave his thoughts another path to track. Spending too much time with his memories in the uneventful solitude created its own disastrous outcome—one that made Ben's antics look like a walk on the beach. And recently, he needed all the distractions he could get.

The first two hundred miles after leaving Richmond accumulated with minimal delays or issues. But over the last two weeks, he had to stop more often, rest for longer, and travel fewer miles each day. Pain slithered back into his daily routine, and he laid awake most nights terrified it would prevent him from reaching his goals. More pain meant more anxiety, opening the door for memories to creep back in. And Ben's latest angry boyfriend episode hadn't helped his flailing attempts to control it.

Despite being the only voice of reason and not taking a single swing or blow, the interaction with Ben's sparring partner triggered his first migraine in six months.

Thankfully, he'd made it back to his hotel room before the freight train slammed against his skull and incapacitated him for hours—an unavoidable reminder that his mission could fail if he didn't stay focused and manage his symptoms.

Sunrays peering over the trees and hitting his face brought Jackson's attention back to the road. He'd made it out of the city, and now traveled down a two-lane with a thickly wooded area lining both sides. Blurry silhouettes of the next town could be seen through the morning fog ahead. While some privacy and shade could still be found, he entered the tree line and located a sturdy branch for his first upper body workout.

He drained one of the water bottles in his backpack and checked his watch. Eleven minutes past seven, and he'd already gone eight miles. Since he had it, he'd take extra time to stretch and hydrate before setting out again.

Eyeing a spot on the branch, he jumped and secured his hands around the smooth bark. Sweat began to bead on his forearms after only fifty pull-ups, the southern humidity already near swelting.

"What are you doing?" a little voice asked from below.

Startled, he dropped to the ground in front of a girl about seven or eight years old, carrying a dirty blue bucket. She had blonde, messy pigtails and wore a plain white T-shirt two sizes too big with scuffed and muddy cowboy boots.

"Hi, there. I was exercising. What are you doing in here by yourself?"

"Looking for berries and nuts."

He glanced inside her empty bucket. "Didn't find any today?"

"Not yet." She squinted up at him through the dappled sun shining on her freckled face. "Why are you exercising in the forest?"

"When I run, I take breaks to work my muscles. This tree looked strong enough for pull-ups."

"What's pull-ups?"

"I hold on to a branch like this." He demonstrated with his hands in the air. "Then, I pull my body up until my chin is above the branch."

"That sounds easy."

He smiled. "It is until my arms get tired."

"What's that?" A chipped purple fingernail pointed at the silver chain around his neck.

He lifted the tags hanging from it. "Their called dog tags. They help me remember my friends."

"You're not a dog."

"No." He laughed. "You get these when you serve in the military."

"Oh. Does my grandpa have some? He was in the Army."

"I would say he does."

"That's his favorite tree."

Jackson glanced up at the tall tree he'd used, then back at the girl. "He has a favorite tree?"

She walked around it, and he followed, waiting while she turned the bucket upside down and stood on it.

"He made that when he found Grandma." She pointed up again, this time to a heart carved into the trunk with two letters inside.

"Found her?"

"When they fell in love, silly."

"Of course." He slapped a palm to his forehead, making her giggle. "What do the letters stand for?"

"Their names, Olan and Helen." She hopped off the bucket. "Are you married?"

"No."

"Do you want to get married?"

"I'm not sure."

"I guess you have to find someone you love first," she said, her long lashes fluttering while she thought on it.

"It's usually a prerequisite."

"A what?"

"A prerequisite. You should love someone before you marry them. There's an order to these things."

Sadness clouded her eyes before she looked away. "Yeah."

Kneeling, he bent to see her face. "What is it?"

"My mom and dad aren't married."

"People can still be in love and choose not to get married."

"They yell a lot."

"Well, relationships can be hard. It takes a lot of work, and that might be how they communicate. But it doesn't always mean they don't love each other or you."

"Yeah," she said again, pushing at the dirt with her boot. "Do you yell at people you love?"

He thought back to the times he'd been angry or upset. "No. But I don't yell at anyone. It's not me. Everyone handles their emotions differently."

She raised her gray-blue eyes to him. "I wish you were my daddy."

"Oh, sweetie." Cautiously, he held out his hand and was surprised when she took it. "You don't mean—"

"Callie! Get away from him," a woman screamed, the sound of crushing twigs and dead leaves under her angry steps echoing through the trees.

"Momma."

He stood to greet the frantic mother, and Callie tightened her grip on his hand, heightening his senses.

"What are you doing? You know you're not supposed to wander around the woods, and this is why." The woman threw her hand in his direction, causing her to stumble to the side. Her short black hair fell into her face with the sharp movement as she felt for a nearby tree to steady herself.

"I come in here all the time, and he's nice."

"But I told you to stay out, and didn't they teach you not to talk to strangers in school?"

"I don't know. You don't take me."

His attention snapped to Callie. "You don't go to school?"

"Don't talk to her. Come here, child."

"No. I'm staying."

"Callie." He lowered to a knee and met her panicked gaze. "I *am* a stranger to you. You can't come with me. You have a family who loves you."

She shook her head. "She doesn't. She won't let me see Grandpa or go to school. Please don't leave me."

"Callie Marie, shut your mouth and get over here." When Callie refused again and hid behind him, the woman lunged at her. "Just wait until I get ahold of you."

Contracting muscles shot fire through his veins at the woman's threat. "You lay one hand on her, and I swear…"

"You swear what, tough guy? Are you going to hit a woman? And what were you doing creeping around in here, anyway?" She looked down at Callie, peeking around his leg, then back at him. "Or have you found what you were looking for?"

The woman had slithered closer without his noticing, her eyes glossy and unfocused on his face. As she stood there, challenging him, she swayed and fought gravity like a heavy wind blew against her. She reeked of cheap cigarettes and whiskey.

"You should step back, ma'am," he warned, struggling with how to defuse the situation. "You're scaring your daughter."

"She ain't mine. She's my good-for-nothin' ex's. On second thought." She took a few unsteady steps backward. "If you want her so bad, you can have her. We'll see how Chris likes finding his perfect little Callie gone when he crawls into my bed again."

She trotted off, and Jackson started after her until he heard Callie crying. "Oh, sweetie. I'm so sorry."

Picking her up, she wrapped her arms and legs around him, exposing how critically thin she was. *Now what?* He couldn't take her back to her house. He'd never be able to live with himself.

"I want my grandpa," she murmured, giving him the answer.

"Does he live near here?"

With her face buried in his neck, she nodded and tightened her grip around him.

Some patient coaxing pulled enough information out of her to start in the right direction. Soon, they came to a one-level, brick house outside the town he saw earlier. She unlatched from him and ran toward it, meeting a man with thinning gray hair in the yard.

He bent down, their embrace desperate and long overdue. "What are you doing here, Callie Bug?"

Unlocking her arms from around his neck, he checked her over, the look on his face breaking Jackson's heart. She meant the world to him, and seeing her upset brought fury and sorrow to the man's eyes.

He could relate.

"Who are you?" her grandfather asked him, but Callie answered, whispering into his ear. Shock brushed across his face before he took hold of Callie's waist and held her at arms-length. His eyes pierced into hers with unspoken questions, which she answered with a nod.

He stood, Callie's hand in his. "What's your name?"

"Jackson Vane, sir."

"Nice to meet you, Jackson. I'm Olan Lewis. Can I interest you in some iced tea or water? It's a hot one today."

"Water would be great."

Olan led Jackson to the small kitchen and prepared two glasses of ice water and a bowl of cereal. "Eat," he instructed Callie.

"Can I watch TV, Grandpa? Momma—" She scrunched her eyes closed and shook her head. "I mean Rachel won't let me watch cartoons when she's there."

"Sure, Buggie. But use the coffee table so it doesn't spill." He placed the bowl in Callie's hands and waited for her to leave before giving his attention to Jackson. "The witch wanted nothing to do with that sweet child but forced her to call her momma anyway. It burns my insides to think of my granddaughter suffering in that disgusting trailer."

Unsure of how to respond, Jackson took a long drink, hoping it cooled his overheated system soon.

"She said you saved her," Olan continued, his mood lighter as he leaned back in the chair.

"I didn't do anything."

"Yes, you did. You kept her safe and from getting beat again. I will forever be grateful to you." Olan studied him. "She had a dream about you."

"What?"

"She dreamed a tall man with long, dark hair would be the one to get her to safety once and for all. That he would be the one to end the cycle."

"Cycle of what?"

"Every time she escapes, she goes to a friend or neighbor's house until Rachel sobers up and comes looking for her. She did that a couple of times here around Christmas. But she's convinced all that is over."

"Why?"

"Like her grandma, God rest her soul, Callie believes dreams have meaning and the power to predict the future."

"That's crazy."

"Is it? She knew you were coming. It's why she wasn't scared of you, and she doesn't trust easy."

"I don't know what to say."

"Do you have children?"

"No. But I recently gained a Godson, William."

"That's great. You'll learn a lot about yourself and how infinite your love can be through him. Children can teach us many things if we take the time to listen and observe. Christian, that's my boy, he's always been good at testing my patience, and I had to learn to control my temper. Still working on it." Olan leaned on the table, his sly grin fading slowly. "He's in rehab again, trying to get better so he can provide for Callie. But I predict that when he gets out, he'll be right back where he started soon after. He can't seem to stay away or see Rachel's toxic."

"Does Callie have to go back? Rachel isn't her parent."

"Christian filed to designate her as official guardian before he went into rehab the first time. He was high as a kite when he did it." Olan's eyes rolled. "I think she forced or manipulated him into doing it, so she'd have that hold over him. He loves his daughter, and if she has Callie, she can control him."

"Does he not know how Rachel treats her?" How could Christian leave her there if he did?

"He does, but what can he do?"

"Remove her as guardian," Jackson suggested flatly.

"No judge will listen to an addict who knowingly signed the paperwork. Plus, they think the child is safe. Rachel can play the part, and I have no say in the matter. Believe me, I've tried." With a sigh, Olan leaned back, his arms crossing over his chest. "So, we play the game, over and over, tormenting the poor child."

"But how can they keep her out of school?"

"What?"

"Rachel admitted it. How has that not reached the authorities?"

"They moved back here late last summer, and I haven't seen her much since Christmas break. I doubt anyone here knows she exists. They move around constantly, always skirting the law." He stood and began pacing the small kitchen. "This changes things, Jackson. If I can prove Rachel's unfit…"

"The fact that Callie wanders the woods alone at her age and Rachel—"

"If I call the cops, will you tell them what happened?" Olan interrupted.

"Of course."

"Bless you." He rushed to the ancient, green phone on the wall and dialed 9-1-1. He provided his address and a brief overview of what he'd learned before hanging up. "They're on their way. Callie Bug," he called.

"Yes, Grandpa?"

Surprised, Jackson turned toward her when she rested an arm on his shoulder and absently played with his hair. The tender grin she offered wrapped him around her finger right along with his hair. He wanted to coil around her and protect her forever. Whatever he had to do to keep her from Rachel, he'd do it.

Olan sat in a chair opposite her and took her free hand. "You've told me before that you don't want to live with Rachel. Has that changed?"

Her eyes instantly filled, and Jackson felt her fist tighten around a lock of his hair.

"No, Grandpa. I don't—I can't." She shook her head quickly, sending tears zigzagging over her pink cheeks.

"Okay, sweetheart. Then, I will do everything I can to keep that from happening. And so will Jackson."

She looked from Olan to Jackson and relaxed.

"We'll need your help. You'll have to tell some people everything that's happened. And I mean everything. It won't to be easy."

She nodded. "I can do it."

"I know you can, Buggie. You're so brave." He kissed her forehead and took a deep breath. "Did you finish your cereal?"

"Yes."

"Do you want anything else to eat?"

"I'm full."

"Okay. Go watch your cartoon." Olan motioned toward the living room.

With a nod, she headed that way, then stopped in the doorway. "Grandpa?"

"Yes, sweetie?"

"Can Jackson come, too?"

Melting, Jackson smiled. "I'd love to."

———

The trio watched TV and chatted until a team of officers and social workers arrived. Callie sat in Jackson's lap, both recounting what happened after they met. She answered questions about her living conditions and showed the bruises on her back, sending his blood pressure into a nauseating tailspin. When a social worker and officer left during the conversation, he hoped they were heading straight for Rachel.

"Do you really have to?" Callie asked him later when he announced he, too, had to go.

He knelt in front of her and took her hand, the sight of her emotional again pulling at his heartstrings. "I don't want to, but you're safe now. There's no way I would leave if you weren't."

She threw her arms around his neck, and he picked her up.

"I gave my phone number to your grandpa. If you ever get scared or need anything, anything at all, you call me. Okay?"

She nodded but with sad eyes, snapping his heart in two. Reluctantly, he put her down before she convinced him to stay. It wouldn't take much more.

"What happens next?" he asked Olan on the way out.

"When I get official custody…I'm staying positive," Olan added with an unsteady grin, "I'm taking her far away from here. If my son ever gets his life straight, he can come find us."

"Good idea. She deserves to be a happy, carefree kid, and if there's something I can do to help give her that, please say the word."

"You're a good man, Jackson. You will always be a part of our family."

"Thank you. If you're ever in Richmond, I'd love to see you both."

"Richmond, Virginia?" Olan asked, leaning against the doorframe.

"That's the one."

"I have a sister not too far from there. Maybe that's where we'll go."

"That would be great. Keep me informed of what happens here and where you end up."

"Will do. Have a safe trip."

With the people he loved and the new family he'd gained since leaving Richmond on his mind, he took off toward town. Why had he been struggling lately? The journey had been good to him. Better than expected, and his life was full.

Still, by the time he reached the Town of Winterville, his heart hurt from missing them all. Pressing a palm against the source of the ache, he stopped at a traffic light to breathe through it, his drive to continue down the road wavering with every erratic beat.

Surrendering, he lowered onto a nearby bench and glanced around. Across the street, a lush yard and cascading Oak trees, lining a narrow driveway, drew his attention. The park-like property stood out among the commercial buildings and asphalt parking lots on either side. Time seemed to have stopped there two centuries ago, while the rest of the town progressed around it.

On the left side of the lot stood a small sign advertising a bed and breakfast. Now that he knew what to look for, slivers of a white structure peeked through the trees in the distance. He shot off the bench and jogged toward it.

The wooded area opened at the end of the drive, revealing a massive historic home with wide plank wood siding painted white to match the towering two-story columns and wrap around porches on both levels. Navy shudders framed every window, and the curved front stairs were constructed with the same red brick as the four towering chimneys above.

His eyes shifted to the perky blossoms planted around the shaped shrubbery, and his chest tightened with thoughts of Eleanor. Her focus would have zeroed in on the flower beds and gardens instead of the stunning mid-19th-century architecture. She'd gush over them for hours with the groundskeeper, sharing secrets and stories and boring Jackson into finding something else to pass the time. The vision lightened his mood as he climbed the steps.

Since the front door sat open behind the screen, he let himself in, stepping into a time warp. The furnishings, fixtures, wallpaper, and wood features from floor to ceiling seemed original to the day the first owners moved in. The grand staircase curved around the ornate crystal chandelier in the center of the foyer, reminding him of the one hanging in his father's home.

Correction, *his* home.

He hadn't gotten used to that life alteration yet.

As he admired the black and white photos on the fireplace mantle in the parlor, a woman with dark gray hair, a plaid dress, and apron joined him. Eleanor's name tickled his tongue with the wave of familiarity she brought into the room.

"Hello there, sweetie," she greeted in an unmistakable southern drawl. "Are you looking for a place to stay for the night?"

"Yes, ma'am. I'll need two rooms if you have them."

"That's wonderful. Of course, of course. Would you like to give the rooms a looksee before payin'?"

"That won't be necessary."

"Suit yourself." She waved for him to follow. "I made some sweet tea and cookies this afternoon. Got a plate of chocolate chip in the kitchen and oatmeal raisin in the oven if you're interested."

"They smell amazing, but I'd like to take a shower first if that's okay."

"Anything you need." She led him to a small office by the back door, soon passing him several forms on a clipboard. While he filled in the information, she did the same for his handwritten bill. He paid with cash since credit cards weren't accepted and listened closely to her instructions. "If you need anything during your stay, just holler."

She narrowed her dark eyes when he smiled. "Did I say something amusin'?"

"A close friend of mine used to tell me to holler if I needed her. She was like a mother to me."

Her frown softened into a motherly grin. "Aww. I can tell you miss her."

"Very much. You remind me of her."

"I'm flattered. I'd love to learn more about your…"

"Eleanor."

"What a lovely name." Her hands clasped together under her chin. "Will you tell me about her at dinner tonight?"

"Nothing would make me happier."

After texting Ben the address, he wandered the gardens to gather details and photos to share with Eleanor. Then, he called Olan to tell him he'd be in town a little while longer. Olan invited him back to the house to spend time with Callie, giving Jackson an idea.

"I'll call you back." Sprinting through the sunflower rows, he took the rear entrance steps two at a time. "Excuse me, ma'am?" he called, embarrassed that he hadn't asked for her name earlier.

"Yes, dearie?" She appeared in the hallway, drying her wet hands on her apron, as Eleanor would.

He smiled at the memory. "Would you mind if two more joined us for dinner? I know a little girl who would love to play on the swings out back."

"Of course. The more the merrier."

"Thank you." He turned to leave, then stopped. "You never told me *your* name."

"Oh. Silly me. It's Hilda."

———

Once in his room, Jackson took a quick shower and changed before visiting the strip mall across the street. Callie had had a rough day, and he wanted to give her something to make her smile.

He returned in time to intercept Ben before he went inside.

"What is this place?" he asked, climbing out of the car.

Jackson glanced back at the flowers and Hilda sweeping the front porch. "Home," he answered absently.

"What?"

"Nothing. Help me grab the suitcases. We have dinner plans."

"Since when do you make plans? Did you happen to find a hot bar on your way here because I saw nothing exciting in this sh—"

"Watch your mouth," he demanded and motioned for Ben to open the trunk.

"Why? Is Scarlett gonna whack me with her fan if I curse?"

"Who?"

"Scarlett O'Hara. *Gone With The Wind.* Old movie. Civil War. Any of this registering."

"No."

Ben sighed. "God, this place is—"

"A breath of fresh air. That's all you need to say or think." With a warning scowl, he yanked out both suitcases in one motion.

"Are you blind? There's nothing fun to do here."

"Good. That means you'll stay out of trouble."